ALSO BY LAURIE DEVORE

How to Break a Boy

Winner Take All

A
BETTER
BAD
IDEA

LAURIE DEVORE

[Imprint]
MAKE YOUR MARK

New York

[Imprint]
MAKE YOUR MARK

A part of Macmillan Publishing Group, LLC
120 Broadway, New York, NY 10271

Library of Congress Cataloging-in-Publication Data is available.

ISBN 978-1-250-22595-5 (hardcover) / ISBN 978-1-250-22596-2 (ebook)

Our books may be purchased in bulk for promotional, educational, or business use. Please contact your local bookseller or the Macmillan Corporate and Premium Sales Department at (800) 221-7945 ext. 5442 or by email at MacmillanSpecialMarkets@macmillan.com.

Book design by Elynn Cohen

Imprint logo designed by Amanda Spielman

First edition, 2021

10 9 8 7 6 5 4 3 2 1

fiercereads.com

If you steal this book, you will find: you can run but you can't hide.

*To Drew, who is probably funnier than me
but not quite as good looking.*

EVELYN

REID ELAINE BREWER, 17, of McNair Falls, passed away on October 11, 2018. Beloved daughter to Adam and Helen Brewer, Reid is remembered as a bright, vivacious student and friend by McNair Falls High School classmates. Often seen taking joyrides in her old red Honda, Reid was a great lover of music, board games, and the outdoors. She is survived by her parents, paternal grandparents, and her adoring longtime boyfriend, Ashton. Her cherished grandmother, Elaine Morgan, preceded her in death.

It took them a few days to find Reid's body; they had to drag the lake to recover it. Back then, when it all went down, I couldn't get the image of her water-rotted skin out of my head, seaweed tangled in her hair, all the trash dumped into Victory Lake surfacing with her. But even still, I imagined a look of sick amusement on her face. Reid with wild dark hair flying behind her, sunglasses too big for her face, wearing any color lipstick she pleased. There was a purple one I liked best because Savannah Rykers wouldn't stop talking about it for days. *Tacky*, I heard Savannah say more times than I could count. Tacky and unapologetic and pissing Savannah Rykers off: That was Reid, until McNair Falls took the most alive thing in it and drowned her, sucked the life right out.

She would've found that funny.

I press my fingers to the newspaper clipping taped on the wall next to my beaten-down dresser. The paper has gone that faded yellow of forgotten things.

Sometimes now, I can almost remember what she was. I remember Ashton, always right there beside her, staring at her like she was his earth and he her moon, orbiting around her like he didn't even mind she only paid him attention half the time. I remember Reid looking at me and saying, "Evelyn Peters. Lord bless you, girl, you don't have a clue."

I didn't then, but I do now.

I finally know.

You gotta do what it takes to survive in this world.

REID

Ashton can't stop staring at me, and I know why. When he looks at me, he sees nothing anymore but his own hurt and pieces of a broken girl and the anger we both feel, burning red and hot in our veins, and he keeps wondering how he can set himself free.

But I can't let him go, not now.

I tell myself I love him, and maybe I do, but maybe I love what he makes me. Queen of this shit town. Queen of this shit life.

I could leave or I could stay, and what would it really matter?

The truth is this: I am nothing, and I think I've known that for a while. I mold myself into the shape of whatever is closest to me, cling to it like a parasite. Right now, that nothing is shitty-tasting rum and a cold breeze on colder water and the night sky itself. I'm an illusion. An illusion of music too loud, of carefree summer nights, of racing down dirt roads and taking clothes off and sweat and fights that end in kisses and *pain*. Good pain. That's what he wanted—*this illusion*, right now, is what he wanted. He's staring at me, and he's remembering the girl he saw all those months ago.

It's hard for him to look away when I'm so alive.

But he knows. Deep down, he knows.

He's only seeing who he wants me to be.

ACT 1
KEROSENE

EVELYN

The options flash through my mind like lightning, faster than I can act on them.

Cry. Scream.

Stay. Leave.

Fight.

Escape.

Destroy.

Don't give up, Evelyn.

Please give up, Evelyn.

Please.

Run, Evelyn.

Go.

Tuesday, October 6, 2019, 1:34 p.m.
Ten Hours Before

Smoke is curling up into the crisp October sky over Tyler McBee's head.

It's gray against more gray, a bleak, cool day in McNair Falls, South Carolina. I'd dug through my dresser for an old sweater this morning, pulled it out, putting my fingers through the holes eaten into the knitted navy material.

Tyler's eyes catch mine when he sees me walking toward him, interested. He has a long face, his hair too short in the front, probably work done by his mama's scissors. He's leaning against the cheap aluminum siding on the outside of the gym, facing the trees next to school.

"Can I bum?" I call to him, once I'm close enough. I shiver against the breeze. Weather tends to yo-yo around this time of year, one day hot and humid, the next a chill stealing into the air, wrapping you up in its windy tendrils. I hate the cold. And I hate the weakness of a nicotine craving.

Tyler's already got his box of Salems out, offering me one. He flicks the box toward me with his wrist, shaking a cigarette loose. I grab it, pulling it between two fingers.

Sometimes, when I like to imagine I'm a better person than I am, I think I'm less addicted to the nicotine than to the moments before it hits my lips. Holding the cigarette between my fingers, watching some desperate boy offer a flame to me, and then sucking in the smoke like sweet release. Like a brief twinkle of freedom, control.

I lean against the wall of the gym next to Tyler, looking out over the trees blowing in the breeze. My red lips leave a stain behind on the cigarette wrapper.

"What are you missing?" Tyler asks, not quite looking at me and not quite not looking at me.

"History," I answer, easy. Exhaustion works to drag me down, and I fight back just as hard. *History is death*, I want to tell him, *and there's enough dead things around here without piling on*. But if I did that—said that—I might not ever be able to get another cigarette, so I keep quiet.

I know what to do. Glance over at Tyler, keep my gaze down, my eyes soft. There's not a lot I can get in this world, so I always play nice with those who give.

"You?" I ask, letting smoke escape out the side of my mouth.

He snorts, ashes his cigarette against the wall. "Haven't been to math all week. To be honest, I'm not really sure I have time for all this anymore."

"School," I finish his thought for him, inhale, blow out slowly. I feel the way he's watching me, eyes catching on all those holes in my sweater. I *always* feel it.

"You know the deal. I figure I could at least be working for the Dowds on their land, doing something useful, making some money. Instead of in here"—he gestures at the wall, the school beyond—"learning nothing. This shit's never gonna do people like us any good."

Drag. I roll the words *people like us* around in my mind. "You gotta do what's right for you." I don't really know what that means, but I've gotten used to speaking to people in clichés. Keeps me from saying anything real.

"You still work over at the store?" Tyler asks me. "For Reid Brewer's parents?"

Reid Brewer. The name sounds so foreign coming out of his mouth. Like a thing that only existed before, in the quietest breath of the wind, in the deepest secrets of a soul.

But that's not right, is it? Reid existed everywhere.

"Yeah," I say.

"She's been dead almost a year now, yeah?" he asks.

I shrug. "It's sad," I say because that sounds true.

Tyler thinks on that for a minute and then nods. "That's life, isn't it? Can't escape sad shit."

I can't help but laugh, surprising Tyler and me both.

Tyler drops his cigarette, stubs it with his toe, and kicks it off the thin sidewalk bordering the gym and into the grass. "You wanna get out of here?" he asks me.

I push my fingers through my hair, slow, careful. Glance up, like I'm ready and willing to be offered up to him as compensation. Like a prize pony. "I've got biology. And I'm not ready to quit just yet."

"Aw." He moves closer, head tilted down, eyes hungry like all boys when they look at girls like me. "Maybe some other time."

"Maybe." I toss my cigarette down after his and step on it on my way around him. Once I've turned the corner, I lean back against the siding, breathing in and out slow, letting myself have this moment alone.

I hate when anyone gets too close to me.

But the bell rings a moment later, signaling for me to get on with it. I straighten back up, dust off my too-tight jeans and ratty sweater, and I keep going.

It's not like the alternatives are any better.

Tuesday, October 6, 2019, 11:40 p.m.
Six Minutes After

I can't exactly walk and I can't exactly run, but I am *leaving*—maybe leaving my home, maybe this whole world, running head-first into the wooded terrain behind our trailer, dark and wild and inviting. The lights fade behind me, and it is so hard to stay upright with the pain nipping at my heels. The ground is sloppy or I am sloppy. Either way, I wait for the inevitable fall.

My fingers are wrapped tightly around the neck of a bottle, and my palm is sweating, the earth attacking me with claws, pulling me down, vicious. *Fall*, it begs, *cry and scream and give in at last.* But I won't let it have me.

So I keep going deeper into the woods behind our trailer, to sweet escape, to where screaming and a clanging, broken piece of shit heater don't echo in my ears.

Smile, Evelyn, warn those trailer walls, whispers of Mama's old boyfriends and teachers who know better. *Don't frown all the time. And don't you dare fucking cry.*

I unscrew the top off the bottle and toss it away like so much trash, letting the vodka hit me and hit me and hit me again. At least it hurts in a way that wants to hold me close, rock me to sleep, make me *forget*. It splashes down the front of my navy sweater as I push forward, and I don't stop drinking, heading toward the old moonshine still.

I hear the crash of plates breaking and see welts on pale arms, smell food burning, and I'm lost in then and now and my skin vibrates to remind me I'm stuck in it forever and always, in this prison I can't escape from.

And then I stop. I forget. Because I am here, at the still, and someone is there, in front of me. Someone else is at the still and I have been too loud and they are looking too closely and now

And now.

and now

"What are you doing?" *His voice is warm*, I think, preposterously. Like a blanket in the cold night, wrapping up syllables and words and keeping them safe.

I've always liked his voice.

"Hello?" He's still watching me, and I am exposed. I pat my pocket, searching for a lipstick or eyeliner or *something* that isn't there, like it can hide me. Help me disappear into the only mask that protects me.

It's *him*.

"Evelyn?" he finally says at last, and I know—*know*—he's known who I really am, all along. He's been waiting to say it, waiting to confirm it.

But he sees me. Ashton Harper sees me.

And Ashton, he might've been running in this direction just as hard as I was running from the other. I like to imagine him that way, like he's still hurting, always hurting, a constant ache he can't escape. Neither of us can escape.

God knows we both got plenty to run from.

Tuesday, October 6, 2019, 2:47 p.m.
Eight Hours and Forty-Seven Minutes Before

The final bell rings, and Savannah Rykers is between me and my locker.

It happens like this sometimes because I'll be copying down my assigned reading for English after the bell rings, and then I'll turn out into the hallway and there she'll be at her locker, one row down from mine. I'd never admit it to anyone else, but I try to avoid her, scheduling my trips to my locker when I know she's not there, shrinking away like a scared animal if she is, sometimes just showing up to classes without books.

It's a dance we do because nothing can turn my hardened shell soft quite like Savannah Rykers.

But today, I'm in danger of failing if I don't do my math homework, and if I don't hurry, I'll miss the bus.

I stare straight ahead, walking past her with purpose. But I think she must sense me somehow, connected to me through a link we are both desperate to break, because her head snaps up and her eyes are on me.

"Evelyn Peters," she says. "Do you *ever* go to your locker?"

Most other girls in this school ignore me, like they're afraid they might catch whatever I have. But Savannah can't help herself; she's always got something to prove when it comes to me.

At least before, Alex was always around. He'd offered me some sort of protection.

No more.

"I saw you sneaking around behind the gym with Tyler McBee

during history today." Savannah has this way of projecting her voice so no one around her can miss a word she's saying—and people love to listen to Savannah.

"Did you?" This is my strategy: to pretend I'm not afraid of her, to will myself to *not* be afraid of her. It's my strategy with everyone. So, I keep moving past her and open my locker. She slides up beside me.

"Surely you could do better than that." She says it like a whisper, but somehow her words echo all around us. "I know you're desperate, but even I never expected you to sink that low. Things really that bad since Alex took off?"

"Alex graduated." I keep my head buried in my locker.

"And didn't bother to take you with him. Does he even speak to you anymore now that he's done with you?"

It's a sore subject, but I try not to show it. Alex was my best friend, but even worse, last year somehow Savannah figured out that I'd go over to Alex's house to sleep sometimes, sneak right in his bedroom window. Alex used to laugh about it. "I have always wanted to be in a hetero scandal," he'd joke with a grin.

And it'd been okay then, when he'd been beside me, laughing too.

I close my locker to find myself face-to-face with Savannah. "Why are you so worried about what I do?" I ask her. But it's a stupid question because Savannah isn't worried about what I do at all. She's humiliated by my very existence.

"You purposely make yourself look like a slut in all that makeup," she tells me, shaking her long dark hair as if some new revelation has crashed over her. She's so pretty in an easy way, a cutout from a magazine of Ideal Girl. She can't hurt me, though. The makeup is mine, the only thing I control. *She can't hurt me.*

"I purposely make myself look like a slut so you'll stay away from me."

14

"Why don't you just get out?" she asks me, and this time she actually does drop her voice, a question for me alone—her only real question. I'd answer, but the problem is I don't know where she wants me to disappear from: the locker, the school, her life? It's not like any of this was my choice.

I'm no one to everyone except Savannah, to whom I am everything.

I answer her back in a whisper, too. "I'm not hurting you, Savannah. Leave me alone." I turn away from her, and she hates that, too, when I don't fight back. She shoves past me, pushing me against the locker. It doesn't hurt, not really.

"Fuck you," I say because I can't help it and I see the way everyone looks at me in my ratty old sweater, my mascara dark and lips painted for war.

I look like the scary one, so I must be.

Savannah whips back around, and I know immediately this was too bold by half. "*What* did you just say to me?" she demands.

I straighten up. "That I fucked him. Tyler. That's what you wanted to hear, right? That's what'll make you happy?"

"You're disgusting," she says, and the way everyone's eyes find me, *see* me as something unworthy, it must be true. At least if I'm a villain, I'll be a good one. It's better than the truth.

Tuesday, October 6, 2019, 11:43 p.m.
Nine Minutes After

There's not much left of the old moonshine still buried deep in the woods past our trailer—the spot Mama calls the Old Home Place. Half of a shelter remains; two collapsed wooden poles have caved the tin roof in on one side. Some barrels and pipes rust away. Mama says my granddaddy used to run shine out of here, but it's not like Mama hasn't been known to lie.

I clutch my bottle close to me, aware—so aware—of everything wrong in that moment, from the cold air choking my lungs to the bruise blooming on my hip, right where my sweater meets my jeans.

"You're not supposed to be here," I say.

"Hey." Ashton toasts me with a flask. "That's usually the line people use *after* they get to know me."

Ashton Harper, I think, like the rest of it has been erased. *Ashton. Ashton Harper.*

And then I think, *Reid*.

"Are you"—he twitches back a piece of dark hair that has fallen into his eye—"okay?"

I can't stop staring at him. I watch the way his eyebrows come together. The way he licks his lips.

I take a pull from the bottle of vodka, sitting with the words. "That's a hell of a question," I say at last.

He's watching me carefully, too, and I get a small thrill from it, despite the circumstances. He's never watched *me* before.

"What are you drinking?" I ask him, edging slightly closer.

He almost smiles, like he doesn't mean it. "Tennessee's finest."

"Cheers." I'm close enough now to tap my bottle against his flask, and we both drink, but he's still looking at me.

"You sure you're okay? Your eyes kind of have that look."

"What look is that?" I return, desperate to keep him engaged but afraid to give away too much. Sure, I may have just downed more gulps of vodka than I ever have, but I can't respond with *real* words, can't show myself, especially not now. That's dangerous.

"Wild," he says. He licks his lips again, and I like when he does that. "Seen that look a time or two."

"Tragedy," I tell him, wise and mysterious. *Please like me like you liked Reid*, I think. *Like me, like me, likeme*. "It's always chasing me."

"I know the feeling," he says.

No, he doesn't.

Not like I do.

Here's how Ashton Harper looks: Imagine perfect pale skin and dark hair highlighted light brown in the moonlight, just long enough to be swept back, and a sharp jawline and dark lashes lining eyes like a storm. Imagine someone who looks so attainable but so beautiful all rolled up into one and a voice laced with southern in the best way possible, clipped vowels and forgotten syllables, dipped in bourbon and peaches and honeysuckle.

Imagine the boy Reid Brewer fell for.

Imagine Ashton Harper.

"How long does it take?" I ask him.

"The real question is how *much* does it take," he answers enigmatically. "And the truth is, I still haven't found enough to do it." He rubs his boot across the ground. "Outrun tragedy and all that."

I tilt my head to the side. "Oh."

I stare down at his foot, the only part of him moving, and then

I laugh, almost completely by accident, a sharp sound and then an intake of breath.

"Are you . . . laughing?" he asks me.

"Sorry, it's just . . ." I look up, meet his eyes. "It's a little melodramatic, isn't it? For you?"

"I don't know." He takes a drag from his flask like he's really thinking about it. "I mean, here I was out at this abandoned still all alone, right? Am I being melodramatic if no one's here to see me?"

"If a tree falls in the forest and no one hears it?"

"Exactly," he says. "I am a tree alone in a forest, holding on by a thread. Like, here's what I figure—maybe I am melodramatic as all hell, but if it's on my own time, it's nobody's business but mine. I'm not crying in the hallways at school or church or everywhere. I tried that whole running-around, tearing-the-world-apart thing, and it got me nowhere. Didn't drive the thoughts away any faster and was a hell of a lot less efficient in terms of having other people trying to fix my problems. So here I am."

Because here's what happened to Ashton Harper: He was perfect and he could've had anything he wanted, but he wanted Reid Brewer because she was *not* anything, she was everything. And when she died, he broke because he loved her so much. Of course he did, because she was bright and shining and *wild* and he'd tame her with a look. They were going to be together forever and ever because the sun rose over Reid Brewer and set behind Ashton Harper because they were never looking any other way but at each other.

"That's not really true, though, is it?" I ask.

"How do you figure?"

"Well, you're not alone, are you? You're with me."

He grins, this time for real.

I climb onto the bus and I sit next to my sister—*our* sister, mine and Savannah's, if blood really is thicker than water—and she curls up into my side, falling asleep on the long slow ride through the greater McNair Falls area. Downtown, if you can call it that, is one blinking yellow light, a couple of abandoned buildings, a gas station, and a Dollar General. After that, we reach the open land: trees, pastures, trailers, dirt roads, and more nothing. A ghost town of nothing forever. A population that is dying faster than it's reproducing, with a school where the yearly graduation classes are dwindling into the eighties. McNair Falls is all that's left a town over from where the old mill closed down twenty years ago, though the way people talk about it, you'd think it was only yesterday. I lean my face into the grimy window and watch it all roll past.

Kara breathes against me. She's tiny—only six and small for her age, pretty hair, long and dark and straight, with easily tanned skin that looks nothing like mine. Nothing about her looks anything like me, like we share even less than half our genes.

I tug on her hair right as our house comes into view. "Wake up, little nugget."

"Tired," she mutters into my shoulder. Then she looks up at me, and it's like looking into the sun. Mama's always preferred Kara to me, and I get it—she looks like joy and I look like disappointment.

"C'mon," I say, and we get off at the end of our driveway, taking the long walk down the dirt road leading to our trailer. Kara sighs deeply, slinging her bag around from one shoulder to the other. "What's your homework look like?" I ask her.

"Borin'," Kara says, her accent coating the word.

"Obviously. All homework is, by definition, boring."

"You smell like cigarettes," Kara tells me, annoyingly superior. I know. I smell it in my matted hair. Smells like weakness.

"No one likes when you point out their flaws."

Kara shrugs.

"All right." I push her up the stairs of the caving-in deck in front of our single-wide, the deck Dane promised to fix months ago. "Let's get you started on your homework before I leave for work."

She stops at the door, startled, and looks back at me. "Dane's home."

"*Shit*." I roll up on my toes to confirm what became clear as soon as Kara said it. Dane is at home and not at his scheduled shift. I don't want to leave Kara alone with Dane until Mama gets off.

"Shit is right," Kara says.

I spin her around from two steps below and bend over slightly so we're eye to eye. "Listen, kid. Don't piss Dane off."

"As long as he doesn't piss me off first," she returns, defiant. I stare at her until she deflates, glances down at the ground and then back up to me. "I won't."

"All right, just call me at the store if he gives you any trouble." I take the steps until I'm up behind her. "And stop cursing."

"You started it," she says.

"I know," I say. "But I'm a shit person, all right?"

"You're my favorite person, Evie," she responds with the simplicity of someone too young to know better.

I push open the door and Dane's in the kitchen, chopping something up at the square of linoleum counter. "Hey, girls," he calls when he sees us. His hair's all mussed up, dirty blond and sticking up in every direction, ten years younger than Mama and eight years older than me. He looks handsome like that. *Handsome and dangerous.*

"I was making y'all some snacks," he says. He's smiling, grinning so hard it makes my skin crawl. Grocery bags surround him, meaning he spent money. Dane doesn't believe in budgeting when he's in his moods.

"Kara's got homework to do," I say, biting my tongue so I won't comment on the groceries. I spot several name brand boxes and feel sick. "I gotta get ready for work."

"I'll watch her," he tells me, and our eyes meet for a moment across the distance between. "We'll be fine, won't we, Kara?"

"Sure," she answers, obedient, dropping to a chair at the fold-out table in the kitchen. I reach over, pull a folder out of her bag, and read the assignment written in the front.

"I've got it, Evelyn," Dane calls to me, fatherly—as if either of us would ever need a daddy like him. "Go on. You don't wanna be late."

I keep reading, ignoring him, but I feel him watching me like fire on my skin. When I look up, I can't hold my tongue. "Why aren't you at work?"

I see the flicker of annoyance behind his eyes, read it like a book, but he wipes it away as fast as he can. "There was too much to get done around the house. I woke up and I felt really *good* this morning," he says. His eyes shine bright, genuine. Sometimes, I pretend I'm someone else and I imagine feeling sorry for Dane, for the demons, for the things he may actually hate about himself. But other people fight the same battles, don't they? And they aren't like Dane.

I want to tell him that it doesn't matter how he feels, that no one cares how you *feel* when you're too broke to pay the bills, but I can't say anything like that because any of it could so easily tip the scales the wrong way, lead to the crash that always comes eventually.

I live in silence and don't even get to complain about it.

"Kara"—I bend down to her again—"you be quiet and stay out of Dane's way, okay? He's busy, you heard him."

She nods. "I didn't mean—" he starts, but I turn tail on him and walk down the far end of the hall to my bedroom.

"Evelyn, I was fixing to make you something to eat!" he calls then, trying to win me over, still *trying* after everything. Maybe, sometimes, you just want to believe so badly that you're not a terrible person, that you're more than the monster underneath.

He ain't.

I stop, count real slow.

"I'm good," I say after a minute.

Tuesday, October 6, 2019, 12:42 a.m.
Sixty-Eight Minutes After

We stand in silence after that, next to each other, drinking slowly and then quickly and then slowly again, the night spiraling out around us. Birds in trees sing their sad night songs and coyotes beckon to each other in the distance while mysterious creepers and crawlers rustle leaves nearby.

I'm numb to physical pain by this point. Pretty soon, I'll be numb to any pain at all. That's a dangerous place to try and live, but I've been holding on to all of it for so long, silent, desperate to scream. Because no one wants to know. Not really.

Not since Reid.

I hear them somewhere in the night: the lies I've told, men I've smiled at, words I've held in, just to survive.

This is survival?

"The world is bullshit" is what comes out of my mouth, presumably filtered through several shots of vodka.

"Yeah," he says, barely more than a thought. "Fuck it." He looks over at me, studies me a long minute. "You look different. From normal."

My fingers go up to my bare lips, fingertips sliding across peeling skin there. "No makeup," I say simply.

He doesn't say anything about how I look, how he prefers me, simply nods and turns away again. I'm a noticeable girl, not hard on the eyes I've been told, and he looks at me like a ghost.

I love it.

I hate it.

"Why are you here?" I stand next to Ashton, leaning against a barrel. A mean wind whistles through the trees, clinging to us, to our bare fingers, our skin. I push my curly blond hair out of my face, trying to see him clearer. He looks at me like he's not sure what that means, so I incline my head toward his drink.

"Wellll," he says, drawing it out, "my girlfriend drowned and I've been drinking my demons away ever since. Nothing has to happen. It just has to be night and be too quiet inside my head and here is where I end up."

"I'd love the quiet," I say, the words out before I can stop them.

"You wouldn't if it sounded like Reid." The words are soft, and I bristle at them. Because I wish I *could* hear her again, wish she'd deign to talk to me, even now.

If I were the dead one, I'd whisper to Reid, a voice carried on the wind. But now, in this reality, she'd never whisper to me.

"That reason is bullshit, you know that?"

He chuckles. "You got a better one?"

"I got a lot," I return, lacing my voice with confidence I don't feel. And then I turn the bottle up and swallow and swallow and swallow—goodbye, memories.

I imagine watching myself the way I used to watch Reid, seeing someone else, being someone else. Because I could be. Here in the dark, here with Ashton, I could.

"Take this," Ashton says, proffering his flask, "seems like you could use some of this."

I could.

The store is completely dead.

Mrs. Brewer is grumbling about being out of Budweiser in the height of deer season, and Mr. Brewer has been flitting in and out of the back, loading the cardboard boxes piling up into his pickup and taking them to the dump site.

"Honey," Mrs. Brewer is saying, walking quickly from the back of the store. I can tell she's talking to me because I'm the only one there. "Give me a couple of minutes to count the register and I'll drive you home, all right?" she says. "It's too cold for you to wait for anyone to come pick you up."

Sometimes, she thinks I'm waiting for my ride and the truth is, I'm walking home as soon as she disappears from sight.

Mrs. Brewer never seemed to care much for me before. But that was then, and once Reid was dead—

Well, I guess sometimes, you're all that's left.

Every day, it gets closer and closer to then, to the first anniversary of Reid's death, and somehow, she's still gone. Here, in this empty store, I wonder if any part of her is left, in the air or the walls or the sounds.

Or is it over when it's over? You're just gone.

I hope so. I can't imagine Reid wanting to stick around McNair Falls.

• • •

Half an hour later, Mrs. Brewer pulls into my long driveway, the wind shifting the trees, clouds covering the usually bright starry sky.

"You okay, Evelyn?" she asks me when she stops, turning her dark, kohl-rimmed eyes to me. Her skin is always too orange—going leathery from the tanning bed she frequents—and her eyeliner's always a mess at the end of the day, but you can tell she was someone other women wanted to be once. Now, something about her just looks broken. "You're looking tired, girl."

Mrs. Brewer married Adam Brewer from Columbia after she spent a couple of years down there getting a cosmetology degree. They moved back to McNair Falls, bought a building, started the country store, and had a kid. Mrs. Brewer had been trying to do everything by the book since before I knew her.

But it didn't change anything the other women around town felt about her. She wasn't one of them; never had been.

And things never change in McNair Falls.

I remember Mama saying once, "I don't know when Helen Brewer got so uppity. Back when she was a Morgan, her family were our next-door neighbors. She was older than me, and she got pregnant in high school, you know. Lost it." And then Mama sucked on a cigarette and didn't say any more.

"I'm fine, Mrs. Brewer," I tell her. "Just a long day."

Mrs. Brewer had finally taken to me, I think, because I was so close in age to Reid. After Reid's death, she needed someone to cling to, and I'd been there, always instantly captivated at the sound of Reid's name.

"Do you need a night off?" she asks.

I shrug. "It doesn't matter so much. I've got insomnia." Funny how people screaming all night will do that to you.

"Look, I don't wanna encourage anything you're uncomfortable with, but if you ever need something to help, let me know. Melatonin is a nice little supplement. And if that's not enough, I have some other things I might be able to give you."

Sad people got a drug for everything.

"That's real thoughtful of you, Mrs. Brewer. Thank you."

I can feel that Mrs. Brewer is watching me. Sometimes, I think she knows more than she lets on about me. About my family. Hell, I think pretty much everyone in McNair Falls knows who Kara's daddy is. Not mine—he was a wanderer, Mama liked to tell me. Wandered into her life and wandered right out of it. He was no one to McNair Falls.

Just like me. Half no one. Half infamous. All unwanted.

"I'm happy to talk about anything that's bothering you. You know that, right?"

I don't say anything because there's nothing to say. There's never anything I can say because saying it won't change it.

This is it. This is my life.

"There were so many nights," Mrs. Brewer finally says to fill the silence, "after Reid died, I thought I'd never sleep again. I'd be up, wondering what had really happened—the story those kids told made no sense. And I haven't seen hide nor hair of Ashton Harper since then."

I sit with that, hungry for more. She stares out the window, off into the woods behind our house.

"I know what it's like not to sleep, Evelyn, is what I'm saying. I know what it's like to hurt." A long silence passes before she goes on. "I'll help you in whatever way I can."

"I appreciate that," I say.

"I know she was difficult," Mrs. Brewer tells me, the words spilling out, "but that's because she felt it all so deeply. My Reid. She was always looking for answers."

"She wasn't difficult," I say. "She was strong. That's how she survived it all."

Mrs. Brewer smiles gently, like I'm a child. "She loved the light as much as the dark. A sunny day as much as the rain. And there's nothing wrong with that, Evelyn."

Reid shone brighter than any star in the night, I want to tell her. She *always* did.

But it's not normal to think things like that.

"I'd just like to see her bang through that screen door at our house one last time. Doesn't seem like so much to ask, does it?" She wipes away a stray tear and I think how suffering is a constant ache, pushing down on you.

I wait like she'll give me more, but she doesn't. I've got nothing left either, so I get out, close her car door. Everyone in town knows the Brewers have conspiracy theories about Reid's death. I'd heard them all, collected them, and flipped them over in my mind, but they made me sadder than I already was. So, I hike my bag up onto my shoulder, once, and then walk toward the house, scratching Dane's pit bull, Porky, behind the ears as I go. He's so gentle, it's hard to believe he could belong to Dane.

"Why'd you leave Kara with Dane?" Mama asks me, pouncing as soon as I come through the door.

"'Cause I had to go work. Which Dane didn't do today so sure seems like we could use the money."

"Please don't start smarting off already," Mama tells me.

"Was everything okay?"

Mama pushes her hair back. It had been starting to gray, but she's using some product now. The blond hair dye makes her look more like me. "Dane's just tired. You know how he gets."

I do know. "I meant was everything okay with Kara," I tell her, which is what she knew I meant.

"Yes," Mama says firmly. "I told her to go play in her room for a bit. It was a long time, and you know she doesn't like to be easy."

"She's six."

"He was crying when I came in. Locked himself in the bathroom. It's hard for him."

"It's hard for us all," I can't help but say.

"What do you want from me?" she asks, and it sounds kind of desperate. I grit my teeth.

Nothing at all, I wanna say. *Never let me take anything from you.*

"I gotta take a shower" is what comes out instead, and I walk around her to my room.

"It's almost dinner, Evelyn," she calls behind me.

"Don't want any," I say, and slam my bedroom door.

I'm drunk.

I can tell because the sky's moving and the ground's moving, and I'm no longer cold.

Ashton and I have been standing next to each other, passing his flask back and forth. He left, once, walked back to his car, and refilled it from a bottle there. I had been afraid he wouldn't come back, but he's here now. There is an electric silence between us, and I feel it, and I feel real, which is something that almost never happens. I feel ashamed for letting it in.

"You know," I start, "my granddaddy made shine out here. Mama calls it the Old Home Place."

"No shit," Ashton says. "I like it here. No one bothers me."

That really is a rare privilege, I think. To not be bothered.

"So, you weren't just here waiting on me?" I say, trying to sound fascinating, the way Reid always did. "Guess I really am infringing, aren't I?"

He laughs. "I guess so. Trust me, I get the irony that there's so few people in McNair Falls and I still can't find a way to run away from them all."

"You didn't used to want to run away from them all."

"That's an assumption," he answers me, quick, and I wonder what could've ever bothered Ashton Harper.

Nothing, I answer myself. *He has everything.*

"That's the trick. The fastest way to get people to leave you alone." A beat. "Tell them how you really feel." He takes a deep breath, steeling himself. "If you wanna tell me I got a problem, get in line."

"Oh, Ashton, I stopped trying to fix people a long time ago. Started with myself."

"Ashton." He smiles, the look on his face like a long-lost memory. "What?"

"I don't know." He shrugs, and I think he's drunk, too. "The way you just said my name, it reminded me of someone. I've never heard you say it before."

"Well, I've never had cause to."

He thinks about that. "Guess not."

Out through the other side of the woods, there's a pasture, and I think the cows must be out, lowing in the darkness. Something howls in response, and a dog barks, and it feels safe, the two of us together.

"I used to think it would be scary," I say, "out here at night."

Ashton studies me thoughtfully for a moment. "You're not what I thought you were."

"Which is?"

"Not nice."

I scoff at that. "What makes you think I'm nice now?"

"Not-nice people don't put up with me," he says, sounding very sure of himself. "They'll tell you all about it if you ask. I've broken too many promises, and I'm too pathetic or something."

"I'm not nice. Just bored." *Lie.*

"I'm not convinced," he says.

"Try me." *Don't.*

He tilts his face up, thinking. "Let's see," he begins slowly, "truth or dare?"

"Truth." *Dare.*

Then he says, "No, that's not fair." He drinks his whiskey. "You go first."

Mama's putting Kara to bed in the room next to mine. The walls are so thin, I can hear everything she says. She's humming a lullaby. It's one my granny invented, or maybe someone before her. I don't remember much about her, but I do remember her singing those words to me.

Then Mama sang them to me. Now she sings them to Kara.

Mama finishes and whispers good night, goes to the door, closes it softly behind her.

A knock comes on my door. She doesn't wait for me to say it, but comes right in, and then she stands there and stares down at me on my bed, quiet. She's mere feet from me in the tiny space that makes up my room, just big enough for the twin bed and dresser.

"How was work?" she asks.

"Slow."

"Helen brought you home?" She perches on the end of the bed near my feet.

"Yeah," I say, and she purses her lips. Her eyes flick to Reid's obituary, something I know she has no idea what to do with. "And how was school?"

I think of Tyler and Savannah, and some small part of me wishes I could say it all. Start talking and never stop. "Fine," I say instead.

"We have to be careful, Evelyn," she begins saying, and finally we might get to the reason she's here, "with Kara."

It stings, the reprimand. "I am," I tell her. "I'm always careful." *What about me?* I would never let myself ask. *Will you be careful with* me?

"I'll pick you up from work tomorrow," she says, getting back up from the bed. "I don't need someone else driving my daughter around."

"'Night, Mama," I say as she goes to the door. She stops there, sighs deeply, holding on to the doorknob.

"I'm sorry, Evie. I'm so tired."

She turns back around, makes her way to me, and plants a kiss on my cheek. "'Night, hon," she says, and closes my door behind her.

I touch the spot on my cheek and wonder at it.

The warning. The questions. The tenderness.

I wonder at all of it.

In the silence that follows, as I hear Mama and Dane talking, voices still at normal volume, I reach for my guitar.

Last year, I saved up enough money to buy an acoustic guitar from some guy on Craigslist who lived in Ravensway. He told me he'd bought it to try and teach himself but never found he had much time for it.

I'd had to be selfish to save up enough money. Sometimes, Mama would say she didn't know if we were gonna scrape up enough for groceries. I'd told her fine, I'd subsist off the free school meals so her and Kara and Dane would have enough to eat. I think she knew I was stashing away a little of my Brewers money, wanted to guilt me, but all I wanted was something that was mine.

I told Mama and Dane I'd found it next to a dumpster, and they may be inattentive, but they sure as hell aren't stupid. I'd gotten a nice purple bruise for my efforts, but in the long run, I'd figured it was a fair price to pay to carve out a small piece of happiness for myself.

I strum some of the chords, keeping the sound down. Dane has had a couple of fits where he'd come in and threatened to break my guitar over his knee so I didn't like to chance it. I can hear the low rumble of Mama's voice still, the hum of the television on in the background.

Dane could turn on a dime, but as the quiet continues, I grow bolder, picking at a slow, mournful country song. I hum along with it, watching my calloused fingers work over the strings.

There's something I like so much about those old country songs. The way they weren't constantly asked to swallow their pain, but to turn it into something beautiful. They weren't quite so afraid of unhappiness.

"Evelyn, put that FUCKING GUITAR AWAY!" Mama yells from the den. I hear Kara shift in the room next to mine, almost feel her fear through the wall.

I sigh, laying the guitar down next to my bed. My fingers ache for something to do, and I know no sleep will be found. I grab one of Mama's old paperback romances up from the floor next to my bed and fold the cover back, opening a page at random.

Dane yells something at Mama. Sometimes, she sets him off by yelling at Kara and me because he says she doesn't know how to raise kids. Dane's good at that, poking at your most sensitive spots, and that always sends Mama into a rage and then a breakdown.

I don't read the next couple of lines because a plate goes crashing to the ground. I involuntarily shudder. We haven't had dish shattering in a while.

The cut on my hand from the last one just healed.

I'd known this was coming. Known since I'd seen Dane in the kitchen after school, but still I shiver. The predictability of pain doesn't make it go down easier.

I turn the page of my book, my heart beating in time with the steady sobbing from the den.

Wednesday, October 7, 2019, 1:40 a.m.
Two Hours and Six Minutes After

"So," I say, feeling bold, teetering closer to Ashton, his face aglow in the moonlight shining down on us, "tell me one thing you've heard about me that you think is true."

"Oh, I see you're starting somewhere dangerous." And Ashton wipes his mouth and gazes at me, his eyes clearer than I've seen them. They remind me of before, of him with Reid, his bright, thoughtful eyes taking in every part of her, eager and hungry.

I wonder what that's like, to feel someone watching you. To know their only intention toward you is love. Respect. Or better yet, fear.

That's how it must have felt to be Reid Brewer.

"It's only as dangerous as the next words out of your mouth," I taunt him.

He leans in closer to me, too, in a way that makes it clear he isn't thinking about it but following an instinct.

"I heard . . . ," he says, his voice soft on the wind. Then he looks away from me, like he's realized a mistake.

"Say it," I command.

He runs a hand through his hair, pushing it back from his face. "I heard that you get around."

I snort. "I 'get around'? Are you trying to be polite?" I kick at the forest floor. "Most people just say I'm a slut. Leaves less room for interpretation."

"I wasn't . . . I don't mean anything by it, you know. That's . . . that's what I've heard."

"And you believe it." I stare off into the distance. "Of course. I'm 'different' than you thought."

"I'm sure it all gets exaggerated," he says. "I know the way that stuff does." Then he continues as if he can't quite help himself. "Savannah thinks you need to be saved."

I turn to him, my eyes sharp, my whole life clunking noisily and terribly into place.

No one can save *me*.

"You know Savannah's got no interest in saving me," I tell him.

"Maybe it could help," Ashton tells me with a shrug, "with your tragedy."

I scoff. "Isn't that the thing about this town? They think us wayward girls are sitting around, waiting on someone to save us?" I pull closer, tantalizingly closer. "Think about it. Maybe I don't want to be saved at all. Maybe I love this sin I live in, love it hard and rough and dirty, just like you hear I do.

"I don't need saving, Ashton Harper. I need someone willing to take a risk for once."

He takes a short breath, like one or two passed him by, surprised him. Then he says the thing he stopped himself from saying before. "You sound like her, you know?"

"Who?"

"You know who." He takes a sip, smiles against the opening of his flask, like a thought just occurred to him.

"Reid," he says at last.

I lick my lips as Ashton watches me, not conscious of it at all until I become very conscious of it. He thinks for a moment before he says it: "Why are *you* out here right now? You said you had good reasons."

I boost myself up onto one of the barrels, swinging my legs out in front of me, all casual again, all part of a game. It helps me put my own mind at ease. "I got a . . . what do they call it in polite circles? Oh, right . . . a troubled home life. And I gotta outrun it. You ever heard a nice thing said about a Peters woman?"

Ashton looks at me for a long minute, then shakes his head.

I feel a smile spread over my face. "Like clockwork. Your mama wrecks one home . . ." I sigh. He frowns, something working in his mind, a question on the tip of his tongue.

I level my gaze at him. "The game is called Truth or Dare. You got a question, ask it."

He accepts my challenge. "Why do you do it? If that stuff with your mama bothers you, why would you do the same things she's done? Why would you sleep with all those guys?"

I laugh. "Who says it's only guys?"

"You know what I mean," he returns, undeterred. He doesn't blink, and for that half a second, I feel raw. Exposed.

Because a bad home has gotta be about my mama being a slut. It's the simplest answer so it must be the true one.

"'Cause us Peters women are cursed," I say after a while. Simple. "And there's nothing we can ever do to change it."

That, I believe.

"It's your turn," I say.

"Fine," he says. "Dare."

I stand up from the barrel, dusting myself off. Say the first thing that comes to my mind.

"I dare you to pretend like I'm Reid."

His defined eyebrows go up, almost disappear into his hairline. "That's dark."

I shrug. I don't know who this girl is, but there's nothing stopping her. "Maybe it will help you."

"I told you, I've tried everything."

I walk closer to him, and he tilts his head down so our eyes are level. His face reads only mild interest, but I circle his wrist with my hand, pulling it to my body, my fingers pressed against the most delicate part. His heart is pounding.

I drop his wrist and it falls to his side.

"Well, first," he begins, and he takes a long drink at this point. There can't be much left in his flask, which means this is almost over, but it can't be. When it's over, I go back to being Evelyn Peters, nothing and nobody but a quiet girl with a bad reputation in a nowhere town.

I hate her so much.

Ashton continues on: "You need to say something completely taboo, possibly hurtful, and definitely inappropriate."

I bristle at his words. "Reid just didn't take shit," I tell him.

He half smirks but doesn't answer that.

"Then," he goes on, "convince me it was somehow my fault."

I blink, confused.

"And then"—his eyes pierce mine—"we'll scream until we're too hoarse to do anything except rip each other's clothes off. But"—he toasts his drink to me—"you've seen that whole song and dance before, haven't you? Everyone has."

He fingers a chain around his neck, almost as if he doesn't mean to, and instinctively, I reach out and grab it. Pull it out from under his shirt.

It's a McNair Falls High School class ring. A girl's. I hold it out to him.

"She loved you," I say, defiant, the proof in my hands. "And you loved her."

Ashton reaches out and licks an escaped droplet of liquor off his palm and then takes the ring and hides it back under his shirt. "Your Reid impression isn't really holding up," he tells me. "She didn't believe in fairy tales."

He looks very superior then, like he's proven something to himself and me.

"You say I'm not nice, but you're not as nice as they said you were," I say at last. "'A nice boy like Ashton Harper' is what I used to hear. 'He shouldn't be with a girl like that.'"

He laughs, cold and hollow. "That's the thing about people, isn't it? They only ever disappoint you."

Tuesday, October 6, 2019, 11:25 p.m.
Nine Minutes Before

I wait for it to go quiet in the den.

The psychology of Mama and Dane's relationship is what nice people call volatile. What I call toxic. They're either fucking or fighting, but at least they're on the other side of the trailer in Mama's bedroom now.

I feel it all the time. Tired to the core of my being, broken down and wrung out but not in a way that ever offers relief. Constantly, constantly, I feel my life unfolding in this endless, colorless miserable day.

And worst of all, I'm hungry.

I stare up at the ceiling, at the dark and the silence. The truth is, I feel myself losing my mind, a couple more pieces floating away from me every day, and some part of me welcomes it, hopes I'll forget to want anything else. Wanting is such a waste.

After an hour, I get up, slide out my door and into the hall, taking the short steps to the kitchen. I open the fridge, my eyes scanning the just barely expired ham, the leftover rice, and a box of off-brand beer.

I close the fridge, opening the cabinet and grabbing some too-expensive Chicken in a Biskit that Dane brought home earlier, stuffing a few of the salty crackers into my mouth and savoring them. I wish I hadn't skipped my school lunch today, but when you're so tired, your body can trick you into starvation sometimes.

And now, I'm ravenous.

Mama's bedroom door opens, and I stiffen momentarily, as if

caught. But then I fish another cracker from the bag and crunch on it hard, the powdery substance coating my fingers.

Through the darkness, I see the outline of Dane shuffling toward the kitchen. I crunch another Chicken in a Biskit, reveling in it a bit.

"Evelyn?"

"Dane." I eat another even though they're starting to taste disgusting to me.

"Go to bed," he tells me.

"No." I eat another. "I'm hungry."

"You weren't interested in dinner." He stands next to me in the kitchen, opens the fridge, removes a beer. "So you aren't gonna eat everything in the house."

I eat some more. Almost gag. Dane opens and swigs his beer, lit by the inside of the fridge, eyes daring me.

"I'm still hungry," I tell him.

"Why you always wanna make a bad day worse?"

I stick my hand deeper into the box, knowing in some part of the back of my mind I shouldn't antagonize him but unwilling to give up this ground. Unable to turn that part of myself off.

Stop fighting, Evelyn.

I try. I try so hard to stop. But it's this day and it's Tyler McBee's eyes on me and it's Savannah Rykers and Dane and every little thing tearing me down.

Why am I never tired enough to stop fighting?

Dane slams down his beer, sloshing it onto the counter, and grabs on to my forearm still stuck in the box, wrapping his fingers around it tight. I try to pull back but he hangs on.

"Let me go," I say, our eyes meeting. He hangs on tighter, his fingertips pressing in so that I can feel my pulse from every point he is touching.

41

I swipe at him with my free hand, and he shoves me away, into the edge of the counter that stabs into my side. Tears well up in my eyes. The box of Chicken in a Biskit hits the ground, and crackers spill out onto the floor.

"That's all you've got?" I ask him, my voice barely above a whisper.

I've tried to stop caring, stop feeling, I swear I have. But it's just the two of us now and I can't help it. I can't help trying to survive.

Do you know how hard it is to kill that instinct?

"Why?" he begs me. "Why do you do this to me?"

I hear him say the same words to Mama sometimes. I stare back in defiance.

"You don't do *shit* for us. You ruined everything. I paid for these goddamn Chicken in a Biskit because you weren't the one who went to work today."

"I swear to God," he begins, like he has a god to swear to.

"Hit me," I taunt him. "You want me to call Matt and tell him what you did? Because I will. This time, I will." It's an empty threat.

Or at least, on most nights it is.

"Don't you dare talk about that piece of shit Rykers," he says, and strides forward, taking both my arms in his hands before I think to run away because I'm too busy digging myself in deeper. He shakes, shakes like he might shake out of his skin.

"It doesn't even hurt," I spit back at him. *Lie, keep lying.*

"Do you really think I'm scared of you?"

I know he's not.

No one's scared of a girl like me.

Wednesday, October 7, 2019, 1:50 a.m.
Two Hours and Sixteen Minutes After

I'm bleeding.

I don't remember cutting myself, but I guess I did, scraped my skin right over some wood sticking out of the ground out here. I suck on my knuckle.

"What's wrong?" Ashton asks. I bask for a moment in the huskiness of his voice.

I stopped trusting being alone with men and boys a long time ago. Whenever the time came, I'd feel cornered, desperate. My nerves would light, fire burning through my veins, and my mouth would begin lying, doing whatever it took to get away. *Of course I like you. Of course you're funny. Of course I'll give you what you want later if you'll just go away from me now.*

I'd seen what men did to girls like me. I'd seen what they did to Mama.

And I don't *trust* Ashton. But I don't want to lie to him.

Maybe I want him to lie to me. Treat me like someone he trusts, someone worthy of respect.

This night, like a scraped knuckle and vodka and the good kind of pain. I'm not ready to quit just yet.

"What do you care?" I ask. But when he doesn't blink at that, I make my voice whinier than it really is and tell him, "I'm injured."

He takes my hand in his unsure ones, shaky from the alcohol. He studies it closely like he knows anything about bodily injuries, holding his phone's flashlight up to my hand. But he is soft, the hair on his knuckles tickling me. He leans close, biting his lip. His eyes travel up my arm and then land on my face.

"Does it hurt?" His voice is quiet.

"Nothing hurts," I return. Not even my ribs. Not anymore.

His fingertips play with the hem of my sleeve, and I jerk my arm back protectively.

"Sorry," he says, but I feel his eyes on my sleeve, suddenly sharp.

"It's not you," I say. "It's me."

His eyes look so much more sober when they return to mine, like he sees something now that he didn't before.

"Why are you really out here?" he asks me. "That's your next truth. Tell me."

For the first time, I flinch.

I stare down at my bloodied knuckle. "I . . . I can't tell you. Dare me instead."

"Show me your arm," he whispers then. "I dare you."

"You're cleverer than you look," I reply, my voice gone icy.

"You think you make it this far with this much alcohol and this many problems and you don't have to be pretty clever?" He tosses his flask to the side. "Show me."

I swallow, staring ahead like I can see two paths laid out in front of me. In one, I walk back through the woods, back to my trailer, back to my life. Maybe I lie down on the floor once I get there and I wait. I wait for it to sink in that this is forever. That every day, I get to wake up and live this life and go to bed and still be living this life.

I wait to die the same person I always have been.

Or I show him and we both keep playing these roles and I don't let him know who Evelyn Peters really is.

I don't *want* to be Evelyn Peters.

I grab on to the bottom of my sweater, pulling my right arm out of it, exposing my bare skin to the biting cold. It's fine; it's nothing to this version of me. Ashton lights his phone again, and his eyes follow the blossoming bruise up my arm, to my tank top. I watch his face carefully, the way he presses his lips together.

"You got a boyfriend who treats you like that?" he asks, his voice completely different, nervous and charged.

"I would never," I say, my voice unbridled rage. "It's my mom's boyfriend." I haven't said it out loud before, but it comes easy with the help of the cold, dark night. I could spill all my secrets on the floor of this old shine still, and none of it would ever matter again. Because nothing that's happening right now is real. It's whatever I decide it is, and tonight I decide I can't feel anything at all.

Ashton looks alarmed. I know why—there's something visceral about seeing real bruises on a real person's skin. Something that makes a concept into a reality.

I pull my sweater back over my shoulder, shrugging in slowly.

"You should . . . do *something*," he says, desperate for that undefinable *something*.

That's the problem with people who only think they've suffered. They think there's something to be done. Some way out.

"I don't care what he does to me," I say.

"You should."

"I don't care what he does to me," I say again, "but this time, he's gone too far."

A beat. I taste the words like blood on my tongue without realizing I'm the one saying them but feel the power in it. In the night, in the vodka, and finally, in *myself*.

This me—*this* is a girl I could love.

The words become as true to me as the breath in my lungs once I say them.

"This time, I'm gonna kill him."

Tuesday, October 6, 2019, 11:33 p.m.
Seconds Before

Dane's grip is iron on my arms. I kick his shin hard, and that's when he shoves me into the table displaying family photos in the den and it slams violently against my ribs, sending pictures falling to the floor, shattering. I am breathless, pressing my hand against the spot, using the wall for support.

"Fuck!"

It's loud enough to wake everyone, if anyone happened to be sleeping in the house. Mama's voice immediately rings through the house as she hurries out of the bedroom the same way Dane came, already admonishing me. *"Evelyn!"*

I straighten up, don't let myself wince.

"I was hungry," I state again.

"You shouldn't have skipped supper," Mama says, like we are all having a perfectly rational argument here.

"You shouldn't have this FUCKING PSYCHO living in our house!" I scream back, knowing those are the words that will upset Dane the most.

He punches the wall next to my head, leaving yet another hole in the plaster, and I do wince this time.

"Go to bed, Evelyn!" Mama yells at me, and deep down, I hear the desperation in her voice.

Then I sense rather than hear Kara's door open and try to stop the tears from running down my cheeks, but it's too late.

"Kara," I call, trying to soften my voice. "Kara, go back to bed."

But she's dragged her favorite ratty stuffed dragon out of bed with her and is next to me, looking between me and Dane. I twist my head slightly to look at her.

"*Please*," I say, my voice barely above a whisper. I press my hand into my aching side as if to turn the pain off.

"You're hurt," Kara says.

"She's fine, babe. She's not bleeding," Mama tells Kara. "Now, come over here, girl."

"I'm fine." I repeat Mama's words to Kara.

Kara stands still, unconvinced.

"And besides"—I glance up, my eyes meeting Dane's, who is clearly working to restrain himself—"what's Dane going to do? Kill me?"

A lot of things suddenly happen at the same time. Dane pulls back his fist again, but I know this time, it will collide with me and not the wall, so I duck and he misses, reflexes slowed by all the alcohol running through his blood. Mama screams, and Kara runs at Dane, her fists flailing. And then, in precisely that moment, time stops again, and I watch as Dane pushes Kara back, away from him, almost a reflex, and she hits the wall behind her, leaving another dent in it, her head rebounding violently as she falls to the floor, her eyes rolling back.

"KARA!" Mama screams, and shoves past us, crouching in front of her, and then Kara's eyes open and she is crying wild, angry, hurt tears, and Dane pushes me, too, pushes past me and back to Mama's room, slamming the door behind him.

I slump down the wall onto the floor, pained and broken and motionless, as Kara cries and Mama cries, and I close my eyes.

I wish I prayed.

I open my eyes.

Ashton takes a step back, but keeps his face clear. "What did he do?"

I can tell Ashton is scared of my answer, but I don't care about reassuring him. Giving him the comfort he seeks. Because people like Dane hurt people like me every day. And people like Ashton Harper never have to look any of that in the face.

"He hurt my sister," I tell him, not letting myself blink. "And I'll never let him hurt my sister again."

Something dark mars his pretty face. "You mean the one that . . ." But he trails off, unsure how to say it.

"The one that looks like Savannah Rykers? Yeah, that one."

"I see you with her . . . or, I saw you with her. Your sister. I don't know."

"He's never done that before. Hit her. He knew better. She's small for her age. At least when he hit me, he knew I could take it." At least when he hit me, I could convince myself I'd earned it.

Ashton keeps staring at me, and I can almost see his brain working, tell that he can't stand this feeling of stillness.

He swallows, looks around at the mess the two of us have made, the cold emptiness around us. "Suddenly, everything about this feels way more fucked up than it already did."

"Don't do that," I tell him, leaning down and picking up the flask he'd tossed to the side. I drain the rest of it. "Don't act like this changes something. It's all a game."

"Doesn't feel like a game."

He reaches his hand up, and I think he's going to brush his fingers over my face or *something*, but instead, his fingertip finds the ding on my cheek, a divot, scarred into my pale skin.

"I've always wondered how that happened. I noticed it . . . when I used to see you at school. It didn't used to be there, but then, one day, it was. Just like the rest of you. All that eyeliner and lipstick and that scar."

I swallow, my skin hot. He *saw* me.

He saw *me*.

"Don't worry about it," I say, and half grin. "Just a little rough-housing."

"Evelyn, that's bullshit. This *isn't* a game." But I grab on to his wrist as he goes to pull his hand away. I grip it tight between my fragile little fingers and smile up at him, realizing I like the way he says my name, too.

"Dare me. *Please*. Don't stop playing."

Ashton licks his lips and anger is written in his eyes. Finally, somewhere he can direct his anger that isn't at himself.

Finally, something we can both do to escape this hell we've been living.

"Fine," he says at last. He's breathing fast, and I imagine his adrenaline pumping through his body, giving him purpose. "I dare you. I dare you to do something about him. Bring it all to light. Burn it all down."

I stare back at him, determined, the idea appearing fully formed in my mind.

"Let's finish him."

Tuesday, October 6, 2019, 11:35 p.m.

"Mama," I call, my voice quiet. It's dark, and I'm against a wall, crumpled on the ground. "Mama," I say again, stronger.

"Kara," she says. "You've got to quiet down, baby." I hear Mama's tears as she tries to stop Kara's, and they cut through me. I think about being nine and falling off my bike and Mama crying with me, too.

She hasn't cried with me in a long time.

"Why do you do this, Evelyn?" Mama asks me, and part of me thinks I hear the sadness in her words, like even she wishes she wasn't asking me. She scoops up the still-crying Kara into her arms. "Look at my girl," she demands of me.

I was her girl once.

"It was an accident," Mama tells Kara softly.

It was an accident the first time he hit me, too.

Kara watches me, her mouth forming the word *Evie* even as I can't hear her say it. But then Mama's hand is on the back of Kara's head, pulling her teary face into Mama's shoulder, and Mama's grabbed up her keys off the counter, taken off out of the house and cranked the car. And then she's gone, and I'm left in a daze, some sort of disaster, floating above, watching myself.

Dane's in Mama's room.

Slowly, I make my way to my feet.

I grab up Mama's prepay phone from the counter and dial, listening to the ringing on the other end. I won't stay quiet this time, no matter what it costs me.

I'd asked Mama once before, asked her to leave him. Appealed to her. After he'd bruised my face.

She'd held a bag of ice to my cheek and told me not to worry about things I didn't understand.

Someone answers the phone, a familiar voice on the other end.

"Who is this?" she demands.

Savannah.

I start to say the words, start to ask for the sheriff, but I can't quite make myself. Can't ask for his help, still. After all this time.

"Why are you calling my daddy?" Savannah Rykers's voice is sharper still.

And I see it then. Matt Rykers smiling at me. Matt Rykers teaching me to ride a bike. Matt Rykers eating breakfast at our table, and Mama telling me, "You're gonna have a daddy, Evelyn. At last."

I hang up and let the phone fall from my grip, bounce back onto the counter. If Matt wanted to do something, he already would have. Not like I haven't seen enough abusers check into the county jail for one night and bailed out the next day.

A noise from Dane's room makes me jump. Mama left me here with him, knowing what he might do.

I know what he might do.

I open up the cabinet under the sink and dig around, looking for Mama's hiding spot, until I catch sight of her stashed vodka. I wrench the bottle free, and in two quick strides, where I truly feel that I'm somewhere between life and death, I'm out the door and down the steps, and I'm running.

I follow Ashton, shooting through the woods like a beacon in the night.

Something hot runs through my blood, singing in my veins. I am sharp and clean and so very, very determined, and I feel him with me, sharing my purpose. Because this is freedom and anger and finally something at last I can do.

I've been living in the undone for far too long.

The single-wide comes into view. *Home*. Where my grandmother lived before she passed away and where we all lived together, where Kara came home, tiny and so different from me.

Where Dane rammed me into the table. Where Mama brought every man she thought would fix her life. Where my grandmother died, feeling that same old misery we all do.

I stop to stare at it, feel Ashton watching me, feel the words he's going to say—something like *we don't have to do it*, so I laugh to stop him.

Because we do.

Because this spell will be broken if we don't.

"I gotta get something first," I tell him.

I go in through the front door, hear the sports talk blaring from the radio in Mama's room. See the destruction from earlier, Kara's open door, empty room, Mama's missing car.

I sneak to my bedroom and grab my guitar. A romance novel. Reid's obituary. I stuff the last one into my pocket and then grab up the almost empty whiskey bottle Dane must have brought out during the night and a box of matches from the kitchen on the way back out, closing the door behind me. Ashton looks at me greedily.

"You're glowing," he tells me.

And I feel that. The sheer power.

"No one," I tell Ashton, my voice clear, "gets to touch me without my permission."

I grab the can of gasoline from under the deck, check to make sure the dog isn't there. I douse the rickety wooden staircase in gas and most of the whiskey, enjoying the idea of Dane's own weapon used against him.

"Poetic justice," I say to Ashton, who seems to be as deeply seduced by the sight as I am.

I stare up at the single-wide. My home. A prison. Like this town and this skin and like what TJ Akins did to me when I was fifteen.

"I'm done being that girl," I say.

"You get to be reborn," Ashton tells me. "That's how it works." He says it with the confidence of someone who's sung on a Sunday and then seen the dark side of the world.

He says it with the confidence of someone who's ready to leave it all behind.

Our eyes meet, and I want to tell him, *I know you. I know who you are*.

And he's looking back at me, and I see what he's thinking, too: *I've always known you*, and all I want to be is the person reflected in his eyes.

"Today, Evelyn Peters is reborn," I say, standing tall. Reborn as the person she was always meant to be. Who burns down the world if it looks at her wrong. "Let her be somebody worth remembering."

I hand Ashton the almost empty bottle, and he takes a swig. He hands it back, and I do the same.

I strike the match, drop it onto the stairs, and they light like that's what they've been waiting to do for their whole pathetic existence. The fire spreads faster than I thought it would, the flames from the deck quickly licking up the old siding of the trailer. Porky, who's never been tied up, has just woken up from his slumber on the dirt drive, and barks at the sight, retreating farther away from the heat. It consumes the front of the trailer so fast, it seems unbelievable it was ever habitable by humans.

No front door. No escape.

Ashton looks over at me and grins, brighter than the sun. I smile back, warmed by the burning world.

I feel like I could stare at it forever, live inside it. I feel invincible.

My face is wet, I realize, because tears are streaming down it. I let them fall, letting them give me power. They're deserved.

The spell isn't broken until Ashton says the words at last, sounding unconcerned: "We better run."

ACT 2
KEEPER OF THE FLAME

REID

727 Days Until the Fire
Then

Reverberating bass is shaking the dashboard of Mom's old Honda. It's in my hands and my chest and my soul, pushing through me like violence. I want to break something, just destroy it, leave nothing but ashes in my wake.

There's nowhere to go when I'm like this.

I swing around the corner of Fuller Road, its long blank gravel crunching under my tires. I'm pushing the pedal eighty ninety one hundred nothing can stop me. This shit town is just one long line of connected roads with family street names, husks of trailers and homes in disrepair. It's such shit and nothing, I can't believe anyone even bothered giving it a name.

I hate Ashton. I hate him like a disease that needs to be cut out of my skin, my very DNA. I hate him I hate him I hate him. I grab on to that anger, stoke it like a fire in my chest.

No other emotion exists, I'm sure, and then I race around the sharp bend that is Fuller Road and I have to *slam* on brakes, push my foot into the floor so hard, I hurtle toward the steering wheel. Because just around the trees blocking my view, a girl is walking along the road with her back to me, hands in jean pockets, T-shirt tucked in, head down.

There's no one else on this road. There's never anyone else on this road.

I'm stopped now, and my heart's still slamming against my chest. I lean into my horn and the girl jumps, turning to look at my car. I slowly pull up next to her, roll down my window.

"What the fuck do you think you're doing?" I demand of her, my rage still fresh, raw as a new wound.

Her voice replies softly, defiantly. "Walking."

I see her then. "Evelyn Peters." The sharp lines of her face and her wavy blond hair, tangled up in knots. She looks me in the eye at the sound of her name, and I think she might be about to cry.

"Get in," I command, and she does, because I didn't ask a question. I try to never say anything like a question—don't want to leave any room for interpretation. But Evelyn obeys without hesitation, and I start driving again, keeping on the way I was going. The music pounds, and I see Evelyn wince out of the corner of my eye.

I turn it down. I know this is where most people expect someone to put them at ease, but I'm not most people and ease doesn't help girls like Evelyn Peters. "Tell me what happened and I'll take you home."

"No." She says it so softly that she's barely saying it, and she's staring straight ahead like this determination will protect her.

I tap a red nail against my steering wheel. "I didn't ask. If you tell me what happened, I will take you home."

I have her attention now, feel her sad eyes on me. "Or what?"

"Or I'll drop you back where I fucking found you. Don't test me, Evelyn." And then she's staring, like she truly can't believe it, so I adjust the mirror to show how truly I mean it and glance over at her.

"Watch where you're going!" she demands when I momentarily have to jerk the car back over from the middle of the road. Not like I'm gonna run into anyone else on Fuller Road anyway.

That's enough. This is boring.

I slam on the brakes again, and she throws her hands out to stop from flying into the dash. "Get out," I say.

"You can't be serious," she replies.

"I'm dead serious. Ashton Harper has already fucked up my day, and I'm not gonna let you finish it off."

"Ashton Harper?" Curiosity. I almost let it get to me, tell her everything, because I'd like to see her reaction. "What about him?"

She's usually not so mouthy, standing behind the counter of Mom and Dad's country store, looking like she'd try to please you if she only knew how. Like some sort of lost soul begging you to save her.

Screw it. I'll tell her anyway.

"Yes, Ashton Harper," I say, peeling back a little, letting her peek into my life. "We're together but he is also under some delusion that he is making the rules between the two of us."

I wrap my hands over the steering wheel again, watch my red fingernails. I like to say his name out loud, almost as much as I like it when he says my name back to me.

When he says *Reid*, it sounds like a prayer, like the preacher on Sunday morning.

Evelyn's watching me, her eyes almost glassy, shining. "He doesn't need to introduce me as his girlfriend to his parents because I've known his parents since we were in elementary school and why does it have to be different if we're dating and blah blah blah, honestly, I've already forgotten it all because it's so dull. *I* get to decide how things are between us. I always *have* decided, since I set my eyes on him. So now he has to learn," I finish. "He's going to beg."

She watches me like a ghost, an otherworldly creature, intrigued. She knows what the Harper name means in this town, she knows who Ashton is, and she knows who I am, so she knows

I ought to be grateful for anything I can get out of him. We stare at each other for a solid ten seconds, and then she reaches down, hikes up her T-shirt, and fists the fabric until it is tight and high on her body, revealing the smallest sliver of pale white skin, and she ties it off with the hair band on her wrist. She pushes her hair out of her face. And I see then, how she must've looked earlier this afternoon, when she'd surveyed herself in the mirror, felt confident, ready to impress anyone who might love her.

Evelyn has a role she was born to play, whether she wanted it or not.

"TJ Akins invited me over," she finally says. "He told me his parents were out of town and him and Luke had a bunch of beer and were drinking in his basement. He said he'd come pick me up and everything."

I study my nails, jaded. "And how'd that go for you?"

She shrugs. "I thought it was cool—him and Luke are juniors, and they talk to me sometimes, but never, like, about anything important, so I was surprised he invited me over. People at school like them, you know? They could've asked anyone over, and they invited me. I thought I was special."

Nobody's special to TJ and Luke. I take a deep breath. "What'd they do?"

She licks her lip. "We were sitting around drinking or whatever, and it was weird. TJ was asking me a bunch of questions about myself and my mama and the store. And then he asked if I wanted to walk upstairs to the kitchen with him, and I said I did. We got up there, and he told me I was pretty and kissed me."

I'm not sure I want to know, but some sick part of me is endlessly fascinated by how some girls fall into this shit like a video on loop. She's Evelyn Peters, but she could be anybody, and how do boys like TJ Akins always know that?

"And?" I press on.

"You know, TJ's cute. When he kissed me, I kissed him back." She's helpless.

"And then, somehow, we were in his room, and I thought—I don't know—like, this is the beginning of something big. He really likes me and now we're kissing. Only then"—she takes a deep breath—"he started taking off his pants and he was trying to grab my hand and I pulled it away and it was okay for a bit but then he grabbed my hand again and I pulled it away again. Then he started trying to undo *my* pants. So, I had to, like, push him off. Pull away to stop him."

I look up at her, feeling like I should do something to fix her and knowing I can't. "What happened?"

"He said . . ." and here, her voice quivers ever so slightly and I want to tell her to stop being so weak because they'll turn that against her every time, "'Oh, come on, it'll be fun,' and I said I didn't want to. But, I don't know, I almost just *did it* because I wanted him to like me and I was so afraid he'd be mad. I keep flashing back to it, wondering if I did the wrong thing. Like I should've let him have his way so he'd keep acting interested in me."

"I bet he *was* mad," I say.

It takes her a minute to answer, but then, "Yeah. Yeah, he wasn't really being nice after that. He goes, 'That's what girls like you do. Why else you think we'd want you here?'

"Then I heard Luke laughing outside the room like he'd heard the whole thing and realized that he was waiting for his turn with me, too. I thought they'd wanted to hang out with me, and there I was with my pants half-undone and TJ was still staring at me, *waiting*. He thought I would do it anyway, like no matter what he said, I'd know what my job was. I guess because of who my mama is or whatever. So I took off, ran away from the house. I started sprinting, like I was escaping, and you know the Akinses live out in the middle of nowhere so I knew it was gonna take forever to get home, not that they were gonna chase after me or anything. I got tired of running after a while so I walked instead."

"Why didn't you call your mama or somebody to come get you?" Tears are gathering in her eyes. I look away because I can't stand it. Can't stop myself from being mad at her for crying over TJ Akins.

"What would I say?" she asks, so soft I can barely hear her.

She's so outrageously tiny and sad. I think back to Ashton, to his pretty mouth, the way he was begging me not to leave him when I got in my car. The way he screamed after me when I almost ran him over pulling out of the driveway. The look of envy that will be on all the other girls in school's faces when they realize that I *have* him. I have him locked down and all to myself at last.

It took so much work. Mom will be so proud.

I could be Evelyn instead, though. I could've been someone just like her if I hadn't figured out the game when I did.

And that's the worst thing I can imagine.

I start the car back up. "I know you live over there off Drafton somewhere, but you're going to have to navigate for me," I tell her.

She swallows audibly. "You won't tell your mom, will you?" My mom, her boss. Mom doesn't think much of the Peterses as is, so I can't imagine it would change her opinion.

"This is between you, me, and the good Lord, Evelyn," I return. For as much of a secret as the good Lord can keep. I tap my fingers again at a stop sign, thinking. As I turn, I finally say, "Your body belongs to you. Definitely not to TJ Akins—no other man either. That decision is yours. No one gets to touch you without your permission, you know?"

She doesn't reply, and it's dumb, but I want to save her from herself. I don't know, like, throw her a lifeline because she so profoundly doesn't get it.

"And listen, no one cares about your feelings, Evelyn," I say, slowly so she hears every word. "No one cares about most girls' feelings, but you in particular, they care even less about. Because you're poor, because they'll call you trash. So if you wanna survive, you better wear that like a badge of honor."

Out of the corner of my eye, I watch Evelyn pawing her bitten-down nails through her hair all slow, pulling the knots apart. She moves like no one's watching her, and I think that's part of her problem.

Girls like us—no one's seeing us until they do. Then they don't look away until they get what they want. You either control it or get destroyed by it.

"Take the right up here," she finally says. "It's a little bit down the road."

I oblige, waiting for her to say something else. She doesn't, though, quiet as a church mouse. And then finally, I ask, "That's everything that happened, right? They didn't hurt you, did they?"

She shakes her head, once, hard.

"You're all right, Evelyn," I say.

"I'm good." Her voice sharpens, fine edges. "The dirt road."

I almost forget what we're doing, the long driveway leading to her trailer sneaking up on me. I stop just in time to make the turn, us both grabbing on to the overhead handles to hang on. I laugh out loud, unable to stop myself, and I see the way she looks at me as if I'm crazed.

Finally, I pull to a stop, my eyes roving over her single-wide. The side of the trailer faces the woods and the siding is peeling, but the yard is tidy. Some Fisher-Price toys peek out from under a set of steps leading up to the front door. I glance back to Evelyn, who's watching me scrutinize her house. "They're just boys," I say to her. "All it takes is a couple of words, a couple of touches, they'll do anything you want." I keep thinking on it. "You gotta make sure they're playing by your rules."

She looks down into her lap and then up at me. I almost see some understanding there. "Thanks for the ride, Reid."

"Thanks for the distraction."

"I'm pretty good at that," she answers, and then opens the door and turns her back to me, walking to her trailer, her jeans hugging her pretty little body, ready to be eaten alive. I can't save everybody.

Or anybody.

Best not to try.

I turn the music back up loud as it will go and take off.

EVELYN

363 Days Since Reid's Death
Now

I jolt awake with my mouth tasting like the inside of a dirty tennis shoe.

The sun is glaring off the windshield, and I raise my hand to shield my eyes, squinting against the light.

I imagine this is what it feels like to be dead. Dried out, hollowed, torn apart. Asleep in the back of an SUV.

Someone shifts beside me and I start, pulling away. But I look down and it's the shape of Ashton Harper and my ribs ache and my arms hurt and I'm so miserably *hungry*.

"Ashton," I mutter. "Ashton, wake up."

He blinks a couple of times and looks at me. I see the way I come into view, clarify, for him. Because at first he didn't know who I was and then he forgot who I was and then he remembered with perfect clarity.

He half sits up, glancing at the time on his phone, then drops back down and closes his eyes. "How do you feel?"

"Empty," I say, which causes him to open his eyes again, examining me closely, before deciding this is nothing more than a hangover description.

"Rise 'n' Shine Diner off the bridge has a pretty good cure for that," he tells me with the confidence of someone who knows that place and this feeling equally well.

"You've talked me into it," I respond, mesmerized by the curve of his cheekbone. By this sick feeling of possibility that is filling me up from the inside out. I should be at McNair Falls High right now, going through the motions.

I'm not. I'm finally *not*.

Ashton climbs over the console like a giraffe who doesn't quite know how to use his limbs yet and flops into the driver's seat. I get into the passenger's seat beside him, pulling my curly hair out of my face, and pick up his sunglasses from where they sit in the cup holder of his car, putting them on. He gives me a sideways grin.

It's no time at all before we've pulled into the parking lot of Rise 'n' Shine. Ashton opens my door before I get to it, and it's shocking to me in that moment, the idea of someone being kind to me without motive. I hate myself a little for caring so deeply.

We sit across from each other in a booth, a sticky table between us. An enthusiastic young waitress approaches our table.

"Shouldn't you two be in school?" she asks, slightly suspicious. Her name tag says *Andi* with a heart over the *i*.

"Probably," I say, and she laughs.

"What can I get you?"

"Coffee," I say. "Lots of it."

"And eggs and bacon?" Ashton says.

"Same."

"Be right back," Andi tells us with a smile. When she goes, Ashton's eyes catch mine and it's like nothing has changed from last night. I love that, the idea that the darkness, the liquor, the circumstances, did not control us: We were a destined meeting across any version of our lives, colliding in the night and starting something that can't be stopped.

"I didn't used to drink coffee," Ashton tells me. "Not until I started drinking everything else. Reid did, though. Black. Not sure she even liked it. I used to imagine she just liked the way she looked drinking it."

I love coffee, maybe more than anything. When she can afford it, Mrs. Brewer always keeps creamers stocked in the office because she knows how much I like them. She'll leave me the festive flavors around the holidays, and I imagine they taste like other people's happiness feels. Like cinnamon and candy canes in the dead of winter, like pumpkins when the leaves turn cold.

"Her mama drinks black coffee," I say then. "Maybe that's why."

"Maybe so," he answers.

Andi drops our drinks off at the table. We go quiet, but in an uncomfortable way—in a way designed to make us take stock of our current situation, so I scramble desperately for something to say, to fix it. "You came in the store and talked to me one time, remember?" I say. "When Reid was in that accident."

Ashton blanches. "I remember."

"Do you remember me?"

He looks across the table at me. "That was a bad day," he says, which is the same as a no.

"She told me before then about you and her."

"Yeah," Ashton says, "we were together then, but not like . . ." He sucks in a breath. "I was afraid how people would react. Afraid how my parents would react." He picks up his coffee. "And when Reid got hurt—let's just say, I didn't know what I wanted until I did. One day, you're floating along in space, convinced you're doing everything right or at least *trying*, and the next, you're in the

69

most intense relationship of your life." He swallows. "But we know all about that, right?"

He means us, I realize. Because we were nothing and now we're here and we killed Dane. It hits me again or for the first time, and something inside me threatens to crack open, but I push back against it. I open my mouth to answer him, but quicker than I can, Andi is placing plates full of eggs and bacon in front of us. And then we both dig in, leaving the topic far behind.

I know true hunger, but this feels different—like being famished. I feel like I ate those Chicken in a Biskits years ago. Like lifetimes have passed since then.

"Where will you go next?" Ashton asks me through a mouthful of bacon.

I hadn't thought about it. I'd only thought about this food and coffee. This feeling of escape.

It hadn't even occurred to me that there was no home left to go to.

"Alex's," I say then, easy, like I've always known.

"Where does he live now?" Ashton asks, plastering ketchup all over his plate.

"In a suburb right outside Atlanta."

Ashton nods and chews and doesn't say anything else.

Alex's. Stupid. I have no way to get to Alex's. I'm not even sure Alex wants to see me; communication between us has become sparse since he drove out of town last May. My chances of getting to Alex's are as small as my chances of getting to the end of the world.

I got caught up in the moment and forgot reality.

Ashton looks up every now and then, watching me as I demolish my breakfast. I feel like I haven't enjoyed a square meal like this in months. And I realize the food tastes so much better because I *know*. I don't have to go back to that house, back to that life, back to the sight of Dane, afraid of what he might do to me or Mama or Kara. Dane is gone.

That single-wide represented nothing but misery for me, and I don't have to go back.

Whatever else might be true, this—*this* is so worth it.

I finish up the rest of the meal and look at Ashton, who's watching me expectantly. He nods at my plate. "Want anything else?"

Before, I would've tried to split this meal into thirds, make it last as long as I could—I let myself not feel the shame of that. I let myself enjoy it. "Maybe later," I return.

He nods with a look like satisfaction and tosses some cash on the table. Standing up, he grabs his coat and shrugs it on.

"Let's go," he says.

"Where?"

"Alex's, right?" He heads toward the door, walking out into the chilly morning, the bell clanging against the door frame behind him. I hurry to follow. He's already in his car, the engine cranked. I get in. He's going to Alex's. He's going with me.

It hits me fast what that means. Leaving this behind. Leaving *Kara* behind, along with everything I never wanted her to be.

Kara's safe now, though, and she doesn't need someone like me. A nobody like me, a constant reminder of the path I want her to avoid. This town is a slow death on a long day. This town is my prison.

Somewhere between nowhere and anywhere but here is in my grasp.

Last night can last forever.

"Wait," I say. "Are you really okay with this? With leaving?"

Ashton watches me. "Am I okay with leaving?" he repeats, and it sounds like a promise on his lips. I hear the yearning, the bone-deep desire in it. Like he's been waiting all these years for someone to say it to him.

It calls out to the deepest desire of my soul, the one I'd been afraid to say out loud.

When I answer him, my voice is low, determined.

"Let's go, Ashton. Let's get out of this shit town before it destroys us both."

He bites into his lip, still looking at me. And then he points his car west and goes.

It only takes ten minutes for us to see the town limits.

REID

244 Rides to School Left
Two Years Before

"You need a ride to school?" Mom asks me, shoving a banana into my hand as I tear into the cramped kitchen. I peel it, hardly stopping.

"Ashton's coming to get me," I return. Mom practically glows. "That's so thoughtful of him."

"Well, he wants in my pants so—" I bite off the top of my banana.

"*Reid*," Mom chides me. "Don't let your daddy hear you talk like that."

My daddy has heard me say so much worse.

Mom tosses a paper bag onto the island for me. "Your car should be out of the shop soon."

I crashed it two weeks ago when the brakes acted up, and all Dad could talk about was how much it was going to screw up his insurance.

"But if you'd rather ride with Ashton, that's fine, too," she continues. How touching.

"It's out of his way," I tell her, breaking off another piece of the banana. I don't even want it, but I need something to distract my hands. My brain is off and running wild.

"He wouldn't mind," Mom says. "The boy can't take his eyes off you." She touches my hair lovingly. "He couldn't stop shaking when he came to see you at the hospital. I thought he'd have crawled into the bed with you if we wouldn't have been there. Moms notice these things, you know."

I know, Mama. That took blood, sweat, tears, and time.

But I see it in her eyes, what she won't say:

I know, too, Reid, and you did good.

A horn echoes from outside, and that's my cue. "Bye, Mom," I say, and I go to kiss her cheek. She grabs my chin with her fingers.

"Be nice, Reid," she tells me.

I jerk back, away, grab the paper bag from her hand, and tail it out the door and into Ashton's Range Rover. He stops when he sees me like he does every day and unbuckles his seat belt, pushing his torso over the console to get to me, our mouths colliding like two trains speeding from opposite directions.

I revel in that moment like I have an addiction and am filling the emptiness left behind from my Ashton-less night.

Finally, miserably, we break apart and he reverses out of the driveway.

"What took so long?" he asks, hitting the gas pedal harder than necessary.

"My mom was giving me lovemaking tips," I tell him, a lilt in my voice. And then I laugh so hard and so loud that it's more like a shriek, and I watch his eyebrows go up and I keep laughing.

He laughs, too, flicking me in the arm. "Your laugh," he tells me, "it's like lightning." He pushes a loose strand of hair back from his face.

I stop. "Lightning?"

"Yeah." I watch his profile, his features perfectly defined. "Sharp, quick, electric. I don't know." He grins at me, self-conscious.

"I guess I just feel like lightning is striking me or something, whenever you laugh."

I watch him, amazed. My whole being had been so focused on getting Ashton Harper for the past year. Not only *getting* him—not sleeping with him or going on a date or spending a drunken night screaming into his voice mail so he'd tell me he was sorry—but *having* him. Because Ashton Harper was everything in McNair Falls and I'd be damned if I wasn't having that.

Call me white trash again, Savannah. I'll have your dream.

And he'll look at me like this.

He'll tell me my laugh is lightning.

"What?" The tips of his ears turn red.

"Nothing." I reach out and rub away imaginary dirt from his face with my thumb. "I just like you, I guess."

Ashton turns into the school parking lot and slams on the brakes so he doesn't hit a girl crossing the road. He swears, loud, and I lock in on the girl. She's skinny, all tight jeans, flimsy top ruffling in the breeze. Eyeliner thick, lips dark, unforgiving red. Her eyes find mine.

Evelyn.

Ashton lays into his horn, and she stares at the both of us for a minute before she continues on. I watch her go.

"Who is that?" Ashton asks me.

"That's Evelyn," I say, looking at him in disbelief. "She's in your class. You know, she hangs out with Alex Reeves. Don't you know her?"

He shrugs. His hand snakes over, fingers looping through mine. He pulls my hand to his mouth and kisses it.

I watch the eyes watching us and sit back and smile.

EVELYN

Seventy-Four Miles to Go
Now

The adrenaline of escape carries us out of the county and across the state line to Georgia. Ashton cranks the music, and we sing along, laughter coming easily between the two of us. The sound washes over me; my fingers move of their own accord, finding the chords.

"You play, huh?" Ashton says, eyes briefly on my hands.

"I guess," I say. "Yeah. I'm not bad." I'm better than not bad, I'm pretty sure, but that feels too personal and I don't miss the irony in that.

"I used to sing in the choir at church," Ashton says.

"You got a nice voice?"

"They needed volunteers and I was easily persuadable." He smiles to himself, some long-ago joke only he knows. Then he says to me, "I didn't know that about you—the guitar thing. You don't really talk to anyone since Alex left."

I laugh. "What do you know about who I talk to?"

"Reid liked you," Ashton tells me. Goose bumps prickle my skin at the sound of her name. She could be here between us, watching us, judging what we're doing.

I wonder what she thinks.

I wonder how many times she sat right in this seat where I'm sitting and stared over at that boy.

"I always paid attention to what Reid liked; it wasn't very much."

"She didn't like me," I say, which I believe. I know.

"Well, you fascinated her, and to Reid, that was the same thing."

I put my hands in my lap, wrap my fingers around each other.

"Fascination and pity aren't the same thing."

"No, they aren't," Ashton says.

"She warned me," I say. "Taught me that sometimes you have to play games with people. Keep control."

Ashton blinks a couple of times. "She was good at that."

It doesn't sound like a compliment.

As we pass by a mile marker, Ashton changes the subject. "Does Alex like living near Atlanta?" he asks.

"Yeah," I say. He'd at least made that clear to me.

"I know you never slept with him." He says it matter-of-factly, throws it right into the open.

It takes what feels like a full minute for me to process what he's said. "Slept with who?" I ask, and I don't even know why I pretend.

"Alex," Ashton returns casually.

"I—"

"It's not a big deal or anything," Ashton quickly says. "I mean, it's whatever." He's flustered, like he said more than he meant to.

"It is whatever. But what do you know about me and Alex?" And then, I can't help but add, "Besides that we didn't sleep together."

He smiles with only one side of his mouth. "Nothing."

"Tell me," I say, "how you know."

Ashton cuts his eyes at me like he wants to say something, but then he just responds: "I know, all right? Alex is gay. I know that."

I feel panic kick in, unsure how to respond. It feels like betrayal to confirm, after years of hiding it, but ridiculous to pretend. Alex's boyfriend lives with him.

Maybe I should tell him we're coming.

But what if he asks why?

"I didn't sleep with him," I say. "So what?" And then, "You haven't been going around, like, telling people Alex is gay, have you? His mama doesn't know."

"I'm not a complete prick," Ashton replies, and his voice is darker.

"You're not a prick," I say. "Everyone loved you." And then immediately wish I could take it back because he hears the *loved* as clearly as I do.

He blinks, shakes his head, and doesn't say anything else, eyes focused on the road. The music fills up the gaping hole left behind.

REID

Three Drinks In
Two Years Before

Ashton's friends are bad at parties.

To be fair to them, which I don't have to do, all parties suck. If parties were as great as everyone made them out to be, people wouldn't have to get so stumbling drunk to enjoy them.

But here I am, at a party at Allen Jay's house, watching this tragedy unfold.

There's a bonfire in the backyard, and all the very important persons of McNair Falls are gathered around it with Solo cups, basking in what will surely be the best years of their lives.

I observe Ashton with them, where he is perfect with his shy, innocent little smile. He seems to shine in the firelight, more golden than the rest of them. The future burnouts and has-beens and Ashton. Surrounded by soon-to-be teen moms and overmedicated PTA presidents. *Mine*.

I'd decided at a party just like this one. I'd been there with Shelley or Kayla or one of those uncomplicated companions who didn't bother me too much, and I'd come to this startling realization.

Ashton Harper was the golden ticket in this boring-ass town.

I'd watched him that night, from the kitchen, the easy way he captured happiness with his smile, the gap in his two front teeth, the way people warmed to him. He was like a bonfire himself, safe and secure and so blissfully uncomplicated.

But sometimes, I caught that look on his face, when he thought no one saw him. Staring off into the distance, searching for something.

Something else.

"Ashton," I'd said the next day at school, "can you help me? I've got a flat."

He'd given me this look like he'd never seen me before, a girl materializing in front of his eyes. He was a good boy, class president, a grade below me. Never missed Sunday school, ran on the track team. His parents owned Harpers Restaurant, a place too nice for the likes of McNair Falls.

He'd known he was all those things that shouldn't interest me at all, and there I was, looking right at him.

I remember him studying the old piece-of-shit Honda my mom had gifted me on my fifteenth birthday, testing out the tire with his toe, then bending down next to it, his fingers playing over the rubber.

I surveyed him from where I was leaning on the neighboring car. "Can you fix it?"

He looked up at me, a sheen of sweat on his brow. "I can, but there's probably a lot of people way more qualified than me for this kind of work at school."

I let my hair fall into my face. "But I didn't ask them. I asked you."

I could've fixed my own tire—Daddy didn't send his girl out in the world without the essential skills. Ashton was too indoctrinated in the McNair Falls reality at the time to even consider that, though. I was a girl, and I needed help. I was a girl who didn't need anyone's help, and I needed *his* help.

I remember he asked me, when he was done: "Why don't you ever talk to me, Brewer?"

And I smiled at that and said, "Because you're so good, Harper. You're *boring*."

He glanced down, as if he knew it was true, and then bit into his lip. "You know, I can actually be really interesting if you ask me the right questions. In fact, it's common knowledge that I am universally loved by everyone."

"Everyone except me, I guess."

"That's what I like to say," he continued. "Universally loved by everyone except Reid Brewer."

And I knew. I knew, right then, that I had him.

After, I'd be standing by myself next to the snack machines and I'd catch his eye as he walked by and he'd step apart from his friends to come talk to me. Then I'd gotten bolder, pulling him away when I wanted him, at school, at parties, at church.

And when Ashton kissed me, I knew Ashton was exactly who I'd thought he was all along, staring at him across the party that night.

I'd freed him.

But right now, the only thing I wanted to free him from was this shit party at Allen Jay's.

"He's a real pretty boy, ain't he?"

I turn around to face Savannah Rykers, McNair Falls's resident self-proclaimed saint. Savannah's mean in that church girl way like if she hasn't been able to save you yet, there's no way in hell God will be able to get the job done.

"Can't complain," I return, lacing my voice with venom.

"Here, you want this?" she asks me, holding out her cup. "I don't really like the taste of alcohol and it's too fruity."

I glance down at the cup in her hand.

"Oh, come on, I'm not trying to poison you," Savannah says, as if that's such a ludicrous thing. "We should make nice. Ashton's my friend, and I know . . ." She takes a deep breath, bracing herself. "I know how he feels about you."

I grab the cup and take a drink, blanching. It's more alcohol than fruit. "I don't wanna be your friend, Savannah," I tell her.

"You might, one day. In case you've forgotten, I've known Ashton a lot longer than you have."

"Reid!" Ashton comes slamming in through the back door, completely oblivious to us talking about him. His hands are instantly on me, the way they always are, and I don't even have to feel smug about knowing it makes Savannah sick. It's so obvious I have him. "I was wondering where you were."

"I was holding her up," Savannah says with a smile.

"No," I correct her. "I was waiting for you to come to me," I say.

Ashton, with his you'll-give-him-anything-he-wants shining eyes, pulls me out into the backyard with all the classmates I've been trying to avoid for years. I don't try to make nice with any of them because I never do. They try to make nice with me because of Ashton, and it makes me hate them all a little more than I already did. Allen is talking to me when I see the blur out of the corner of my eye. Courtney Braden runs into me with the force of a raging bull, spilling my drink all over my clothes. Courtney steps back, looking guilty, and Savannah smirks behind her.

"Reid, I'm sosorryIdidntmean—"

I immediately launch myself at Courtney, but hands grab me back. I know it's Ashton holding on to me, hear the way he says, "*Reid*," like he can't believe what I've done.

"She ran into me!" I yell, fighting back against Ashton to get at Courtney, who is backing away, scared. Her face has totally given her away, bright red. She'd never have the nerve to do that without direction from Savannah. "She did it on purpose!"

"You're being *crazy*, Reid," Savannah says, looking at me like I'm so unbelievable. "Courtney did not mean to do that."

"Reid, it was an accident," Ashton whispers into my ear.

"Let me go," I demand of him. Everyone is staring at the two of us, enraptured. I meet all their eyes, glaring back, daring them to say anything.

Ashton unwraps his arms from around me. I look daggers over Courtney's shoulder at Savannah.

"You're right, Ashton," I say at last. "It's obvious that Savannah didn't *mean* to make Courtney run into me. Savannah's family is known for their accidents. Like when her daddy accidentally knocked up Evelyn Peters's mama. That sure was an embarrassment for all of us. But he didn't *mean* to do that."

Savannah changes colors slowly. From some slight tinge of green to bright red to purple. No one says anything.

Then Savannah turns, shaking her head hard, and walks back toward Allen's house. I see her bend her head down and I know she's crying because everyone knows to never bring up the Peters girl around the Rykerses.

"Savannah, wait, she didn't mean—" Ashton goes running off after Savannah, trying to grab on to her shoulder, a little puppy dog begging for forgiveness, but she shoves him off and then she runs inside and I stand there, simmering with rage like a missile about to leave the planet.

Ashton's gaze burns on me. "*Reid*." His voice is sharp as a knife, but I don't flinch away.

"I'm leaving. Don't *touch* me," I spit out, heading toward the fence and yanking it open to walk around to the front of the house. He follows me.

"It was an accident," he calls from behind. "Why would you say that to Savannah?" That's his problem—he doesn't understand that for girls like Savannah and me, there are no accidents.

I turn on him in the front yard, clenching both of my fists at my side. "Don't be such a *pussy*, Ashton! They're mocking me! They're mocking *us*."

"Why are you like this?" he asks me.

"Why are *you* like this?" I retort. "Every *fucking* time Savannah or one of those other sycophants come around, you're tripping over yourself to make sure their feelings don't get hurt, but do you know how they treat other people? Do you know how they treat *me* when you're not standing right there playing Mr. Fucking Perfect Ashton Harper?"

"I never claimed to be perfect."

But he is *to me*, and that's what makes it all the more fucked up.

"If you don't want to be with me, *don't*. Run back to them if you miss it so much. You always did look so nice in your button-up shirts and ties."

He half laughs, unable to stop himself. "I think that's what you told me when you were trying to get me out behind the worship hall that first time." He takes a tenuous step toward me. "I'm sorry if I embarrassed you, Reid."

I love the way he sounds apologizing to me, so I snake closer to him. "It's true." My voice comes out almost in a whisper. "About the button-up shirts."

"But, Reid, you don't have to flip out like that. You don't have to flip out on *me*."

I trace the lines of his face, pulling his head down to me so I can see him in the soft glow of the lights from Allen's house. "They're always going to treat me like you're too good for me," I say, pressing my face against his chest, trying not to let him see me vulnerable.

It's always a mistake. No one ever likes me after they see me like that.

He tilts my face up to his, eyes on mine. He's an open book, a mix of anger and lust and lust and anger, his fist a ball he keeps curling and uncurling.

"I don't care about that shit, okay?" When my expression doesn't change, he pulls me closer. "None of that matters to me. Not all the stupid politics of this town or our parents or everyone else. It's just you and me." He wants to believe it so bad. Believe it really doesn't matter. "Okay, Reid?"

I push my body against him, our eyes aligned. I'll give him this illusion if it's what he really wants. "Okay," I say.

And just like that, he forgets about all the rest of them and says to me, "Let's get out of here."

EVELYN

139 Days Since Alex Left
Now

The sun is high in the sky when we get to Alex's. It's crossed my mind that he might not be home, but I triple-check the address he'd sent me a few months ago, trying to will his presence into existence.

The townhomes are all lined up with greenery growing outside. They're not the nicest, but they have the air of people who are doing the best they can. People who *care*.

I tell Ashton to hang back as I go to the door and knock.

It takes a few moments for Alex to answer, and when he does, he flings open the door and immediately grabs me into his arms.

"Evelyn? Jesus Christ," he says, his voice garbled.

"Hey," I say, and suddenly I remember so vividly what it is to be known. I bury my face in his plain white shirt and listen to the sound of canned laughter on the TV in his apartment behind him. "Goddammit, I missed you."

He pulls away quickly. "You missed me? Evelyn, I thought you were dead." The word hits me like cold water. *Dead*. Alex's eyes are red rimmed, I see now, like he was crying. "You almost gave me a heart attack. I've been trying to get in touch with your mama for an hour."

My gaze flits to Ashton's car parked on the curb, and I almost bolt right then. But this is *Alex*, my best friend. "What?"

"People have been texting me all morning—people I didn't even know had my phone number—telling me your trailer burned down last night and you were in it as far as anyone knew."

My face goes blank, and his eyes narrow. "What are you doing here, Evelyn?" He glances at his phone, reading a message off the screen to me. "'She's missing. Heard earlier: presumed fatalities.' My mama sent me that, Evelyn."

The words hit me hard, guilt searching for anywhere to take hold in my body. Mama. Kara. I watch a carefully controlled rage under Alex's exterior grow.

"I had to see you," I say weakly. "But you can't tell them."

His eyes search mine.

"I'll explain, okay? Can we just come inside?" I ask, gesturing to Ashton's car. He steps out when I motion for him.

Alex looks from me to Ashton and then says, "What the fuck."

Ten minutes later, Alex and I are standing together in his den while Ashton runs water upstairs, cleaning himself off. Alex is watching me carefully, and I think of the thousand questions he could ask, but he chooses the one I least expect. "What are you wearing?"

He surveys my ratty sweater, my dirty tennis shoes and tight jeans. It's what I've always worn.

"Clothes," I tell him.

His frown deepens like that is the most concerning thing I could've said. "You're *dirty*, Evelyn. What happened? How did the trailer burn down, and what the hell are you doing here with human train wreck Ashton Harper in tow?"

Train wreck. It didn't seem so inaccurate, his out-of-control kinetic energy taking down everything in its path. I remember the day he'd stumbled back into school after Reid had died, the opposite of a ghost—a body with nothing left inside. Alex and I had watched him run into a door, drunk off his ass, and hit the ground without trying to break his fall at all. Allen Jay had put an arm around him and hauled him to the bathroom.

It had made me unspeakably sad. Alex had scoffed and muttered that Ashton didn't even go to Reid's funeral.

"Let me explain—" I start to say.

"Babe, I'm home!" a voice calls as the front door closes in the distance. My heartbeat speeds up.

Alex's boyfriend sticks his head around the corner, and then the rest of him appears, holding a plastic grocery bag. He is tall and thin with light brown skin and hair sticking up wildly.

"Alex? Hey! Who . . . is this?"

"Trey, this is Evelyn—you know, from McNair Falls. Evelyn, Trey."

Trey sets the bag down and strides forward, grabbing my hand in his. "Evelyn, I've heard so much about you. Great to meet you! Sorry, I didn't know we were expecting any guests," Trey says apologetically.

"Neither did I." Alex shoots me a look. "But now we have two of them."

"Two?"

Ashton Harper in all his Ashton Harper glory walks in at that moment, tousling his wet hair absentmindedly, his white T-shirt damp and sticking to his body in an unsettlingly attractive way. He is hungover and shit and beautiful all at the same time, like perfection dipped in pain.

"Ashton?"

My eyes go back to Trey, who is staring at Ashton openmouthed. My pulse quickens again, tension soaking up all the atmosphere in the room.

Ashton pushes his hair back. Every line of his body screams that he doesn't care about anything. "Hey, Trey."

"What are you doing here?" Trey says to Ashton, his formerly kind eyes now home to something much darker.

"He came here with Evelyn," Alex says, gaze traveling from Trey to Ashton to me, confused.

"Alex," Trey says, cocking his head toward the stairs, "we need to talk." And then he walks upstairs from the way Ashton came without another word. Alex glares at me as he goes by in a way that makes me feel small and follows Trey, presumably up to their bedroom.

"Shit," Ashton mutters under his breath.

"What the fuck?" I demand of him because there's nothing else to say.

Ashton looks remarkably calm for someone who just cleared an entire room. "You didn't tell me Alex lives with Trey Watson."

"Because I didn't know. He told me he lived with his boyfriend. How do you know him?"

Ashton looks at me through his lashes in the most practiced way. I wonder if, after Reid, his friends fell for him over and over again every time he apologized for ruining something for them. A car that never stopped crashing but that promised you it would change every time. I want to give him everything; I bet they did, too. "We kind of used to date."

I stare, the word *date* rolling maddeningly around in my mind. Date. "You're . . . gay?" But Reid never would've been a placeholder. No one could ever look at Reid and not want her.

"I'm not gay," Ashton says then. "I like girls." He shrugs. "I also like guys."

"So, you're bi, then? Right?"

"Sure," he says. "Anyway." He shakes his head, water droplets flying.

"Did—did Reid know?"

He chuckles darkly. "Yes, Reid knew. Reid knew everything. That was always fun."

"You told her?"

"No one told Reid anything," he bites back. "She figured it out herself."

"But she didn't care," I say, because of course not.

"Sometimes, she cared," Ashton returns with a humorless laugh. "Sometimes, it was a delightful game to her. And others . . . well, she used to ask why didn't I just admit I wanted to suck dicks and stop stringing her along. But that was Reid."

Was it?

"Anyway, as fun as this has been, I think I need a drink. Enjoy . . . whatever this is."

And he leaves through the front door.

REID

Eight Slow Dances Before the End
Two Years Before

Sometimes, at night, with nothing better to do in McNair Falls, Ashton and I just roamed the roads in his SUV like creepy southern vampires, trapped in the middle of hell and eternity. But we did it with confidence. With purpose, driving from McNair Falls to Ravensway and back, down roads we knew like the back of our hands and roads best forgotten, together and talking and knowing each other better than we knew anyone.

It's probably not a revolutionary thing to say, but there's a whole lot of unplanned pregnancies in small towns because there's nothing else to do.

But then again, maybe there's nothing else to do anywhere.

We're creeping down one of the dirt roads that connects two families through a copse of trees when I turn to him.

"Let's go to the dance," I say.

Ashton's eyebrows almost disappear into his hair. "You mean the Halloween dance? At school?" We hadn't planned to go because of course we hadn't, but I want to surprise him. Surprise myself.

"You know any better ones?"

He stops the car and turns to look at me. "Are you well?"

"Ashton," I say, crawling over the console and close to him, "take your girlfriend to the dance." He grins, and I peck him on the cheek, falling back against the seat. I know what he wants. Dances and pretty girls and happiness.

I can be all those things.

I can be everything. Galaxies. The perfect girl.

And I can bring it crashing down just as fast. But I won't. I promise myself I won't.

The Halloween dance is, unsurprisingly, a travesty. Savannah Rykers has somehow managed to wear something both tasteful and suggestive, which I would commend her for if she wasn't already wearing a human suit as a costume twenty-four seven.

The difference between Ashton and me is everyone loves him and everyone fears me. In fact, I think they fear me even more now that we're dating. Because before I was just a bitch and now I'm a full witch who put him under a spell they don't understand and they're slightly scared I'll do the same thing to them.

They all think they're his friend, and they know nothing about him at all.

"Let's dance," I say, and he's looking at me then like I am magical. A bolt of lightning crashing into his life where before there had only been mind-numbing boredom.

It was so nice to have a challenge for a change.

I grab his hand and loop myself under his arm, then spin again and again. His arm pulls me warmly against him.

I close my eyes, swaying my hips to the beat, and then I open my eyes and glance past him to find Evelyn Peters looking at me. She blinks once quickly, and turns away.

"What are you looking at?" he asks, and I grin back at him.

"You," I say. "Always you."

His hands are on my hips and through my belt loops and

desperate for every part of me, and I think about how he's so wrong for all of them now but so right for me.

"Promise we'll never become anything like the rest of them," he says then, his eyes alight.

"What do you mean by that?" I ask him.

"Predictable," he says to me. Like he's terrified to go back to that.

I press my hand against his cheek. "That's a given."

He leans his face close to me, a chaste kiss, but still I feel it in my toes. *Let's tear the world apart and hold each other close.*

We dance that one and then another, and I start to think some of his golden may be rubbing off on me, the way the eyes follow us.

I wonder if that might be dangerous. If I'll lose some of me in that process.

"I'll be right back," I tell Ashton, squeezing his hand as I walk past him, over toward the side of the gym to where Evelyn is standing in her jeans with her punch.

"Evelyn," I say, walking right up to her, "why are you here?"

She shrugs, as if she didn't even end up here on purpose. As if she didn't have to carefully plan her attendance.

"It's a Friday night," I say, "you could be anywhere and yet you're here."

"Alex thought it would be fun," she says. "I didn't want to be here."

But of course she did. Otherwise, she wouldn't. No one wants to be here and be fine more desperately than Evelyn Peters.

"Do you want to dance?" I ask her. She blushes and that makes me laugh.

"With you?" she asks.

"Well, you could try Ashton, but I'm a much better dancer," I tell her with a smile.

She rolls her eyes. "You don't have to fuck with me, Reid, seriously."

"Oh, come on, Evelyn. Surely you don't care what they think?"

She glares back at me as if insulted, and I know she fiercely cares what they think.

"I like the new look," I tell her, reaching up, my finger skimming the side of her face, down the foundation hiding her clear skin to under her chin, just below her dark lips. I pull my hand away.

She glances down at the floor. "Why are you here?" she asks.

"Because I was bored," I tell her, narrowing my eyes with interest.

She doesn't respond.

Alex Reeves appears at her side. "Hey, Reid," he says suspiciously. Alex's expression is a challenge, and when I look back at Evelyn, I see relief on her face.

It bothers me, something about it. That I might scare her.

Doesn't she remember how I tried to save her?

"I guess I'll see y'all later," I tell them, shaking it off, and then I pick my way through the crowd to Ashton. My eyes find him, lost in the crowd of people who love him, who would happily get lost in him themselves.

I watch him when he catches sight of me, his steely eyes flashing up to my face and his tousled hair falling down onto his forehead—the little gap between his front teeth.

He's exactly what I want him to be.

Allen Jay is talking as usual because he loves to hear his own fucking mouth run. Even Ashton is ignoring him. Ashton holds out a hand to me and I take it, like a girl in a fairy tale.

He pulls me into him, his skin warm as his other hand goes to my back, his body slow and sure on mine.

"You like this song, don't you?" he says, so close to my ear. I shiver. "It can be ours."

My eyes find his and I can't help but laugh. I want to say no, but instead I say, "Okay." I lean closer. "Just promise you'll never tell anyone."

"I won't," he answers. "You'll always know all my slow dances are only for you."

EVELYN

162 New Messages
Now

I follow Ashton outside, and he's in his trunk, fetching a bottle of Fireball. I stare at him, but he doesn't look back. "Ashton," I say, and that gets his attention. "Are you really going to leave me?" I want to say *after everything*, but everything is just words and murder.

He thinks about it, takes a pull from his bottle, and winces. "Last resort," he mutters, brandishing the bottle of amber liquid. "I wasn't going anywhere. It's been a while since I've seen Trey is all."

I cross my arms over my stomach. "Before or after Reid?" I say. It's none of my business.

This almost makes him laugh. "Are you kidding? Do I look like I have a death wish? After." He wipes the back of his hand over his mouth. "Trey hates me." Ashton takes a shot. "And I guess he's with Alex now."

"Do people know about this?" I ask him.

"I know you're not exactly part of the McNair Falls in crowd, but do you really think if people knew about it, you wouldn't? Again, I have a little bit of self-preservation. Guys like us in McNair and Ravensway—we have our ways of finding each other. I told you, I knew you'd never slept with Alex."

"Guess you did," I say.

"It's not my fault Trey hates me," Ashton tells me then. "Just like everyone hates me after a while. It was bound to happen. I think he thinks I was, like, self-hating or wanted to piss my dad off or something, but that's stupid. I was the same piece of shit I have been since"— he shakes his head—"I don't even know when."

"You're not a piece of shit," I echo, and he gives me a pitying look.

"You only remember before," he tells me, and it sounds like he's homesick for it, too.

"They think I'm dead," I say to Ashton then, and his eyebrows rise precipitously.

Alex's front door opens and he calls out, "*Evelyn*, get in here. And bring him with you."

I take the bottle out of Ashton's hand and screw the top back on, tossing it into the trunk. He follows me inside Alex's apartment without comment.

Alex sits us down on the couch in front of him, and I remember how arrogant Alex can be, like he always knows better than you do. His gaze flicks between the two of us. "Well, I might as well ask at this point. Did the two of you do it? Are you the ones who burned down the trailer?"

Trey's walked back in the room, and he's pacing; he's lithe, tall and skinny, more legs than person, bouncing around like he can't contain himself. I imagine Ashton with him, the way I imagine him with Reid, and ridiculously, it gives me comfort.

At least Ashton wasn't always so alone.

"What did you *do*, Ashton?" Trey asks. "What did you do now?"

Ashton rubs his fingers over his knuckles, staring down at his hands. "Her stepdad was hitting her. What do you want from me?"

"He's not my stepdad," I snap.

"Dane?" Alex says, and I hear how sharp his words turn.

"He didn't hit me," I say, even though he did. "He hit Kara."

The memory races through my veins like ice, and I shiver. I see Alex's hand curl into a fist. Trey shoots Ashton a look that almost reads like affection, but Ashton's face doesn't change at all, and I wonder if he's completely forgotten how to feel.

I want to fix him. The most cliché way I've ever wanted to fix anything. I want to fix him.

"You can't just fucking *burn people inside their house*, Evelyn," Alex says. "What kind of vigilante justice bullshit do you think is going on here?" He's an intimidating six foot three, but not much bulkier than Trey.

"What choice did I have? Who was gonna help? Matt?" I ask. I see Matt's round face in my mind, staring at the remnants of my trailer, and I feel sick.

Maybe he'll think I'm dead, too. I wonder if that will hurt him.

"How the hell did you manage to get involved with this, Ashton?" Trey asks, the words of someone who cares too much.

"It's kind of funny," Ashton says, and I turn my eyes to him abruptly because I don't remember much being funny about it, "but I said to burn it down. And she did. I didn't mean it literally."

"What the fuck do you mean, you didn't mean it literally?" I demand of Ashton.

"*Look*," Alex cuts over both of us. "Who did what doesn't matter at this point. This is going to be fine. You go back. You say Dane set the fire. No harm done, right? It's fine."

"Go back," I repeat.

"We're not going back," Ashton says, reading the words from my mind, and saying them with such confidence, they must be true. He glances at me to confirm, and I smile despite myself.

"No, we're not," I say. "Not when I'm finally free from that godforsaken place." Because going back is nothing and going forward is nothing but possibility.

It's *something*.

"I swear to God," Alex says, "I will call the police and report you."

He's bluffing. Some of his reactions may be foreign to me, but this one isn't.

"He's dead, and we're free," I say, and they all wince when I say it, a knee-jerk reaction, because you're not supposed to talk about killing someone with so much ease. "Would you really do that to me?"

Alex twitches, and I see right through him, familiarity coming back that easy. "Evelyn, I need to talk to you," he says.

Alex doesn't grab me, because he knows what it would mean to grab me, but he waits for me to walk past and then we go out into the October air and he looks me over and he looks sad. He gazes at me until we both get lost in each other's faces, and then he says, "What are you doing?"

"What Reid can't," I say, which even I know is insane.

"Reid Brewer is dead, and Ashton Harper is unhinged," Alex tells me. "You've been obsessed with them for longer than I can remember, like there is something special about them, but all they've ever been is two more losers in a town full of them. This has to stop. What do you think you're going to prove?"

I remember sophomore year: a day where we sat on the bus together, watching the two of them. Reid was in front of Ashton right on the sidewalk in bus pickup, her hands resting on Ashton's shoulder, thumbs pressed into spots just above Ashton's collarbones, talking to him seriously. "She's so perfect." The words had slipped out on accident, but they were true.

"She's cheap, Evelyn," Alex had responded, his eyebrows arched. "She acts like she's above all this, but you know what will happen to her? She'll get pregnant and she'll be here forever, just like all the rest of them. You think she's pulling off some magic trick? If Ashton's smart, he'll break up with her before he ends up being the guy who makes that mistake." We watched them disappear. "Then again, that's probably her plan," he said with a laugh. The memory runs through me like ice water.

Maybe that's all I ever was to him, too.

"You were fine to leave me there," I tell him. "You were fine to write me off as another loser lost to McNair Falls."

Anger flashes in his eyes. "You can't stay here. You're acting crazy, and I can't stop you. I won't rat you out, but you can't stay here, not after what you did. He *definitely* can't stay here." Even though his expression is neutral, I can tell how much it hurts him to say it. *You burned down a house, and I'm your only friend, but you can't stay here, Evelyn.*

It feels like the opposite of *I love you.*

"I don't even want to stay here. Not with you."

"*Stop it,*" Alex says. "Stop chasing whatever this is. Let broken people lie. Tell them Dane was drunk and hit you and started a fire and *go home.*"

"Fuck you, Alex," I say, and for the first time since Dane hit Kara, I feel like I might cry. "You *left* me. You know what it's like for me there, and you left me. And now you want me to go back? *Fuck you.*"

"I spent eighteen years there. I did my penance," Alex tells me, trying to justify it to himself.

"Yeah?" I respond. "I can't remember the last time I wasn't afraid in my own home. When I wasn't trapped. Is that not enough penance for you? I'm not going back. I won't let you condemn me to that because it's more convenient for you." Then I push past him back into the house. "Ashton!" I say. "We're leaving." I glance at Trey and continue: "Lovely to meet you."

I go back outside, where Alex is still standing.

"Wait, wait," Alex says, and I see him clearly for a moment. The bony kid who used to let me crawl into his single bed at night and look at my bruises and kiss me on the cheek and tell me it would be all right. That we'd protect each other.

Maybe I do know why he'd want to forget that part of his life.

"You can stay tonight," Alex says. "I'll talk to Trey."

"You don't owe me any favors, Alex," I say to him, and he stares down at me.

"Of course I do," he says, and he leads me back into the house.

● ● ●

I'm on the couch, not even a little asleep, and Ashton is sleeping on the floor, snoring softly.

Ashton's phone buzzes on the coffee table and, unable to help my curiosity, I pick it up. The message is hidden but the backlit screen tells me it's from his mom.

Mama, it reads. 162 new messages. The phone doesn't open its home screen for me. I gaze at it, mesmerized, unable to stop thinking about it. Someone loving you so much that they send you 162 messages, even when you won't open any of them.

I hear footsteps and quickly drop the phone back down, my heart pounding.

"Evelyn," Alex's voice hisses, "it's just me."

He creeps through the den and gestures with his head toward the back patio. I nod, climb out from under the blanket, and follow him.

The back patio is more of a five-by-five slab of concrete overlooking an untidy shared courtyard, closed in by rows of town houses on three sides. Cigarette butts litter the grass, and a couple of nearby apartments have set their trash out by their back doors. Alex and I sit together in the rusty patio chairs, and he lights up a cigarette.

"Trey wants me to quit," Alex says. "I'm trying."

"Aren't we all?" I return, and hold my hand out to him. He hands over the cigarette, and I take a long drag and hand it back.

"You know," Alex says, grinning in the dim light of his cigarette. "Trey used to tell me all the time about how his ex was an alcoholic, emotional vampire. Of course it was Ashton Harper. How'd I not put that together?"

"Did you know about him?" I ask.

Alex shrugs. "You hear things. Vague mentions of a pretty boy in McNair Falls, but listen. If someone is in the closet, I wasn't about to try and drag him out of it."

"He says Trey gave up on him," I tell Alex.

"Well, he doesn't exactly strike me as the most reliable narrator, Ev. I'll help you figure this out if you want. But I don't know him and I don't trust him and Trey doesn't like him being around, so."

"I'm not going to abandon Ashton," I say.

"Why?" he asks, and I don't really have an answer.

"How's Atlanta?" I say instead, and Alex doesn't push me. That's one of the things I've always loved about him. He's fine with letting something sit.

"Not bad. The garage I work at pays pretty well, and Trey is going to the local tech school. I feel a hell of a lot closer to happiness than I did before, but that's all part of the struggle, isn't it?" He takes another long pull on his cigarette.

I tilt my head back, my face toward the night sky. "Just trying to get as close as we can to what we imagine that feeling is."

"What about Kara?" Alex says then.

"What about her?" I ask.

"Your mama ain't exactly the picture of stability, Ev."

"There's people who'll look after them. Mrs. Brewer for one."

"Ah, our patron saint, Mrs. Brewer," Alex says. "She would've sold your soul for a bag of chips before Reid died."

"Don't do that, Alex. Don't mock me. Don't try to make me feel more unloved than I already do."

He smokes his cigarette. "I love you, Evelyn," he says after a minute. "Don't pretend not to know that."

"It's easy to forget," I say. "When I didn't hear from you . . . I've been conditioned to think that way."

He nods in acknowledgment, but doesn't try to justify himself. And then it's quiet between the two of us. I watch his profile, his sharp nose and chin, the way I watched it so many nights.

He never said the words all those times he'd patched up my hand or put ice against my face. He never said *let's kill him*, and some stupid part of me wonders if that's its own kind of betrayal.

"You're going to get hurt," he tells me at last, and I hate him for how sure he sounds about it.

"Good thing I'm used to it, then," I reply, combing back my hair. "And Ashton hasn't even tried anything, if you think . . ."

"I don't," Alex says. "I just—" He sighs. "Be careful, okay? To Ashton Harper, we're nobody, the two of us. Look how he acted after Reid. He didn't even show up for her *funeral*, Evelyn. We don't matter to him at all because he's always got something to go back to. Don't forget that you've got everything to lose. Or maybe you already did."

And then he throws his cigarette down, crushes the filter with his foot, and goes back into the house.

REID

Thirty-Six Bags of Chips Down
One and a Half Years Before

Ashton pulls into the empty lot of Brewers Country Store and stops. I smile over at him, wrapping my hand around his wrist.

"Come on, you're going with me," I say.

"Your wish is my command," he replies, eyes sparkling, and yanks his keys out of the ignition, following me. I unlock the door of the store and then turn and close and lock it behind Ashton. I spin around and focus in on Evelyn, and something wild overtakes me.

"Evelyn, I'm here to lock up," I tell her. She is restocking one of the aisles, but her eyes find me and Ashton, my prize, and I see how carefully she watches the two of us.

"Oh . . . ," she says. "Good."

Mom told me I *had* to go lock up. She didn't have time. *I need your help, Reid. I need you to do what I tell you.*

Mom tells me I have to come home at a decent hour and sit in the third pew at church with her and *for goodness' sake, Reid, can't you just do what everyone else does.*

Because what matters more than appearances in this miserable town.

"It'll only be . . . a minute," I tell Evelyn, grabbing on to Ashton and pulling him into the back office, slamming the door shut and shoving him hard against it and kissing him, hot blood rushing through my veins.

He pulls away. "*Ow*, Reid." He touches the back of his head. "What are you doing?"

"Whatever I want." I press my mouth to his neck, my fingers climbing up the back of his shirt.

He lets me kiss him for a moment, my hands wandering, before he asks, "What about that girl?"

"Evelyn? She could use a little excitement in her life. C'mon." I try to kiss him again.

"Let's get out of here, Reid." He practically sighs my name out. "You told your mom you'd lock up." And his eyes seem to accuse, *after throwing a fit.*

I pull away. "*Fine.* If it's really *that* hard for you to do what I want."

"Don't be ridiculous."

"And if you'd been listening, you'd know I told my mom to fuck off."

"But. Why? Is all this really necessary? I don't bitch incessantly when my parents ask me to help at the restaurant."

"That's so like you, isn't it? Because you're perfect. But we only get to have sex when it's convenient for you, when you want, because you're Ashton Harper and I'm just the girl Ashton Harper likes to carry on with. That's what your daddy says, right?"

He stares down at me, eyes full of disbelief, the same way my mom looked at me earlier. "What does that even mean?"

"So, when you get sick of me, you get to discard me, right?"

"Reid, I would never *discard* you." He pushes his hair out of his face. "Who exactly do you think I am?"

Incensed, I tear past him back out into the store and pick up the first package of chips Evelyn has restocked onto the shelf and throw it at the wall next to Ashton as he comes out of the office.

"Reid, *what are you doing?*" Ashton hurries over to me, puts his hand on my shoulder to stop me from grabbing another bag of chips. Holding me back. Wanting me to be nice.

I swipe my arm across the entire shelf of chips, clearing it.

"*Reid!*" he says.

"What? If my mom wants me to close up the store, close it, I will. Right, Evelyn?" I smile at her because I want to give her a thrill, something to remember. Give them all something to remember. "Isn't that right?"

"Jesus Christ, Reid. She just put these up. What is with you tonight?" Ashton reaches down, trying to pick up a couple of different bags of chips and stuffing them haphazardly back on the shelf.

"Why won't everyone ever *stop* telling me what I *have* to do?" I ask Ashton. "Is there something *so wrong* with me that none of you know what to do with me? Am I embarrassing you?"

"Right now, yes," he retorts, grabbing up another handful of the chips. And it kills me, the way he says it.

Of course I'm embarrassing him.

"It's fine," Evelyn mutters, her mouth barely moving. "Leave it."

"We're not going to leave it," Ashton says. "C'mon, Reid. *Please.*" And I can tell he wants me to be normal, too.

Suddenly, I feel tired. I glance over at Evelyn. *Who are you?* I think desperately, staring at her blank face. *What do you want?*

And I care so much in that moment and hate myself so much for caring.

"You leave it, Evelyn. Tell Mom I did it."

Evelyn nods. I know she's lying. She'll clean it up herself, first thing in the morning.

I'm as terrible as Mom and Ashton think I am.

Deflated, I fall into Ashton and twist in his arms to face him, kiss his cheek.

"Please don't be mad," I whisper. "I'm sorry. I don't know what's wrong with me." He frowns, confused.

Evelyn is watching the two of us, and Ashton averts his eyes from hers. I feel him do it.

"Can we just . . . close this place down?" he asks Evelyn, still not exactly looking at her, like that would be too much work for him.

She nods and hurries to lock up the register.

Later, we wait silently next to Evelyn until her mama's boyfriend drives by to pick her up. Ashton and I climb together into Ashton's car, and he looks over at me.

"Don't give me that shit about being mad at your mom. Why are you carrying on? What the hell was that?" Ashton says because he knows me now. Knows when I want to impress somebody because I never want to impress anybody. "Who is she?"

I gaze blankly out at the parking lot, not looking at him. I remember him not knowing who she was all those months ago, too. But she's Evelyn. Why doesn't he see her?

She's the most interesting person in this godforsaken town. She doesn't give in to it. She *never* gives in.

"Nothing," I say. "She's nobody."

EVELYN

$12,000 Credit Limit
Now

I wake up to the sound of pans clanging against each other in the kitchen. "Where is it, Ashton? Where the *fuck* is it?"

Something falls and bangs against a counter, clattering as it hits the floor. I sit up straight, wipe my bleary eyes. Someone is mumbling.

"You couldn't even do *this* right, could you? Just not fuck up everything for one night?" That's Trey, I think.

"Please, Trey." And that's Ashton, quiet, the sound of despair.

Footsteps are on the stairs. It's dark outside, the sun not up. I pull the blanket off me and rise. Trey and Ashton are standing close to each other, Ashton with his head down, Trey practically rippling with anger.

"Ashton, get the hell out of my house," Trey says.

I step forward into the kitchen. "What happened?" I ask him, and Trey looks at me but Ashton doesn't. Alex appears behind me.

"Tell them," Trey says, staring at Ashton.

"Trey," Alex says, and he steps around me and closer to Trey, drawing the line.

"I finished off a bottle of vodka I found," Ashton finally says, looking up at Alex. "I thought it would be okay."

"The fuck you did, Ashton. It was *one* night," Trey responds, sounding like he's continuing an argument he thought he'd finished a long time ago. "Get out."

Alex's eyes flit over to me.

"You heard me," Trey says. "I have to get ready for class." He doesn't look at me as he walks through the kitchen and up the stairs, slamming a door behind him at the top. My eyes water, stupidly. Ashton runs a hand through his hair, slowly, shakes it out, and makes his way to the front door.

That's it.

Alex and I gaze silently at each other across the space of the kitchen. I know him like I know me, broken and lonely and wondering where it ends.

"I guess this is bye," I say to him. He grabs me into an embrace, practically clawing at me as he pulls me close, and I try not to falter. We stay like that for a few minutes before he pulls away, stuffs a twenty-dollar bill into my hand.

"Don't go where you can't come back, Evelyn," he says to me, and I see the tears he tries to stop from falling. Before I can look at him any closer, he wipes both eyes and hurries around me and back upstairs.

• • •

The sun rises up in the sky as we sit in the Atlanta traffic. Cars are at a standstill as far as the eye can see—lanes and lanes of human misery.

My mind keeps running over what Alex said last night. About Ashton having something to go back to.

That's the thing about being the right kind of person. There's always more chances for you.

"You've barely said anything since we left," Ashton says, breaking the silence. I startle.

"What do you want me to talk about?" I ask.

"I don't know," he tells me. "Anything at all. You're easily the most interesting person I've met in the past year."

"But you didn't just meet me," I say, my words slow. "You've known me for ten years."

It takes him a moment before he answers, "Right."

"You couldn't," I finally ask, "control yourself for one night? Not break into their liquor?"

He has the decency to look cowed. "I really didn't think Trey would freak out like that," he says. "I'm sorry. Really. I know Alex is your best friend."

"Yeah," I finally say, still with a feeling that he *did* know. "It's okay."

It's quiet in the car before Ashton starts moving again. He's fished some protein bar out of the console of his SUV and is ripping the package with his teeth. He bites into it. "God, I'm so hungover."

He proffers the bar to me. "Do you want some of this?"

"Yeah," I tell him mechanically, and he breaks off half and hands it to me.

The bar tastes like a tire. A peanut butter tire. I chew it like the world's most essential substance.

"Where are we going?" Ashton asks me, like I have any idea.

We're running. Because whatever Alex said, there's nowhere for us to go but away. We're driving wide open on a highway to nowhere, and I'm riding shotgun. "To hell?" I guess.

"There's a Four Seasons in Atlanta," Ashton tells me.

"What?"

"Let's get a room," he says. "Have you ever been to a Four Seasons before?"

"I can't afford a room at the *Four Seasons*," I tell him. I can't even afford one season.

"Well, I've got a pretty high fucking limit on my credit card and you're dead at the moment, so. What do you say? Why don't we make the most of it?"

"How high?" I ask. I can't help it.

"I mean, high enough that I've never hit it."

"You don't know?" I continue on. "Oh my God, you're so rich, you don't know how much money you have?"

He laughs. "We're not *rich*, Evelyn."

"Your house is huge," I can't help but say.

"It's"—he shrugs—"got a lot of land, but we're just, like, *average*. My parents have debt, and, like, a mortgage." He fiddles uncomfortably with the steering wheel. "If it weren't McNair Falls, you'd get it. We're getting by like everyone."

You might think you're just getting by, I don't say. *But you're not everyone.*

"Well, if I prayed every night, that's what I would ask for." I put my hands together, mocking him. "Dear Ashton's God, please make me average, just like him."

"I'm gonna get you a room at the Four Seasons, Evelyn Peters. And you're gonna be so average, it'll be a night you never forget. One day, you'll look back and say, 'Remember that mind-blowingly average night that Ashton Harper gave me?'"

I laugh, watching him, and his easy smile suddenly matches my own. He said I was dead, but by that, he means *free*. Who cares if I don't have money—I have him. As if emboldened, he turns up the song on the radio, playing through the Bluetooth on his phone.

"I like this song," I say after a minute.

He half smiles. "Me too."

REID

Fifteen Fights In
One and a Quarter Years Before

"I've found the perfect song." Ashton says it with the confidence of someone who has, like, solved world hunger. He flips through a playlist on his phone, finally stopping at the song, and some man starts crooning because of course he does—everywhere in America, there's some man crooning like he understands pain. Ashton drives in silence for a few moments and I see him watching me, like he's expecting something, like there should be some fucking epiphany and I don't even know why it drives me so crazy, his surety, but it does. I hate him for it like I hate everyone for everything.

"That's so like people, isn't it? To decide there's some objectively great song and inform you of that fact like their musical taste is so superior to everyone else's."

Ashton hits the next button on his phone.

"Jesus. Fine."

It was stupid. If I was smart, I would take it back. But, honestly, it frustrates me so much sometimes, to have gone from being a *me* to a *we* so quick that I barely saw the transformation happening. Like now I should just agree with him on his great song choice and congratulate him for being himself, the way everyone else does every day.

He pulls up in front of the school, his car skidding into his spot as he slams on the brakes. He turns off the engine and puts his hands back on the steering wheel, staring straight ahead.

"What the fuck," I say.

Finally, he unbuckles his seat belt and turns to face me. "Okay. What's wrong with you?"

The same thing as ever seems like too obvious an answer.

"I'm *bored*," I say.

"Fine." He shrugs. "Be bored, then. Choose to be bored."

I want to tell him to fuck off, but I don't, and then I don't know why I didn't. He scrapes his hand through his hair once twice three times and stares out the window in front of us again.

Outside in the parking lot Courtney Braden is hanging on to Dante Martinez and they are both laughing at something and I see the way Ashton's eyes are narrowed in on the two of them and their stupid fucking happiness. Courtney is smiling up at Dante, whose eyes are glinting like firelight. I watch them and I watch him and it burns through me like gasoline.

"Why are you staring at her?" I demand. I'm raring for a fight.

And he jumps. He does jump like he was caught doing something he didn't realize he was doing, heat rising up his cheekbones, and I can't believe it. That he was staring at someone else when I'm *right here*, and it's Courtney, of all people, and she's so fucking dull.

"Reid, why do you do this?" he finally asks. "Why do you hate my music? What's the point of hating everything?"

And I hate that he asks me the question Mom is constantly asking me, and I hate that sometimes I ask myself that, too.

I open the door and grab my bag, holding his eyes as I do, and

I scream at him like I mean it, abuse him with every terrible word I can think of. *You're such a fucking prick* and *I swear to God* and *I wish you'd just stop*. Courtney and Dante look at us and in the distance, so does everyone else.

I slam the door and stalk away.

EVELYN

Ninety-Three More Messages
Now

Ashton's mom's name is on his credit card so he books the room as Pam Harper, and we check in on his phone before we even pull into the parking garage.

He looks at home as we stroll into the lobby, but I'm amazed by it—the tiny flutes of bubbly *something* handed out to guests as they check in, the man in the tux playing the piano. It's easy for Ashton to ignore since he looks like he could belong anywhere, to anything.

"I'm going to tell them I need a new key card at the front desk," he says, handing his things over to me and nodding toward the elevator. He puts his phone in my hand and grins at my surprise. "Saw Allen pull this off in Myrtle Beach one time. They don't ask questions if you have the same last name as the person who booked the room."

"Devious," I say, and I can tell that he likes that. He goes toward the front desk, and I flip the phone over in my hand, seeing it's unlocked, signed into some social media app. Message after message lights the screen.

Where are you???

are you ok, man

call me

The names are endless as I scroll. Ashton Harper never does anything right, but people still care so desperately.

And I stop when I see the wall of messages that have come through from Allen Jay.

Sheriff Rykers came by my house asking about you and Evelyn Peters.
You need to get home now.

"Here you go." I jump and hit the phone's home button, blocking it with my body, as Ashton approaches, handing me a plastic bag. "You good?"

I nod, quickly handing the phone back over to him.

As we wait for the elevator, I notice a felt board next to it that reads GREENVIEW CHARITY SOCIETY MASQUERADE BALL TONIGHT. I reach out to trace the letters.

"What does that mean?" I ask Ashton.

"Some rich people are having a masquerade ball," he tells me.

"I thought those were made up." I feel Ashton watching me. "It doesn't feel real," I say.

"What?"

"All of it." I look at him, smiling. "Being here. Not being in McNair Falls."

"Do you want to go?" he asks, the idea apparently as simple as the words leaving his mouth. "To the masquerade ball thing?"

"Go?" I repeat.

He smiles at me, bright. "Unless you got a better bad idea."

I wonder if he's trying to make up for last night. I wonder if he's going to abandon me and go back, just like Alex told me.

This will end, and he'll leave me for dead like the rest of them.

At least this time, I've got a head start on the dead thing.

"Fine," I say. "Let's go, then."

REID

Two Minutes After the Bell
One and a Quarter Years Before

It's so stupid, but I don't realize it for a few days.

He wasn't looking at Courtney; he was looking at Dante.

It hits me as I stand there, gazing down at them from opposite the parking lot, watching Ashton talk to him. His eyes alight, his body turned into Dante completely. That's how I'd known, the first time, known how much he wanted me.

It's how I'd known how much he didn't want Savannah.

I watch them for a moment more, until Dante turns away with one last wave of his hand. And then Ashton stands there, a beat too long, the way you do when you are desperately analyzing a conversation, and he gets into his car, too.

I don't move from my spot on the hill, where I'm standing, overlooking the school. I'd skipped my last class and taken a walk, the incessant hum of thoughts running through my head finally too much to take. Ashton will sit in his car for a while, waiting for me, wondering where I am.

He drives me to school almost every day now. We never talk about how it's out of his way.

I watch Evelyn Peters in the parking lot, too. She always rides the bus, so I wonder if she missed it. Ashton should ask her if she needs a ride.

He won't, but he should. He'd never think of Evelyn. She knows that; I know it.

He'd never think of either of us at all if I hadn't forced him to. He would've done exactly what was expected of him. Never missed Sunday school and married Savannah Rykers and boxed up his thoughts about Dante into a place he'd never have to touch again, at least not *now*.

I wonder if that would've made him happy.

Evelyn's still standing there in front of the school, and Savannah's dad pulls up in his police car. Savannah isn't around yet, and I watch Sheriff Rykers, the way he slows and stops. The way he inches forward again and rolls down his window, talking to Evelyn.

No, I imagine she's saying. *No, I'm fine. I'm fine. I'm fine, really, it's fine.* And finally, she turns and goes back into the school just to escape from him. Not long after, Savannah bounds out and climbs into the car and they leave.

The parking lot is clearing out fast. Ashton's car sits there, standing sentry.

I decide to walk home.

EVELYN

One Soul Down
Now

I hear Ashton through the wall in the bedroom, watching TV at a low volume. I can't stop staring at myself in the beautiful bathroom mirror, turning ever so slightly to check how I look from the smallest of different angles.

I showered, dried my hair, put on a big fluffy white robe. Used shampoo and soap that were made for people more important than me. Every item here is the nicest thing that I've ever touched, and somehow, it makes me look more beautiful and more dangerous; even the lighting itself, like a hidden power, is alive now, emanating from me. I love the transformation.

You killed Dane, I think, and then I shiver.

The thing is, you take enough hits over the years, you think they've stopped hurting. You open up the same wound enough times, maybe it gets a callus. Maybe you become invincible, your skin thick.

But the other parts of you—the real parts—they don't heal. They get bloody and raw and angry until you want to see something else.

See someone else.

See someone who did something. That's the girl looking back at me. The girl who made sure what happened to her could never happen to her sister.

Wouldn't I rather be her?

Mama never took us to church, but I know enough to know one of the major rules is not to kill people. That it damages your soul, and that's the most important part of you.

I don't care so much about my soul anymore. I've already chipped away enough of it.

Ashton, though. I think he might care about his soul.

Mama will be upset because she loves Dane and she thinks he loves her. Mama's been short on that since Matt left her all those years ago. I think that's when she lost the energy to love me, too. Everything else in her life was so time-consuming, I can't help but somewhat forgive her for forgetting me. Besides, I'm not sure I even love her anymore, as much as I want to. Kara is easier, but me, I'm complicated. A reminder of too many bad times, too many men she regrets. And she dived into that regret a long time ago, decided to live there.

Dane was easy, too, until he wasn't. But still better than me—cleaner than me.

Maybe she can finally figure it out for Kara and her. People in town are churchgoing. They'll pity her. She could sell the land, or maybe she'd get enough money for a new trailer—that one was starting to fall apart anyway. And if it's only Kara she has to look after—well, that puts the complications down to one.

I look at myself, and I think it's for the best for everyone. There's nothing so important about me as to be missed.

Dead, I can be anyone. I can be *this*, this dangerous girl who laughs freely, crashes balls, burns down what hurts her, and runs without looking back.

This girl, who Ashton Harper can't get enough of. I bet Reid would've liked her.

Finally, I go back into the bedroom—where Ashton and I have littered every surface with things. Clean T-shirts and makeup from CVS, a dress and makeshift menswear from a thrift store down the road, and cheap masks from a pop-up Halloween shop we found. I've never seen anyone spend as much money at one time as Ashton just did.

Ashton is half-asleep on one of the double beds. I grab the dress and the rest of the CVS bag and take it back to the bathroom. I dump the contents onto the counter, carefully organizing them in the way I like, the way I always did at home. I crouch down, sort through my clothes dumped onto the floor. Clothes made for my skinny arms and legs, my bra gone a faded color. I look back up at the girl in the white robe, and I pick up the foundation and spread it over my face, watch the way I fade.

It doesn't take long to make a skinny, insecure girl disappear, I've found. Hide yourself. Arm yourself. Turn your flaws into strengths, highlight your inadequacies until it looks too intentional not to be beautiful. Paint yourself dark and angry and pretend you could be.

Don't be who you are. Be someone better.

I step back and give myself a cold, anemic smile. The girl in the mirror gives it back, but somehow it looks fuller.

I like her, I decide. I've always liked her more than me.

She doesn't look like a killer. Or maybe she looks exactly like a killer.

Maybe that's why I like her.

I slip off the robe and slide into the dress, and I could be anyone but me.

I brush my fingers through my wild hair, surveying myself one last time, and then I go back into the other room. Ashton has gotten up, dressed. He glances over at me, straightening his tie. "Look at you," he says, which is not a compliment, and I start to wonder if he's lost the ability to say anything kind.

"Look at me," I repeat, and that makes him smile, like he knows. "Masks, I believe," I say, and toss one over to him. He catches it, and we both tie the black masks over our faces at the same time, twin bringers of darkness.

"You ready?" he says, and he offers his hand then. I take it, and together we leave into the night.

REID

Forty-Three Minutes Before the Rain
One and a Quarter Years Before

The sky is hazy.

I stare up at that dull color, at the clouds barely containing the rain, and wait for nothing. I brace my toes against my shoes on the porch of Ashton's house and pet his dog. He sits one step above me, stretching out his long, bare legs, a crappy old pair of athletic shorts riding up over his thighs.

"Why are you so quiet?" he asks me.

"I'm tired," I say.

"You're never tired, Reid," he says, like someone who knows me better than I know myself. I settle myself on one of the lower stairs of the porch, leaning back against his legs. He checks his watch. "I need to get ready for work soon."

"Boring," I say.

"My parents probably won't accept boredom as an excuse for not showing up for my shift." The dog licks my face so I push him away. He goes to Ashton. So much easier to get love from. Typical.

I glance back at him. "You're not going to, like, work there forever, are you?" I ask.

He shrugs. "I don't know," he says. "I guess it depends. Maybe after college, I'll decide that's what I want." His eyebrows go up. "Why?" he asks. "What do you want?"

"Nothing," I say. I smile at him. "That's the beautiful thing about me."

"Reid," he says, nudging me with his knee, a playful tone in his voice. "You have to have some idea of what you want, after all this is over. You're going to graduate next year."

I'll graduate without him, he means. The year before he does. And what do I do with that? Sit around for a year in McNair Falls and wait for him to finish high school? Go to the same old shitty parties and drive around the same old haunted dirt roads, waiting for peace of mind? The two of us come back one day and run Harpers Restaurant and live in a house and send our kids to McNair Falls High?

That's the ultimate victory here, isn't it? That's winning.

I don't say anything, and he doesn't push. A few more long moments pass. "Do you know who I like?" I say, staring up at the sky. I rub my hand up and down his leg, playing against the dark hair on his white, white skin.

"No one?" he guesses.

"Don't be cute." I pinch him with my nails, and he jerks away. *"Ow!"*

"I like Dante Martinez," I tell him, rubbing his leg again, feeling the tension in it. "He has sharp features, you know? High brows and a strong chin."

"What the hell are you talking about?" Ashton asks me, suddenly annoyed.

"Don't play stupid, Ashton," I say, my voice like a whip. I look over my shoulder at him until he cracks, breaking eye contact. I turn back around.

"Great," he says, his voice flat. "You caught me."

I glance back one more time at him, and he is determinedly looking anywhere but at me.

"What do you think it is about certain people?" I ask him. "That we always want what we can't have." I swallow. "What about me?"

"What do you mean?" Ashton says, still not looking at me. "I looked at someone else. Like you've never done it. I love you, Reid. I want you. Only you. The rest is just"—he shakes his head, as if shaking the thoughts away—"noise."

I think about it. Lean my head against his leg, turn my face and kiss the inside of his knee. "I love you, Ashton Harper. You know that, right?" I tilt my head back to look at him, his eyes staring down at me, dark and angry and confused because it's what I haven't said before. But now—today with a storm about to fall—I can't stand the idea of him wandering. I hang on to him tighter. "You have to promise not to leave me."

His hand tangles in my hair. "I won't leave," he says, and it's so stupid, but I believe him.

EVELYN

Six More Glasses of Champagne
Now

Sneaking into the masquerade ball isn't hard. Look the part and you are the part. Before, I'd been so determined to color inside the lines drawn for me. I'd felt completely tied to that enforced reality, to surviving, even if that meant suffering. But now I see that whole construct was waiting for me to grow into someone better, to tear it all apart with my bare hands. That I was one lit match away from the rest of life.

And if this is the way it feels, why would I ever look back?

There's no reason for a place like McNair Falls, and the people there don't even know it.

"Champagne," Ashton says, and grabs two glasses off a tray that floats by. I take a sip and shiver from the shock of carbonation, setting it down on the nearest table. Music plays—a loud pulsing beat—and drunk adults laugh, carefree.

"I've never seen anything like this," I say to Ashton, and decide not to feel stupid. The mask shields so much of his face that I have a good chance to look at his eyes, the way they're dark and stormy and so, so distant, even when he's looking right at you.

"Enjoy it," he tells me. "You deserve this." I think he means it. Then he downs his champagne. "Let's dance."

"Okay," I say, and he puts down his empty glass and grabs both my hands, leading me to the dance floor, and I like that the song isn't too slow, that he spins me around and around like a top without ever getting too close.

The distance fades, though, as the songs go on. Near, but not close. Close, but not touching.

He makes me feel not so afraid.

I remember him and Reid one time, at that Halloween dance Alex had dragged me to, the way they'd shown up halfway through in T-shirts and shorts, danced together with abandon. I hadn't been able to take my eyes off them.

Maybe that's what it could be like for people when they see us.

The women's dresses catch the light as the waiters carry around the trays of drinks, pale gold and pink and amber.

It's like a secret. A fairy tale world. Walk through the wardrobe, burn down the evil king, and here it was on the other side. Smiling girls and beautiful boys and dresses that twinkle like stars in the night.

Happiness.

Maybe it was always this easy.

• • •

I keep snatching up hors d'oeuvres as the waiters bring them around. First a delicious stuffed mushroom, then a tiny pimento cheese finger sandwich, and lastly, a small perfect crunchy bite of something I've never seen before. I make it my mission to taste every hors d'oeuvre in this building.

At the table next to us, a woman is not fond of her friend Phyllis, from the sounds of it. Ashton has crashed from his dancing fast; now he steadily drinks his feelings away and sometimes I catch him looking over at me.

A slow song comes on, something sweet and simple about

loving someone, living a life together, and I see the couples get closer to each other.

"What about another dance?" I ask, elbow on the white tablecloth, chin in my hand.

Ashton listens, then shakes his head. "I don't do slow songs."

I return my gaze to the dancers and don't say anything.

Another drink down and I can't stop myself from saying the thing that's under my skin. "Did you only want to come for the free drinks?"

He's quiet, swirling the liquid around his glass, not meeting my eyes. "No. I wanted to come because of you," he says finally. "I thought it might make you happy." He swallows. "And I guess—to see if we could do it again?"

"Do what again?"

He stays focused on the white tablecloth in front of him. "Forget."

I don't look away from him. "And?"

"It worked for a little bit, but—" He shrugs, finally catches my eye. "I'm scared. About opening myself up because really bad shit happened last time I did that, Evelyn, and now we're here."

"So," I say, "talk to me."

"I can't."

I push in closer to him. "Why not?"

"Because you talk and you fuck and you change." He sighs. "And it's never possible to go back to who you were before."

"I don't know what that means," I tell him. "That's not what this is."

"I know," he says. He stares at his champagne glass, as if somewhere inside it, there might be an answer. "I know. So let's just leave it be."

REID

Ten-Point Buck
One and a Quarter Years Before

"Evelyn," I say, leaning over the counter of the country store. "Daddy told me to bring you some venison. He shot a ten-point buck last week."

"That's nice of him," she says, head down.

Daddy hadn't strictly *told* me to do that. He'd said he was gonna donate some of it, so I figured I'd do it for him.

I'd thought of Evelyn and her wide eyes and how she needed someone.

Isn't that absurd?

"How are you?" I ask. She looks up, confused at the question. "Fine?"

"Are you not sure?" I lean farther forward, getting closer to her.

Those same wide eyes find mine and I see the way her mask drops ever so slightly for a moment and she finally says, "I'm never sure."

"Y'all got enough food?" I ask, and it's too personal and she's too proud to say otherwise, but I still stare, running my fingers over the counter.

"I'm standing here, aren't I?" she says, which we both know is a non-answer.

"Want me to buy you some cigarettes?" I ask. It's what I do. Press and press at the bruised spot, waiting to see what will happen. "I've seen you smoking them out back."

"What do you want from me?" Evelyn says like a sharp-tongued little thing. It's the first time I consider she might see through me, but I brush that aside.

"Look around," I say. "It's not like I've got a whole hell of a lot of other people to talk to around here."

Her eyes actually briefly traverse the store like she can't believe that there isn't even one person more interesting to talk to in here than her.

"Alex is cute," I say, and when she gives me a blank look: "Your boyfriend?"

"He's not my boyfriend," she responds without offering up any further information.

"*Ev-ve-lyn*," I say, drawing out every syllable of her name. "I mean no harm. Really." I hold up my hands. "I just wanted to talk."

She half shrugs, hiding her face behind her hair.

"I know how much shit Savannah Rykers gives you at school. You know I don't think anything of it, right?"

"Do you think anything of anything anyone says, Reid?"

A total bullshit question. It sounds like something Ashton would say. She reminds me of him in some ways, while being nothing like him at all. "No."

"Tell your daddy thank you," she says. "For the venison."

"You don't need to be scared of me," I say. Wonder if it's a lie.

Maybe fearing me is exactly the right thing to do.

"Why shouldn't I?" she says. Her eyes are like staring into a window, the kind boys like. And they take me all in. Find me.

"Because you're not like them."

Her answer is defiant. "Yes, I am."

Liar. She knows. "This town is shit," I tell her because I know she agrees.

"It's empty," she tells me. "Like me. You're not."

She says it without a trace of irony; like a fundamental truth. I don't know what to say and I don't know what to say and then I say, "You can talk to me, you know. I never told anyone. About TJ. You know that, right?" *I can help you*, I don't say because I can't.

She stares, and it's like she's looking at me for the first time, dark eyes and dark lips and all. "I know," she says.

And I leave, feeling like I probably shouldn't have said anything to begin with.

EVELYN

Three Kisses
Now

The party is getting loud. A woman falls into me, splashing me with her drink, and forgets to apologize. Ashton hands me a napkin. I desperately want him back to before.

"Why are they like this?" I ask him.

"Because they hate their lives just as much as we hate ours," he tells me, and it sounds true. "We're all miserable. Some people wear it better."

This was supposed to be fun. Welcoming me into my new life. Not *this*.

I nod at the new drink in his hands. "You've got a problem, you know that?"

"Yep," he says.

"You didn't do that before, did you? Before Reid died?"

"Drink?" He blinks. "Not really."

I can't stop myself from saying it: "What would make you right again? Like you were before?" I ask him. "If Reid were alive?"

He almost spits out the drink he's sipping. "If Reid . . . were alive?" he finishes.

"That's what started all this, right? The self-loathing, self-destruction tragedy thing?"

He rubs his face with his long, slender fingers, pressing them in so hard to his forehead, it's almost violent. "I don't know, Evelyn," he says, words coming out like the longest sigh. "I think it started a long time ago, way before Reid. Maybe it was always inside me. Everything was right, supposedly, but I didn't *want* that. I was never happy.

"I was always broken. Reid was just the wrecking ball that brought it all crashing down."

I frown. I hear what was unsaid. Reid being alive wouldn't make him happy.

And something inside me shifts.

"It's not that I just didn't sleep with Alex," I say to him. I look down at the table, pressing my dirty fingernail against the pristine white tablecloth. "I didn't sleep with any of them. I didn't even kiss most of them, not unless it was the only way to get rid of them. I . . . lied and pretended I did because I thought it would be easier that way.

"It was only three of them actually," I say, my voice going low. "I only kissed three of them." It flashes back through my mind, each and every one. I close my eyes against it and open them to Ashton's pretty face.

His brow creases. "What are you talking about?"

I recover, continue. "I know it made a nice story for Savannah. I was a slut, just like my mama before me, but . . . I guess I'm not. A slut. Whatever that means. I never let any of them touch me. Just let them think that maybe they could."

Ashton licks his lips. I can tell he doesn't know how to respond.

"It was exhausting. Faking my way through every boring conversation, pretending with every idiotic face."

"You've . . . ," he starts to say, then goes red, "never . . ."

"God, no. I've seen what it does to you. Men are a fucking

drug you get addicted to, and if I'd let myself even wonder what it's like, I'd be as doomed as everyone else in my godforsaken life."

Ashton looks up at me from under those dark eyelashes. "Even now?"

"Now?" I ask, pretending to be as carefree as I want to be. "I can do anything now."

I almost wish I could snatch the words out of the air as soon as I say them, stuff them back in my mouth and swallow them. Because I don't even know what I mean. I don't know what I want.

I'm still scared to want.

But, Ashton—he doesn't look like he thinks anything about anything at all. "This is so fucked up," Ashton says to me, the words long and drawn out in his beautiful accent, "but I think, since Reid died, this is the first time I've really felt . . ." His eyes shine. "*Anything.*"

And that's it. That's why he's here with me. To *feel*, even though that still hurts.

"They're really letting anyone in this year, aren't they?" A voice interrupts the thoughts running through my head. It's not Phyllis's friend. It's a girl in a flowing black gown that I would guess is significantly more expensive than my secondhand dress, staring over at me openly.

My heart is pounding from the conversation with Ashton, and I don't want him to look at me, to see what she sees, some girl faking a life that doesn't belong to her.

He wants to be back in the woods again. I do, too.

I stand up from my chair, walk over to the girl. "Hello," I say, taking a deep breath. She jumps back, a manicured hand flying to her chest.

She'd meant for me to hear her, but I was supposed to take it.

135

I always have before. I smile at her, like I've been practicing for a long time. Like smiling at Tyler McBee. "I don't think we've met."

The shock is clear even through her mask. "No, I don't believe so."

I grab a glass of champagne from another one of the endlessly circulating trays that just keep coming, like magic. I sip it.

"I'm not sure what you want," the girl says, and she glances at her friend. I'm not sure what I want either. I keep chasing fearlessness, a feeling outside myself.

If everyone looks down on me, I'll remember what I did.

How powerful I can be.

The girl maneuvers around me. I hold out my arm.

"Wait," I say. "Don't go—"

The girl blinks rapidly. I dump out the glass of champagne on the floor right in front of her, right onto her perfect shoes.

"What the fuck?" she demands.

"Now what?" I ask the girl in the black dress, a dark cackle escaping me. A man seems to appear out of thin air beside her, staring down at me. I lose my nerve just as fast, backing away from him, as if by instinct.

"Get over here and get your bitch!" the man calls to Ashton, who pushes himself up from the table faster than I've seen him move in two days, and then he's next to me.

"What did you say?" he snarls.

"Ashton, please don't—"

"I said, take out your trash," the man says. I suck in a breath. Ashton launches himself at the guy, shoving him. He almost topples over in the process, clearly too drunk to fight. The guy takes a swing, and I try to grab Ashton and pull him out of the way. "Please pleasepleasepleaseplease," I hear myself saying.

A hotel employee runs over, putting himself between Ashton

and the man, who is red faced and breathing hard. The woman is crying now. And of course this is her fault, but in the world we live in, it's never her fault.

"Apologize," Ashton keeps demanding, yelling over the employee's arm at the man, who glares back, unmoved.

The hotel employee puts Ashton into an armlock and escorts him out of the ballroom and into the hall. I hurry behind, and the employee tells us not to come back as he slams the door in our faces, leaving us alone in an empty hallway.

"What"—I put my hands on my knees, breathing deeply—"is wrong with you?"

"*Me?*" he demands. "What the hell were *you* doing?"

"Don't ever do that again. Use violence to solve a problem." I shudder involuntarily. "It scares me. It fucking scares me, all right?"

He stares back at me, down at me, and has the decency to look ashamed. "I didn't mean to do that," he says. "I've never been in a fight in my life. Just—what he said was bullshit."

"Maybe I am trash," I say, finally standing up straight. "What's so wrong with that? I've been called worse."

"Evelyn." He rips his mask off, and my eyes trace the outline of his cheekbones. I fall back against the wall and start laughing.

"What next?" I say. The adrenaline is running through me now, and he allows a smile to creep onto his face.

"Whatever we want," he says.

REID

433 Days Before the End
One and a Quarter Years Before

I remember the day Ashton Harper fell in love with me.

It wasn't the first time I knew he wanted me. That day had been a few weeks after we'd started talking, when he used to stand there next to my car for half an hour after the final bell rang, lost in our conversation.

This time, I'd caught him between classes. "I can't stay late today," I said. "I have to go work for my mom in the afternoon." It was a lie. I hated filling shifts at the store; it was one of the reasons Dad had hired Evelyn in the first place. I just wanted Ashton to miss me.

"Mama will be grateful I'm getting to the restaurant earlier," he'd said with a smile. "She keeps asking me what's taking so long."

"But tonight," I told him, leaning in closer. "When I'm all alone and can't stop thinking about you, I'll do to myself what I wish you were doing to me."

His face changed so fast, I wished I'd had it on video. He went red and then closed his eyes, almost as if in physical pain. He'd taken a long moment, blown out a breath, and swallowed, his Adam's apple moving up and down.

When he'd opened his eyes, he was completely mine. "Reid," he said.

I smiled wickedly and turned away from him, waving back over my shoulder.

That had been the easy part. Boys, no matter how good they think they are, are easy like that. Predictable.

Love had been harder. Love had been after stolen kisses and falling asleep with legs entwined and nights spent sneaking around under the stars.

It had been after he'd dismissed me that day I picked Evelyn Peters up from the side of the road.

I'd lost control when I was driving, and I'd gotten a concussion. My dad had said it was amazing the car wasn't totaled.

Ashton said he'd thought at first that I was still too angry at him to answer his texts, but then he'd heard I had been in an accident. When I'd woken up in the hospital, he was there and I remember the way he looked at me.

He loved me.

"I'm sorry, Reid," he'd said, and he'd grabbed my hand and said it over and over again. "I'm sorry I'm sorry I'm sorry," and he'd pressed his mouth to my bruised knuckles so softly.

After that, he didn't want us to be apart. Since then, life had played out like a montage: of hands splayed across skin and kisses exchanged in the rain and fights that ended in tongues lashing out against one another. It was chaos, and we thrived on chaos.

And that look he had that day in the hospital—that's how he's looking at me right now.

I'm leaning against his passenger's door with my bare feet in his lap over the console and he's absently touching my skin as if he doesn't realize he's doing it and there's so much intimacy in that.

He brushes his hand slowly up my leg to my thigh, his fingers pressing into the soft flesh there. Maybe it's nothing more than a moment in time, but he loves me.

He loves me.

"So," I say, "who else besides Dante? Who else do you like? You can tell me. I can keep a secret."

He frowns. His hand stops moving against my leg.

"My sexuality isn't, like, a toy for you to play with. You know that, right?" Ashton says.

It's funny he pictures toys and not playing cards. Like there's no strategy involved in this whatsoever.

"All of you is a toy for me to play with, Ashton." I press my toes into his jeans.

he loves me he loves me he loves me he loves me

He pulls his hand back, and he doesn't go anywhere, but he retreats.

"It's not a joke," he says. "I just want peace and quiet."

"Then get a new girlfriend," I tell him.

He focuses on his fingers, drumming them across his steering wheel, releases a breath.

It reminds me of the day at school, the one when he stared longingly at Dante. Even Dante, here in McNair Falls, seemed easier to him in that moment than me.

He'd imagined himself happy with someone else, and that was treason.

"Is that what you want?" I ask. I shift so I can reach out and thread my fingers through his hair. He licks his lips in that nervous way he does.

"Just say the word," I continue, my voice light. "Savannah's been waiting forever." I sigh. "But then again, she's never held much interest for you, has she? I can see why."

I scoot closer to him, to his mouth. I press my lips to his and pull back so our eyes are lined up with one another's. So he can't look away from me.

"I only want you to be happy."

He swallows. "Sometimes, it doesn't feel like it."

The thought of it makes me breathless. Of losing him. And I hate that. The exposure.

"Do you want it all back?" I ask because I can't help it. "Were you happier before?"

He sucks in a breath, too, like the question surprises him. "Of course not."

Stupid, sweet relief floods through me.

"Who I was before. It was always missing something. Some essential part of me. I had it all, and I still felt . . ."

"Empty," I say, thinking of Evelyn Peters.

"Lay off the Dante stuff, okay?" he says, his voice going colder again. I missed the passion in it already. The surety in this. In us.

The necessity.

We go quiet. We don't touch. A breeze is trying to roll in, cut through the September heat. I roll down the windows on either side of us, turning up the radio until it's so loud I can't hear myself think.

"Are you insane!" Ashton yells at me. He reaches for the volume, but I bat his hand away. I smile back at him and nod my head to the clearing in front of us, getting out of the car. Ashton follows me.

"You promised me all your slow dances," I say. "Don't you remember?"

His voice changes, softens. "Of course I do."

I wrap my arms around his neck, pulling him close, and that old mischief dances in his eyes.

"Sometimes," I say, "it's like we barely know each other at all."

I stare up at him. "But we do, don't we? Like we were born under the same moon in the same fucking spot, right? Like we're two parts of one whole."

"We are." He says it like a promise he wants to keep.

I close my eyes, and we dance there in the headlights of his car, barefoot over the leaves and dirt.

"Reid," he says, and his voice is so rough, so textured, so *mine* that I feel like I could die in that moment; give it all up in a perfect beat in time to never let anything spoil it. "You don't have to be anyone but who you are for me."

I hear the lie, but I want it. I need it, a weakness so blatant I feel like it's branded on my skin for anyone to see. "Okay," I say, and press my face into the fabric of his shirt.

The stars shine so bright overhead.

EVELYN

$0 Credit Limit
Now

We go back up to the room and order a small fortune in room service. It amazes me, the way the plates are brought up, covered, with the most beautiful sauces and delicate vegetables.

Ashton and I sit on the same double bed with the room service plates spread between us to share, plenty far apart. We eat our way through them, eat so far past being full, watching some cable show where everyone has a British accent, and then Ashton flips over to the Braves game at one of the West Coast stadiums and makes me try his chocolate cake.

"It's good," I concede. "But Mama's was better. God, I haven't had it in so long. She used to make it all the time when we were younger."

"Why'd she stop making it?" he asks, watching me.

I shrug. "She liked to make it when Matt came over."

"Jesus," Ashton says. "What a dick."

"Yeah," I say slowly. And then, because it suddenly seems important, "He was kind of like my dad, though, back then. I still find it hard to hate him, even though I do. I try. For her, I guess. And for me."

Ashton's eyes catch on me, and they stay like that for a beat too long.

"You're—" He swallows. "You're so different than I thought."

"People usually aren't what you think," I say, but I hear myself speaking in nothingisms again, so I add, "It's funny that you ever thought I was anything. I always thought I was no one to you. That's how it felt." Sometimes, that's still how it feels.

Ashton licks his lips. "I was kind of shit," he says. "Not paying attention to people who I didn't deem—worth noticing, I guess. And I—" His hand comes up and I think he'll try to touch me and then he doesn't. "I know you don't want to be touched. I shouldn't have, in the woods."

"I don't—" I start to say. And then, "I'm not scared of it . . . of being touched."

I swear his eyes dilate slightly, but he goes right past it.

"I really am sorry about shoving that guy," he says. He's sitting up straight, and I see the way he tries to hold himself together. Convince himself he's okay. "Are you scared of me?" he finally asks.

My curly hair falls in my face. "No," I answer, wondering if I should be.

"You're not trash," he tells me.

"Maybe it doesn't matter if I am." I shrug. "Why should I let them hurt me with something I'm not ashamed of?"

He frowns. Words seem to be fighting to come out. "Can I see something?" he asks me at last. "I just. I want to know."

"What?" I ask.

"Can you . . . come here?"

I slide off the bed to my feet and stand in the space between our two beds. He moves to the side of his bed, putting his bare feet on the floor, in his dress pants and a T-shirt. He stares up at me as I drift toward him until we're close. So close, my body is positioned between his legs.

"You remind me so much of her." And he whispers it like it's a secret, and it's the first time I've seen something like adoration in his eyes when he talks about Reid, like the way I used to always imagine him looking at her, and I reach out and roll my thumb over his cheekbone and he's so hollowed out but still so, so beautiful.

His breath catches and he pulls me closer, his fingers sliding up my legs and resting on my hips. I feel as if I'm under a spell, my fingers tracing the contours of his face. I lean down, closer, closer, so our lips almost touch, but they don't. Not quite.

"I won't do it," he tells me, his warm breath on my skin. "Not unless you want me to."

I do, I think, but I so desperately can't. I lean my forehead against his, and he pulls my hips even closer and breathes like he can't catch his breath, not really.

"Ashton." We breathe in the same oxygen, from his mouth to mine, and I can't tell which of us is more scared of what might happen next. This was stupid, diving headfirst into cold water.

We could kiss. We could kiss right now, and there would be *more* somehow. More in the best way and more in the worst.

I tilt my head, just barely.

The phone in our room rings, startling us both apart. Ashton reaches for the phone, pulling it to his ear as I turn away.

"Yes," he says, listening to the other person on the line. "I'll be right down."

And then he slams the phone down and hops up from the bed. "My parents know," he says. "They got an alert on the credit card. We have to get out of here. *Right now.*"

REID

Two Hymns Until Noon
One Year Before

Mom has a nice voice. She's singing from her hymnal, her gaze trained on the preacher. I'm standing next to her, listening, and it's not so bad. I close my eyes and I hear her voice and I understand religion for a minute and then I open my eyes and Savannah Rykers is staring at me and I hope hell is real.

The preacher holds up both arms and says some words, sends us on our way.

I check my watch. 11:55. Not bad.

I take Mom's arm and steer her out as fast as we can go, fighting through the many congregants to reach Mom's car. She stops in front of Savannah's mama, Alice Rykers, and comes to a halt, resists my maneuvering, so I sidestep the preacher and go out into the parking lot.

Mama likes to pretend. To talk to Savannah's mama and all her minions, but I know the truth. They don't like her and they never will, because Mom's family didn't play by the McNair Falls rules, and then she went and got herself married and had a kid and tried to be respectable, but they never forget.

And they definitely never forgive.

It's okay. Neither do I.

Savannah is talking to Ashton, so I make my way over to them. He's laughing, and I can't imagine why because I know she didn't say anything funny.

"Hey, babe," Ashton says, and he leans in to kiss me so naturally, it's like nothing could ever be wrong. I smooth back his hair, just to rub it in a bit.

"Hey, Reid," Savannah says, muted.

"I've gotta run for Sunday dinner service, but I'll call you later, okay?" Ashton says to me.

I glance at Savannah, gauge her reaction, her desperation for that same promise. "Okay," I say, and he kisses my cheek this time, gives Savannah a hug, and jogs to his car, taking off his suit jacket as he goes.

"I'm surprised you didn't burst into flames when you walked through the door this morning," Savannah says, still waving at Ashton's back. She turns to me with a smile.

"Flame-retardant pantsuit," I tell her.

"You look ridiculous."

"But I feel great." I smile.

"Your mama must think she's finally made it," Savannah says. I turn around to see what she's looking at. Mama, in a group of the First Baptist Women's Club members, chatting away.

"You know, Savannah, it ain't very Christian to decide who someone is the first time you see them and then never change your mind the rest of your life."

"It's worked so far," she retorts. "And I sure wasn't planning on asking you for advice on how to be a good Christian."

"We may solve problems in different ways, but we both like to be on our knees." I shrug. "And the Bible says God loves us equally."

I wait for that to sink in, watch her fury rise. "I could make your life very difficult, you know that?"

"No, you can't," I tell her. "Sometimes, even, I bet he's talking to you and all he's thinking about is me."

Savannah manages not to take the bait on that one. She grins back at me. "And maybe sometimes, he's fucking you and all he's thinking about is once this phase is over, once he's done with the white trash girl who makes his blood run hot right now, he can settle down with me." She raises her eyebrows and starts to turn away. "You've never been very good at the long game, have you, Reid?"

And then she disappears into her mama's Camry, her dress and then the rest of a long leg sliding out of sight, and I feel the rage building up inside me.

"Reid!" Mom calls. "It's time to go."

I clench my fists until my nails dig a crescent moon cut into my palm, walking back to the car and sliding into the passenger's seat.

Mom is checking her reflection in the mirror, touching up her lipstick. "You all right?" she asks.

"I hate this place. I hate this town. I hate everything it does to people."

"Surely you aren't letting Savannah Rykers bother you," Mom says. I don't answer as she blots her lipstick. "You're smarter than all those girls combined, you know that, right, honey?" she asks, pursing her lips.

"Yes," I say.

"Savannah Rykers's own dad didn't even love her enough to stay with her," she says, her kohl-rimmed eyes meeting their own reflection. "You'd never lose Ashton to a girl like that." She watches me, her eyebrows raised. "I know you know how to handle him."

"Of course I do," I say back, defiant. "But Savannah Rykers's daddy went back."

"Different circumstances," she says. "Though it would probably help if you didn't spend time with Evelyn Peters at the store. That kind of reputation rubs off on people."

"You're right," I agree. She throws her makeup back into her purse.

"You're a good girl, Reid," she tells me. "Don't let people like Savannah treat you like you aren't worth it."

She puts the car into reverse and pulls out of the church parking lot, gravel flying behind her.

EVELYN

$578 Left
Now

Ashton and I start throwing all our scattered supplies into plastic bags. I hurry into the bathroom, changing out of the white robe as I go.

We're both lacing our shoes up when it happens—the knock on the door.

Our eyes meet across the room.

"Mr. Harper?" the voice asks. "Miss Peters?"

I almost collapse onto the ground. We're fucked.

They know I'm not dead now, and we're fucked.

Ashton and I don't say anything to each other, barely seem to breathe.

The person politely knocks again. I hurry over to the door to peek through and see a man in a Four Seasons uniform standing at the door.

"It's an employee," I whisper, going back into the bedroom. *Not the police*, I don't say.

The man is talking loudly outside the door, on the phone with someone. "I mean, it's just a couple of horny teenagers, I don't see how we can hold them in custody." His voice drops. "Oh yeah, some bumpkin sheriff I'm sure." He sighs a deep I-don't-get-paid-for-this sigh. "Yeah, let me know when I'm authorized to use my key card."

Ashton's expression is grim. "Why make him wait?"

He begins walking past me, his body slumped. Resigned. But I put my arm out, holding him back. Take a deep breath. Hurry over to the hotel phone, pick it up, and dial 9-1-1.

It rings once before someone answers. "Nine-one-one, what's your emergency?"

I take a deep breath, and I start lying with everything I have. It doesn't take much more than lying to any boy.

"He's not breathing," I say. "Oh Jesus, he's dying! Please, honey, please wake up!"

Ashton's eyes catch on mine, going wide.

"Ma'am?" the operator says. "Ma'am, I need you to calm down. Can you tell me where you are?"

"Oh God, he's not going to make it."

"Ma'am."

I take a deep breath, struggle mightily with it. "The Four Seasons," I say. "Third floor. It's, uh . . . it's room 312." The level below us. "Hurry," I say. "*Please*."

"I'm dispatching someone right now, ma'am. Can you stay with me?"

I hang up the phone and hurry over to grab my bag. "We've only got a couple minutes," I say.

"What the hell did you just do?" Ashton asks me.

"Do you want to go to jail?"

I put my ear against the door. The employee is still on the phone. After a moment, though, I hear the sirens out front, and the sound of the man as he takes off running toward the imaginary emergency in the room below us.

"Let's go," I say, and grab up my plastic bag. We take off out the door and down the stairs, the past never seeming far enough behind us.

• • •

The tires turn and turn through a dark night.

I wish we would've slept, at least.

"Shit," I say, behind the wheel after Ashton's bender. "Shit, that was close."

Ashton swallows but doesn't say anything. He ditched his credit card in a trash can as we ran to the parking garage, along with his phone. We stopped at the first ATM we saw, and he withdrew all his money in his account before tossing his debit card out the window.

In some ways, there's nothing left of Ashton Harper.

"They know you're alive," he says. "That means they're looking for us."

"And you were ready to turn us both in."

Lights blur past in the windows as we speed out of Atlanta. "I can't have any more blood on my hands," he says after a minute.

"Oh, what, I'm white trash so I must be violent?"

"We killed someone, Evelyn," he says, and then releases a breath. "We killed someone and they know we killed someone."

"So you want to go home?"

He blinks, eyes glued to the road. Finally, he says, "I want whatever you want."

Whatever I want. My whole life has been one day bleeding into another of getting by, of teaching myself not to dream. There wasn't money for college, so why imagine what it would be like? There was no respectable person who would want me, so why indulge in imagining someone else's skin on mine? There was no happiness or freedom or simple. Only survival.

Whatever I want.

"Nashville," I say. "I've wanted to see the Opry my whole life. Walk the streets where the greats did."

"Nashville," he echoes, and reaches forward, cranking the music up loud like it will give him strength. It shakes the car, shakes me down to my soul, and I swallow.

I watch Georgia roll by. The dark rural roads should be melancholy, but instead I think about how there is so much majesty in utter darkness. The night sky gives you everything in a place like this, a place like home.

"I only had to call nine-one-one once in my whole life, you know?"

I don't know. "Why?" I say, but as soon as the words are out of my mouth, I know.

"The boat," he says. "Reid went in, and . . ." He trails off. That's it. The end of the story.

"I did what I thought would save us," I defend myself, even though he didn't ask for it, and he doesn't argue.

"I'm sorry," he says, "about the hotel. Before. On the bed." He shakes his head. "That was fucked up."

"It—" I start to say and then trip over my own thought. "It's not a big deal." And then just to stop him from saying anything else: "I was thinking about Kara. My sister. I'm glad she won't think I'm dead."

"Do you think she's all right?"

"She's tough," I say. "She'll hold Mama together. She's been holding me together for long enough."

"You don't need anyone to hold you together, Evelyn," he says then, and maybe I'm prickling at the idea he knows me, after a drunken night and an almost kiss. Like that's all there is to know. "And your mama was never doing enough to protect you."

"People aren't that simple," I respond, not entirely sure why I'm defending her. "Something got broken inside her, I think. After a while. The world beats you down long enough, and you give up."

"You didn't," he says, and I'm a story he's telling himself. That's the easiest thing to do—heroes and villains, right and wrong.

I do it all the time.

"Of course I did," I say. "Anyway, Kara will be fine. She always is."

He lets it all sit there, knowing he's picking at an open wound, before he continues, "I know this sounds weird, but I used to kind of think of Savannah as my sister. Before . . . before Reid, I guess."

"Savannah?" That doesn't seem right. I knew what Savannah had wanted from him, and very little of it had to do with sisterhood. I always thought there was something there between them; everyone did. Everyone was always waiting for *something* to happen, back before Reid.

"She used to cry a lot, when we were younger," he says. "We'd sit on my porch and drink Yoo-hoos. God, I'd kill for one of those right now."

"You mean that she cried over her dad." I don't look at him, but I feel him looking at me.

"It wasn't your fault."

"I know," I return sharply. "Thank you."

"I just meant—I know you didn't want to see Savannah hurt," he says.

"You think I ever gave a shit about Savannah?" I reply easily. "I used to kneel down by my bed every night and pray to God that Matt would finally stay forever. That he'd be my dad." Ashton is now staring intently at the road. "I remember this one time, we went to a middle school assembly and Mama came and she told me not to look at Matt or speak to him and I understood, Ashton. I understood we'd always be his shame. And Savannah tortured me for that.

"So, you know what? I'm glad she used to show up at your house and cry over her miserable fucking life. That comforts me."

"I didn't—" he starts to say, but he never finishes. We both decide that the quiet is better than digging up any more of our graves.

• • •

I pull into a gas station an hour outside Nashville. When Ashton goes in to pay, I open the console, for no particular reason at all, an old habit, a need to do something with my hands. I almost close it without even realizing what I'm looking at.

He has a gun. A small pistol tucked into the console.

It doesn't surprise me—lots of people back home do. He probably got a permit when he turned eighteen, along with a present from his parents.

But Ashton, *Ashton* of all people shouldn't have a gun.

I look up just in time to spot him headed back out toward the car. I slam the console shut and try to clear my face.

He slides into the passenger's seat.

"You okay?" he asks.

I smile reassuringly back at him, at the first words we've spoken in an hour. "Fine," I say. "Hey, Ashton?" I continue as I start the car back up. "You ever gotten in trouble for anything? Besides drinking."

He raises an eyebrow. "Before this?" he asks, sarcasm in his voice. "Just Reid."

REID

Three Miles till Home
One Year Before

I remember the day Ashton Harper fell out of love with me.

Sometimes, I think I can almost track it down to the precise, inescapable instant. Because there was so long when I could tell he was just hanging on, despite himself.

The bell rings, releasing us for another day, and I loiter by the vending machines, watching people walk by.

"Dante!" I call as soon as I see him, and he cocks his head, swerving to come over to me.

"What's up, Reid?" he asks, unsure. I've never given him the time of day before. I can't help but think back to not so long ago, when it had been Ashton I'd waited for by the snack machines.

"Good game the other night," I commend him. He's on the football team, and he's not one of the best players, but he's a starter. "Three tackles for loss and a reception, right?"

He smiles hesitantly. "I didn't know you were such a fan."

"I dabble."

Ashton walks across the parking lot then, and his eyes flicker to us and away and then double back.

Dante grins for real. "I could see it."

I'm a chameleon like that. Everything comes just easy enough that he has no trouble imagining me appearing anywhere and fitting in. Mom taught me well.

A blessing and a curse.

"You around this weekend? I heard Katie is having a party."

He laughs. "You're going to Katie's party?"

"Don't you think this town could use a little excitement?"

"Every day," he says.

"Good." And with the smile that's gotten me everything I've ever wanted in my life, I glance at him one last time and walk away.

Ashton is waiting by his car.

"What exactly are you trying to do?" he asks, barely looking at me.

"Nothing," I say. "I'm being friendly."

"Nothing about you is friendly," he shoots back, ice cold, and then he does look at me. "You've never said a word to Dante Martinez in your life. Why the sudden interest?"

"Does it so shock you that the things that interest you also interest me? I want to know about your life."

"You want to torment me. You want to torment me, and you said you wanted me to be happy."

"Just because you hate yourself doesn't mean I do, Ashton."

"Of course you do. You hate me more than anyone else does. Otherwise—"

My heart pounds. "Otherwise, what?"

He meets my eyes for a beat too long, then shakes his head, looking away. "Otherwise, nothing. Let's go."

And we don't speak at all on the ride home.

When we pull up at my house, I know he won't say anything. He waits for me to get out.

I reach over and grab his hand, dragging it to me, resting it between my own hands. I spread his fingers apart, tracing each one of them before I pull his hand up to my mouth and press a kiss into his palm, finally resting it on my cheek. I turn to face him.

"What do you want?" I ask.

He blinks once, twice, eyes on mine. A tear steals down his face. He's wearing his McNair Falls Track sweatshirt, too oversized for his coltish body, and he doesn't look quite so golden as I remember, because he's just a boy. Not an answer.

He's my boy.

"Nothing has changed," I tell him, reaching over and wiping away the tear with the pad of my thumb. "Nothing ever changed, Ashton. We're the same old us." We *have* to be. I can't lose that.

"I—" and he chokes on his own voice, tripping over himself, and I think I might cry and that's so fucking stupid. "I love you, Reid. So much, it feels wrong, and you *do* this. You keep doing this. This isn't who we were. I'm losing you to whatever *this* is."

That was the moment. He said it out loud and he heard it and he realized it, I think. What I was. What I am.

"Please leave," he says, looking away from me.

I close my eyes, bend my head, almost like I'm praying, and I want to give him whatever he wants and I want to take whatever I want from him.

"Okay," I say. "Okay."

EVELYN

NOT 21
Now

We make our way into Nashville as the sun rises.

We find a motel on the outskirts of town, and I am asleep in my double bed before I have fully hit the pillow. When I wake up, I find Ashton staring out the window, watching cars in the parking lot. I know nothing about Nashville's geography, but I can tell we're in a part of town where most people wouldn't be happy to find themselves.

I'm not scared of people who don't have money, though.

"What are you doing?" I ask Ashton, unsettled by the idea of him sitting there fully alert while I was vulnerable asleep in bed. It's not that I think he'd hurt me; it's just that bone-deep fear that he could if he wanted to.

"Trying not to think," he says, running his hands up and down his arms, almost like he's fighting off the cold. It's starting to get dark outside, night creeping in like an old friend. It seems like I've seen nothing but night recently. "You ever feel like you're fading away? Losing some part of yourself?"

I don't answer because he looks so sad. Instead, I tell Ashton, "Dane looks like you do sometimes." *Looked*, I amend silently. "When he hasn't had anything to drink in a while."

"You saying I'm like him?" Ashton asks me.

I swing my feet off the bed, staring him down. "I'm saying you have a drinking problem."

His eyebrows go up. "Groundbreaking." He grabs his coat. "So let's go, then."

"Where are we going?"

"I don't know," he says. "Anywhere. Not here."

I don't want to go, but I don't want to stay. "Ashton, they're looking for us."

"Yeah," he says. "In Atlanta. I doubt we've topped America's Most Wanted. We just won't do anything stupid like back there."

"Won't we?" I challenge him. "They know your car."

"It isn't that serious," he says.

"It's *murder*."

He shudders, and I can tell the truth of it. That he'd die for that drink, get arrested, anything.

"You're the one who wanted to come here," he says.

"You're right," I agree. "We'll only stay through the four days we paid upfront. Make a plan for where to go next."

"Should we, like, get out of the country?" Ashton asks me, looking as overwhelmed by the thought as I feel.

"I don't know," I say, feeling stupid. *Nashville. Why Nashville?* "Whatever we do, we need to keep a low profile. We have limited money and targets on our backs. Okay?"

He crosses his heart. "Swear," he says. "We'll go to the grungiest grunge bar we can find."

Somehow, that doesn't make me feel better.

I reach into the mess of clothes we stuffed in plastic bags on the way out of Atlanta and throw on a long-sleeve shirt Ashton picked up from the drugstore yesterday.

"Why don't you bring your guitar?" Ashton asks, looking

down at the case. I've carried it everywhere we've gone, hauled it from place to place like a talisman containing my very soul. "You can play it."

A cold chill runs up my spine. "In front of people?"

"I thought that was a given."

I recoil, wrapping my arms around myself protectively. "I don't play in front of people." Because then they might see me. Might see me for real.

It's already too much.

"Yeah, well, I don't burn down trailers," Ashton counters. "We're all trying something new this week."

"That's the opposite of keeping a low profile," I say.

"This is Nashville. It's more conspicuous if you don't have a guitar." He doesn't wait for me to agree, just picks up my guitar and away he goes, out the door with the confidence of an alcoholic boy who's been running from his demons for a day. I hurry behind him, scurrying to keep up.

Ashton deposits my guitar into the back seat of his car before going back in to get local recommendations from the guy in the lobby. When he returns, we get in the car, and he takes off out of the parking lot like a bat out of hell.

"Where are we going?"

"Little Red Bird Café," he tells me, a lilt in his voice.

"Like Bluebird Café?"

"Exactly like that except we can get you on the stage at this one." He keeps his eyes on the road, a determined expression on his face as he studies the street signs we go past.

Little Red Bird Café is not close. It's a good twenty-minute drive from our motel; Ashton's Range Rover reads the directions to him as he goes.

Finally, we turn into the parking lot of a little old decrepit brick building. We have no IDs to show to the bouncer, so he stamps both our hands with a giant red NOT 21 stamp. Ashton frowns at it as we walk in.

It's still early, and a few families dot the seats, parents with drinks in their hands while children run amok. A man is onstage, and he has a voice too sweet for pain, countrifying some John Mayer song or another.

Ashton's still staring at the stamp on his hand. "I'm going to the bathroom," he tells me. I sit down at a table, alone with my guitar, and try not to let anyone notice me.

It takes Ashton forever to get back, and when he does, his hand is clean, he's holding a drink, and he looks particularly smug.

"I signed you up," he tells me, falling down into his seat. "You're up in a few."

I clench my fingers together on the sticky table. "Why are you doing this?" I ask him.

He leans forward, the happiness the drink has given him falling away like it had never been there at all. "Please," he says. "Please play."

"Why do you want this so much?" I can't help but ask him. "What do you think it's going to do?"

He's quiet, swirling his drink around in the cup. "You know, when I was ten," he says, "I got baptized. And all my sins were forgiven or whatever, right? They dunked me in the water but at the last minute, I panicked, and I breathed in at the wrong time, like almost drowned myself."

I blink at him, lost.

"But, after, when I stopped coughing, I just felt this clarity. This surrender."

"Ashton."

"I'd do anything to feel that again," he says. "My heart." He shakes his head. "I'm not clean, and I—I can feel that I *need this*."

He stops his fingers just short of touching mine. I swallow, looking up at him, our faces too close. "What's wrong with you?" I ask.

He half laughs, and I almost think he's going to cry.

"Don't ask questions you don't want the answer to."

REID

Four Siblings to Love
One Year Before

The truth is that Dante is too nice.

He's too nice for Ashton is the first thing I determine.

It bothers me that Ashton could even like someone so nice. Because Ashton is supposed to want *me*, and his interest in someone so simple and milquetoast has to be the first sign of a coming storm.

I'm not nice.

Dante is hard to pin down. I have to get a couple of beers in him. He has a shiny glint in his eyes, I notice, and I like that.

"Tell me something, Dante," I say to him, leaning back against the railings running down the side of the stairs, sitting across from him. We're on Katie's back porch, and a bug is sucking on my leg. The music is pounding, and we're angled in too close to each other. "Tell me something about you."

"Why?" he asks.

"Because you fascinate me," I tell him. "Isn't that enough?"

The thing is, Dante in particular doesn't fascinate me at all. But his appeal to Ashton—that's something I have to understand. I have to dissect it, take it completely apart and put it back together for myself.

"Well," Dante says, taking a long breath, "I'm kind of exactly who you think I am. I show up at school every day, play football, go home, and hang out with my mom and my younger siblings. I got two, and then two more half brothers who live over in Ravensway. My dad split on all of us."

"Tragic backstory built in," I say.

Dante looks thoughtful. "Yeah, I guess. Or, you know, just my life."

I take a sip of my drink. "What do you want to do after high school?"

His brow creases, as if he finds the question surprising but also somehow too invasive. "What do *you* want to do after high school?"

"Run away," I say with a grin, "and never stop."

"Ashton wouldn't like that too much, would he?" Dante says, and that hangs in the air between the two of us. "Ain't he gonna take over his family's restaurant?"

I shrug. "Ashton doesn't know what he wants."

"What's the deal with the two of you anyway?" Dante says. "You fight all the time. Everyone talks about it."

"I don't know," I say. "Ashton won't accept his own happiness."

"Ashton is the one, huh?" Dante says with a smile, and, wildly, for a moment, I think he's way too interested in Ashton.

But of course he's not. Because this isn't a place where you get lucky enough to get exactly what you want—not this nice, athletic boy with his dimples and curly hair.

You get me or you get Savannah, and you don't know which future you hate the sight of more.

And once I let this truth about Ashton even cross my mind, I stupidly almost break myself open.

"Maybe you're right," I say. "It's just life. Maybe none of us can accept our own happiness."

We stare at each other across the darkness, and I know we're both wondering: *What's the point?*

And then I lean in and kiss him.

EVELYN

Four Chords
Now

They don't call my name. They call, "Reid Brewer," and I look at Ashton, and I know. Deep down, in the most broken part of his soul, he's so desperate for her. To fix it all again. Even still. Something so bad happened between them, and he can never look it in the eye.

Closure is a myth coated in gasoline and cheap whiskey.

He hands my guitar case over to me, and I see the desperation in his eyes. I *feel* the desperation in his eyes.

I just wish I knew what he really wanted. The same way I still wondered what Reid had really wanted.

I grab my guitar case from him and make my way to the stage.

There are, at most, twenty people in the café, and that's including the kids back in the corner squealing at each other. But I don't look at any of them. My hands shake furiously as I set the case down and pop it open, fumbling with the clasp. Finally, I manage to get my guitar out—it was so easy at home every night, touching it as lovingly as you would touch the only friend you have—and pull it into my lap, so aware of every strange thing about me. My ugly shirt and the hard stool I'm sitting on, my nervous expression and jagged fingernails.

The music is me, and I'm so afraid they'll see it.

See me. The real me. All of it. *Me.*

I mess around tuning my strings, aware of eyes on me, even as glasses clink on tables and patrons talk among themselves. I look up and it's Ashton and there's nothing but Ashton and his gaze. I avert my eyes back to my guitar.

I strum the first note just to hear it. And I like how it sounds, simple and easy. Something inside that note brings an inner calm I haven't had in days.

Evelyn Peters. That's who I am.

Not someone else.

Call it inner strength or peace of mind or whatever bullshit you want to call it, but in that moment, there is nothing left but a girl and a guitar. Easy notes, obvious and simple and mine without any thought. And I wish I wasn't so hard on this girl. I wish I could figure out how to love her.

I let the words spill out of my mouth, the melody carrying them in the quiet of the café. I keep my eyes down like I always keep my eyes down, but it's quieter now. They're listening to me. They're *hearing* me.

Is this what it feels like? To be listened to. To be believed in.

And then I do it—I chance the glance up and I know I'll look right at Ashton and he gazes back at me and there's nothing cloudy or hesitant in his expression. It's sure and dark and reverent. And I'm singing right at him even though it's so stupid, we can't break that eye contact. We can't let it go.

It's like the moment before a kiss when it's all you've ever wanted, but you're worried doing it will ruin it. That it won't live up to what you imagined, but you see someone else's soul in yours and you're not sure whether to run into it or away from it.

It's like forgetting and remembering at the same time.

So I finish and he blinks and the audience applauds, half-drunk men banging their cans on the table. I finally look away from Ashton, and for that smallest moment in time, I smile at them, at all twenty of them, and then I put my guitar back in its case.

It wasn't so bad, not for a girl who's spent her whole life going nowhere.

• • •

Ashton doesn't say anything about the song. He sips his drink, and some more people filter in, taking the stage and pouring their hearts out to a roomful of strangers.

Bizarre and comforting.

Finally, Ashton says, "I think about Dane and I feel bad and I don't." He stares straight ahead.

"What?" I whisper, pitching my voice low.

"It's eating me up, Evelyn. Having this blood on my hands." He turns to face me. "Isn't it eating you up?"

I shake my head, refuse to let the thought in. "Don't do that."

"But he was hurting your sister and your mom and you," Ashton says, "and look at you," and it's this phrase he says over and over again as if I'll understand precisely what it means. *Look at you*.

As if I haven't spent my entire life trying not to do that.

"Just think, you were right there this whole time. Right under my nose and I was so lost in my own shit and I thought I had changed but I haven't changed at all. I should've seen you. Should've seen you were hurting. And not just assumed, not ever asked myself if those guys were using you or you were using them or who you were. You were right there, and all I ever thought about was myself."

"Why would you have thought about me?" I ask him.

"Because," he says, "you deserved it. You deserved for someone to care."

"People don't get what they deserve," I tell him.

"Yeah," he says after a minute, "I know." He drinks. "I want you to forgive me," he finally says. "I need someone to forgive me."

"For what?" I ask.

"All of it." He gazes down into his drink and goes quiet again. I lean back in my chair, close my eyes, and listen to the music.

The songs go by. The drinks in front of Ashton disappear. I try to ignore him, to stay focused on the stage, the way the music makes me feel, until midnight, when the café closes.

"Let's go," I say to him.

He gets up without a word.

Outside, he stumbles into the night toward his car and I follow behind him.

"Give me your keys," I call to him.

"Keys," he says, feeling around in his pockets. "Keys, keys, keys," he chants. "Where are my keys?"

"Where are your keys?" I repeat.

"Shit," he says, turning out his pockets. "Shit."

I stare at him. He swallows. "Ah, I fucked it, didn't I?" he says, and half laughs. It makes me want to cry. "And we don't have a phone." He stops laughing. "Shit."

I search my own pockets desperately, willing an answer to appear out of thin air, and when it doesn't, I tug on my tangled hair. The café has cleared out, people getting in their cars on the way home. "We need to go back inside, turn the bar over," I say. "They have to be in there."

"Yeah," he says, but as we make our way back to the entrance, a voice comes out of the darkness.

"You kids okay?"

I look up, and a small man in a threadbare coat is leaning against the wall outside the café.

"We're fine," I say. "Just need to find our keys."

He pushes off the wall, tossing a cigarette to the ground. "I can give you a ride, if it'd help."

"No," I say. "It's probably out of the way. We've got this."

"They're not going to let you back in after closing," the man tells us. "Trust me, I'm a regular. You'll have to come back tomorrow. I don't mind."

"We'll figure something out," I say, my eyes locked on the man, who looks back, undeterred.

"Evelyn," Ashton cuts over. "What's wrong with you? Take a favor when it's offered."

I glance over at Ashton and then back at the man, his face shaded in the dark of the night. His chin is squared. It's not right.

"I gotta get home," the man says. "Or the old lady will start asking questions. You wanna go or not?"

"Yes," Ashton says emphatically, relief coating his voice. "Please."

I grab at Ashton, but he follows after the man. Once it's clear there's nothing I can do to stop him, we get in the car, him in the front seat, me in the back.

It smells like cigarettes, and I so desperately crave one, it's like an ache gnawing away at my soul. But I won't ask this man for anything.

He might want something in return.

Ashton gives the man directions to our motel. He looks

completely relaxed, chatting across the console, even laughing, and I wonder who this boy is. Where he came from.

He wants something. And he knows how to get it.

I stare out the window, but don't lean forward, afraid to touch the glass.

"Actually"—my heart drops as Ashton says it—"it's the right up here."

"Oh, really?" the man says, making no move to turn again. "Maybe we can just go around."

"Ashton," I say, my voice coming out like gravel.

The man pulls the car into a parking lot of a closed-down gas station. He kills the lights. My heart pounds.

The man turns toward Ashton.

"Let's make this quick," he says. "I saw all the cash you had at the bar. Hand it over and no one gets hurt."

Ashton freezes and I say his name again.

The man looks back at me. "Would you shut up?"

"But you said—" Ashton begins. My mind flashes to the gun in his car, so fast it surprises me, and I wish for it. I wish for a way to protect myself.

I wish for a way to stop this man from ruining everything the way they always do.

"C'mon, kid," the man says. "Let's go."

Finally, slowly, Ashton reaches into his pocket, pulls out the wad of cash. All of it. And he'd showcased it like the pampered idiot he is.

I no longer want to cry. I'm angry.

Ashton hands the money over. The man lifts up the console, and Ashton glances into it, swallows.

"That all of it?" the man asks. "The pretty girl got anything?"

Ashton shakes his head. "That's it. It's all my cash. Let us go, please."

The man is jumpy, I can tell. He doesn't do this; just spotted a quick way to make cash off some morons.

My anger grows.

"Get out," the man says. "Get out. And if you tell the cops, I'll come to that motel you mentioned and kill you both. Her first."

Ashton quickly opens the door, but I can't help but say, "No, he won't." Ashton has opened my door and is pulling me out of the car as fast as he can, and the man takes off, so fast his old beater barely makes it over a speed bump.

Ashton throws up on the ground, from nerves or alcohol, what difference does it really make?

"Great job," I say, my voice coated with venom.

"Please don't," Ashton whimpers, crouching on the ground.

"That was all our money," I say.

"I am aware of what just happened," Ashton says, glancing up at me.

"No one," I yell at Ashton, "gives you anything in this world for free. How fucking hard is that to understand?"

"You can't go through life believing the worst of people. There are good people!" he says, finally standing back up, facing me.

"Only people like you get things handed to them," I say. "And you're not you anymore, in case that hasn't crossed your pretty little mind."

He wipes his mouth, staring down at me.

"I've been fucked plenty of times before, thank you."

We glare across the empty parking lot at each other, totally and completely screwed. And then Ashton says, "Shoe."

"What?"

He looks down at the ground, not meeting my eye. He mumbles, "I put my key in my shoe so I wouldn't lose it."

I should leave him, I think. Right now. He's lost his usefulness to me, and if I'm honest with myself, he lost it as soon as that credit card was canceled back in Atlanta. There's no point in this continued partnership; he's ruined everything for me at every turn, like he promised from the start.

There's nothing but loneliness keeping me here, and I know that.

So, tomorrow, I promise myself. I leave tomorrow. Because nothing could pull me back to McNair Falls, and it's time to start looking after myself again.

It's time to be realistic again.

At least he looks ashamed.

"We better start walking," I say.

REID

Just Six Days
One Year Before

The day is slipping away from me.

Ashton breathes into my hair, that boy smell of his all over me. Our legs are tangled up in the sheets of my double bed, and I turn around to face him.

He has these eyes, always a little dark and troubled. He's the kind of person who will never forgive himself for anything, and it's so sad.

"What are you staring at?" he asks.

"You," I say. "Always you."

"Don't tease me, Reid," he says, but he's smiling with that perfect small gap in his teeth. I asked him one time why he never got rid of it, and he smiled just like now and told me "because it's me," and he was right, because without it he's someone generic, but with it, he is beautiful.

"There's nothing about you I don't love," I tell him, and it's true. It's so true, it hurts sometimes, down to the bottom of my feet.

"I'm sorry," he says, "that I get so mad at you sometimes."

"It's okay," I tell him. "I get mad at me sometimes, too."

And I see it. The way his eyes study my face, all of it, memorizing it. Ashton's penchant for worship is always there. He never lets me down.

"Let's go get food," I say to him.

"Okay," he says. "I'm starving."

We throw on our T-shirts and shorts and get in his car, making our way over to Subway, the only fast food restaurant in McNair Falls. We order our food and grab a table, where the bright sunlight shines in on us through a window.

I play with my food, and I feel the mood shift. The darkness creep back in.

Earlier, that wasn't real. That isn't who I am anymore.

I used to want him to think that so badly: that I was a happy girl who just lets it all go. That I'd be the girl who'd make his life better, easier, who'd stare at him until I couldn't see anything else.

Why can't I be happy?

"Do you want to go to the lake next week?" Ashton asks me after he finishes his meal. "My uncle said we could use his place. I think Allen and his girlfriend are going to come."

The day is slipping away. People come in and pick up their subs and leave, and my eyes follow every one of them.

"What's at the lake?" I ask him.

"Water, boats, all that shit. A good time, presumably." Ashton picks up the remainder of my uneaten sub and starts eating it, and I hate that. It's mine. He didn't even ask if I was finished. "Or do you not like the lake now, too?" Exasperation coats each and every one of his words. He doesn't even give me a chance to fuck up anymore; he already knows it's coming.

"It's fine," I say. He doesn't deserve this. Me.

"What's up with you?" he asks. "You're the one who wanted to come here."

I look out over his shoulder, distracted. "I kissed Dante," I tell him.

It crackles over us, a bolt of lightning. Ashton drops the sub on the table. He opens his mouth a couple of times like he can't get the words out, but how hard can it really be?

"I just wanted to see," I tell him reasonably, "for you. I wanted to do it for you so I can tell you about what you can't have."

His voice goes low and deadly. "Are you completely out of your mind?"

"No," I say.

He scrapes his chair back across the floor, grabs up his keys, and heads for the exit. I roll my eyes.

"Ashton, wait."

He doesn't wait. He hits the door and then he's out into the parking lot and I'm so pissed I have to run after him. That I even want to.

I follow him into the parking lot. "*Ashton.*"

He turns around. "No, Reid. Fucking *no*. We're done here."

"You're being ridiculous," I tell him. I know he's not being ridiculous. I know what I did was incredibly fucked up. I know. *I know.*

Shit.

"Reid, I cannot do this anymore. I cannot love someone who treats me like this. It hurts."

"But who are we without each other?" I ask him.

"Better people," he tells me. "I used to be a better person."

"You were never even yourself before," I tell him, and he shakes his head, tries to shake it off because he knows it's so disgustingly true, he's terrified of it.

"Fuck you," he says.

"C'mon, Ashton. Didn't you want to know?"

"No, Reid," he replies. "I just want to live my life without *this* all the time. I want happiness and love for myself. I want to fucking breathe again without you next to me, plotting how to take it away."

"You're not happy," I tell him. "You're not. We're the only ones who really see each other. Don't you know that?" Maybe he already did know that because he slams the door and drives off and then I'm there. Alone.

I pick up a rock and throw it after his car. It misses, completely and desperately, and trails sadly after him.

EVELYN

$120 Left
Now

When we get back to the café, Ashton hands me the key and I pull myself up into the driver's seat of his car. He practically falls into the passenger's seat, burying his face in his hands.

"Are you okay?" I ask him. "Are you going to be sick again?"

He closes his eyes, pressing the heels of his hands against them. "I'm fine," he says at last.

"If you want to talk about—"

"I don't."

"Fine," I say. I plug our hotel back into the navigation. Soft music plays out of the speakers from one of the local stations. We don't say anything as I take off.

A few minutes pass in silence. "What happened to you, Ashton?" I finally say when I can't take it anymore. "How'd you end up here?"

"This car my parents bought me," he tells me, looking out the window.

"No," I say. "Why are you like this? And don't say Reid Brewer."

I don't think he's going to answer me at first, but then he shifts slightly and I hear him: "I didn't know who I was," he says. "And this is where that ends up."

"That's not good enough," I answer. "Stop speaking in riddles, please." I don't look at him as I say it. "I used to be so jealous of your entire life. I'd see you at school, and you were so beautiful and perfect and fucking happy. All I wanted was to be that happy."

"And now you've seen my full misery in action: getting robbed and vomiting up my night's consumption." He half laughs. "Shit."

"And the Reid thing," I tell him. "Do you know how much of my time I spent thinking about her? How charming and smart and *alive* she was, but then you tell me that's not her at all." I shrug. "And you're—whatever you are, and it's just like, what's real, Ashton? Was *any* of it real?"

Ashton shifts ever so slightly, pushing back his hair. "Sometimes, when I get into a really dark place, I start to wonder if she knew me better than I knew myself right down to some darkness I never really wanted to examine." He keeps stopping and starting like he's not sure if he should say it all out loud, give it over without a fight. "Like one day, she was there in my periphery and I thought it was so strange for someone like Reid Brewer to see someone like me and think I was interesting or worth her time."

"You?" I say, surprised.

"Yeah." He scratches at the leather of the interior, like he can't bring himself to focus all his attention on this conversation. "At First Baptist, she used to skip service and go sit on the playground. I'd see her through the window sometimes. Like some kind of weird, lonely mirage." He takes a deep breath. "I wanted . . . a taste of that. I wanted to know what it was like because all I saw in front of me was this long, boring life where everyone knew who I was and what I was and that's all it ever amounted to. And then—well, I'm an addict, if that's not obvious. I couldn't lose that feeling once I had it. That feeling that anything could happen at any time with Reid. And she never gave me what I wanted back. What I really wanted."

I pull into the parking lot of our motel and put the car in park. I sit back in my seat. "And what was that?"

"Some proof that she actually saw me. Loved me. Stupid, I know."

"What's stupid about wanting to be loved?" I ask.

"Plenty of people love me, Evelyn. But I wanted the one I couldn't get. That's a stupid fucking tragedy. Anyway, it doesn't matter anymore. It's over."

It isn't, but I don't disagree. As he gets out of the car, I unbuckle my seat belt and follow him into the motel. He goes straight into the bathroom, and I listen as he runs water to clean himself up, carefully unlacing my shoes.

A moment later, he comes back out. "I had a hundred dollars in my bag." He wipes his hand across his face. "That should buy us a couple more days."

"Okay," I say, even though it doesn't matter, and it won't. What's the point in arguing?

He pulls his shirt over his head. I look away.

"You're ridiculously shy," he says, grabbing a T-shirt out of one of the plastic bags. It isn't said in a mocking way, more with surprise.

"Don't tell anyone," I say. "Might ruin my reputation." He snorts, and then we both laugh, and some of the tension dissipates.

"Reid had me out of my clothes the first time we were alone." He says it easy, like a thought that just occurred to him.

"Oh," I say. I feel the skin around my neck flush and try to hide it.

"Sorry," Ashton says. "I didn't mean—"

"It's fine," I say. "It's not like—whatever, I'm not *scared*." I don't meet his eyes, and I feel small. Because he is the fuckup, but now my dirty little secret is out for him, like the fear is so deeply ingrained in me, I have no idea how to hide it.

Pretend. Just pretend you're okay.

"I won't talk about it," he says, "if you don't want me to." But I can tell now that he's started talking, he doesn't know how to stop.

And more importantly, I don't want him to.

"No," I say. "It's fine."

"I just—" He paces. "I fell for her so fast and there was nothing—the whole time we were together, I swear—nothing I ever wanted more than her. Before her, I knew other guys were having sex. But I wanted to be good and do the right thing. Reid was there, and . . ." He shoves a hand through his hair, falling down on the bed across from me. "You get all these confusing messages, you know? Abstain and do what's right, but also don't you want to be a real man? I don't know. Before, I thought about it all the time, about what I shouldn't do or want. Felt completely tortured by it because it's what was *right*. But after—after I met Reid, I didn't really think about that anymore."

"It's like she set you free."

"Did she?" he asks. "Or did she give me someone new I felt like I'd never please?" He laughs without humor. "It changed my whole perspective. I knew God would always love me, but it was a fucking mystery if Reid did. Maybe letting that in is what doomed me."

"Don't be ridiculous," I say, and he frowns at me. Lately, every time I try to reconstruct Reid in my mind the way I remember her, another piece fades from view.

I wish he'd stop doing that to me.

"What about after, then?" I ask. "Trey?"

He smiles to himself. "Trey should've been so easy. I fell for him the first time I saw him, across the room at a party in Ravensway. It was his eyes."

"And you knew . . . that he liked you, too?"

"The more we talked, the more sure I was, so I got drunk

and kissed him. Some people aren't willing to take that chance, but—well, you know, it's not exactly an easy place to be out. For either of us. I was afraid if I didn't do it then, I'd miss my chance at something great, and you'll find that alcohol is a hell of a way to lose your inhibitions." He shakes his head out, shakes memories away. "We made it work, for as long as it could. It was easier and harder than being with Reid, I guess. Easier, because Trey always gave love freely. Harder, because I didn't know how to accept it anymore. I couldn't process anything. And God knows I couldn't stop drinking."

"But you said he gave up on you."

Ashton's eyes go glassy for a minute before he wipes them clean. "C'mon, Evelyn, you saw me tonight. Everyone gives up on *that* eventually. He didn't need something so damaged, not when life was hard enough. I guess I never really give them a choice in the end. I needed someone to pick up the pieces, and Trey wanted more than that. After Trey, I couldn't stand the idea of being heart-broken again. So I decided to be alone instead, as much as anyone would let me.

"Jesus." He runs his hands through his hair. "I need a drink." He gets up from the bed and goes to his bag, digging out the Fireball, a bit of liquid still left in the bottle. Seeing it, I realize he's been drinking it when I wasn't paying attention.

He takes a swig and then hands the bottle to me. I do as suggested and take a small sip, my whole body shuddering as it goes down. I return it to him and wipe the back of my hand across my mouth.

"You make it sound so easy," I hear myself say. I almost immediately want to take it back.

"Becoming an alcoholic fuckup?" he asks, tossing the bottle on the floor and collapsing onto the bed again.

"Love," I say.

"If I made love sound easy, then I really fucked up the telling of that tale."

"I guess, like, feeling love for someone else. *Wanting*."

"Sex?" he asks, his eyes on me.

I shrug. "Intimacy." I lie back on my bed and gaze up at the ceiling instead. "I've seen what it does to people. What it did to my mama. I always thought she was so proud when she was younger, you know? She knew other people looked down on us, but she didn't give a shit, and honestly, I think that's why Matt liked her so much. He'd never had that before, really, and then she loved him with everything she had. Until he left us. Once he did that, she was chasing some unfindable *thing*. I've seen her fall for man after shitty man, and I wonder if that's what intimacy does to you. If it's like a drug, and once you've had it, really had *it*, you'll never stop trying to get it again. You'll look for it anywhere, even while it tears your whole life apart."

I roll onto my side so I'm looking over at Ashton on the opposite bed. His face is clear, but his eyes are doing that thing they do so well now, saying everything, and it doesn't surprise me that someone with so much compassion in his eyes could get himself so desperately broken. "Or maybe it kills you," I say.

"That's why you don't want anyone to touch you," he says, and it's such a simple statement that it cuts to my heart. "Not really."

"I don't want to be used," I reply. "I—I don't want to be hurt. Not any more than I already have been." And I think back to every time Dane hit me, and of how sometimes, I would close my eyes and be right back in that spot, walking alone down the road when Reid pulled her car over and saved me.

"What they do to you, what they want from you, that's not intimacy," Ashton tells me. "Listen," he says. "You don't want to be

184

scared of anyone ever getting too close to you. That's like . . . how I got where I am."

"Do you? Want to get close to me?"

He flinches, visibly, like he hadn't thought about it and now that he has, it's all he can think about. "I'm not sure," he says at last. And then, with a swallow that seems to hurt, "I think so."

His eyes go up to the ceiling, and then he pushes his hair back with both of his hands. "I don't know what I'm doing," he says at last.

"How about another test?" I ask.

"What if we fail?" he returns. "What if it turns out intimacy will kill us both?"

"We've done worse," I answer. I finish this bad idea for him. "Get in bed," I tell him.

He freezes, staring over at me. "Are you . . . are you sure?"

"We'll be careful," I say. "Get in bed with me."

Tentatively, he gets closer, climbs on top of the covers, still as far away from me as he can possibly be.

"Like all the way in bed," I admonish him. "I don't have PTSD or anything. I used to sleep in bed with Alex sometimes."

"It's not the same," he says, and I know that.

"I'm asking you to do this," I tell him, trying to keep my voice steady. "You owe me that much at least, right?"

He looks quickly at me. "This is such a bad—" I silence him with a sigh, and he picks up the covers and slides under them. Since he's clearly not going to get any closer, I move toward him. I wonder if this is what it's like.

"Evelyn," he says, his breath soft against my face.

"What?" I return.

"I'm sorry about tonight. You're right, about me. I never had to think about it before, about everything having a price. I don't know what that's like, and I didn't listen to you. And"— he swallows again—"and I think I do want to get close to you."

"How much closer?" I ask.

The bed is small and our bodies are flush, warm.

He lets out a sigh, can't make himself say it. I press my hand against his face, running my fingertips over the stubble on his cheek.

I used to lie in bed with Kara sometimes, her tiny little body snuggled up against mine. I had known then that I was protecting her.

Ashton isn't protecting me.

"You're the prettiest boy I've ever seen," I tell him, and he blinks and almost smiles.

Finally, I roll over, turning my back to him, so we're still touching. Tentatively, he puts his arm around me; I feel his breath on the back of my neck, subtle and understated.

I should've told him I want to be close to him, too.

Instead, I close my eyes and go to sleep.

REID

Eight Inches Off
One Year Before

I chop all my hair off the next day.

There's something powerful in it. Empowering. Mom gasps when she sees me because it's a little haphazard, and I worry for a minute that she'll cry.

"Reid, what the hell are you doing?" she demands.

"Following my whims like always," I return with a sarcastic smile. "I've heard it's my most charming quality."

"You look ridiculous," she tells me. She stands up and starts running her fingers through the thin hair now falling above my shoulders. "All your beautiful hair."

I'm not pretty anymore, not in the way she likes. Now I'm feral. "I think it's interesting now," I respond.

"Did you tell Ashton?" she asks.

I see the hopeful look on her face and choose not to break her heart in a moment of weakness. "I'm going to the store instead," I tell her.

"Why?"

"I left something there the other night," I lie, and now I'm much worse than manipulative; I'm someone who lies about my feelings for no reason. Who lies to protect other people.

Shit.

I don't drive straight to the store. I drive past Ashton's and I stare at the door and the shape of the house and I think about him and his skin and his gap-toothed smile and wonder if he's there or at the restaurant and if he's thinking about me, too.

Of course he is.

I go to the store then, and there's Evelyn working harder than anyone employed at a stupid family country store should ever deign to work. I go in and grab candy and a soda and take it to the front.

She's who I wanted to see. She watches me. I see her doing it all the time, and I wonder why. I'd had this idea that I could *do something* for her. Help her.

I can't even help myself.

"Put it on my tab," I tell her when I hand the items over to her. "How are you?" I ask when she doesn't say anything to me.

She has a light bruise on her face that I almost can't see through her makeup. She has her hair hanging over it. "Shit," I say, and reach out to almost touch her but she pulls away. "Are you okay?"

"Probably," she says, and gives me a half-cheeky smile. "I like your hair."

No she doesn't.

"Ashton broke up with me and I chopped it all off," I tell her, my voice coming out oddly detached even to me.

Her face falls. "Oh."

"It's bullshit, you know," I say to her, and I can hear myself talking and wanting to stop, but I don't. "You spend all this time fighting for one person, and you lose some part of yourself in the process, and then they just leave you. Even though they promised."

"Reid," she says. "It's going to be all right," she says. She looks at me like someone worth looking at, when I can't even face myself.

"What does love feel like?" I ask her, stupidly. "Maybe I fucked this up. Maybe it was wrong."

"Of course not," she says to me with such confidence, and I've never seen her like this before, never heard her voice, the way it speaks with clarity and purpose.

She's been hiding her whole life.

"The way Ashton Harper looks at you," she says. "That's love."

"Sometimes, I think I love him so much, I don't know what to do but break his heart." I play with my class ring, the one Mom forced me to buy because that's what people do. Even if it's not worth the cost, even if I'd rather die than look down at my hand and see the sign of this town and this class and everything it means, it's what everyone else did.

And I think I wear it because some part of me wants so desperately to make her happy.

"Love is so painful," I tell her, "and raw, and sometimes I just want to be free of this stupid, controlling feeling." I want to cry and I don't and that hurts, too. "It's cruel. It's cruel to feel like another person has all the most important parts of you and to not know how to tell them that."

She blinks and blinks and blinks and I wonder if silence can eat two people whole.

The bell over the door rings as someone walks in. Evelyn wipes away tears of her own, ones I can't help but feel jealous of. I take the food she's rung up, and I leave.

I need to think.

EVELYN

Zero Days Left
Now

I wake up the next morning alone, the memory of last night making me feel a dangerous mix of charged and terrified. I wonder if I'm testing boundaries that I'll never be able to put back up.

Protect yourself, Evelyn.

Ashton is in the chair again, but I don't feel the flicker of fear when I see him this time. He turns to me when I sit up in bed.

"Do you sleep?" I ask him.

"I made coffee," he returns, and points at the shitty coffee maker in our room. "Let's go out," he says. "Actually, you stay there, I'll make you a coffee. You like a lot of creamer, right?"

"Ashton," I say. But then what? *I have to go. I have to go before you make this any worse for both of us. Before you let them catch us.*

"I went and talked to the guy in the lobby, and he sold me some tickets for an Opry tour," he tells me. He's pouring coffee into a thin paper cup and mixing in the contents of two plastic creamers now.

My heart races. "You did what? We only have a hundred dollars."

"Technically we only have fifty dollars now," he says. "But

the whole reason you wanted to come to Nashville was to see the Opry."

"What the fuck is wrong with you?" I ask him. "That was all the money we had left. Things have changed."

"There's nothing we can do with a hundred dollars," he tells me. "So what does it matter? There's no out. There's today and it's going to be a fucking amazing day."

"What does that mean?" I ask.

He doesn't completely look at me. "We'll figure the rest out tomorrow. Let's have this day in Nashville for you. *This* is what you wanted. It's what you deserve."

I breathe in and out through my nose, try to tell myself it doesn't matter. I was going to leave today anyway, and I'd figure it out myself, the way I always had.

So, let him waste his last hundred dollars on my dream of Nashville and then I'll *go*. And he'll go home and blame the fire on me and be fine, exactly like Alex had said.

Besides, I did always want to see the Opry.

"Fine," I say. I don't have the fight left in me. I've already started formulating, planning how I'll get a bus ticket to somewhere else, become someone else.

This is the last thing for Evelyn Peters before I really leave her behind for good.

But something about that thought makes me miss home. Not the claustrophobic-ness of home, and not even really the home I remember.

Home before. With Mama and sometimes Matt, and something very close to safety. Home where I used to be *me*. Where I used to believe I deserved to be happy.

And then I say the thought I haven't let myself have in days:

"Do you think there's any chance he's not dead?"

He seems to retreat. "Evelyn," he says.

"What if we're lying to ourselves?" I say.

He almost laughs. "We obviously are, but I don't know which way you mean."

"We're assuming based on what Alex said, but what if—?"

"Evelyn," he says. "Dane is dead. I know."

"How?"

"Trey," he says.

I feel tears sting my eyes. "You're sure?"

"He won't hurt her again," he tells me, and he knew what I wanted. What I needed. "You don't have to go back. Ever."

He hands me the coffee and kneels down in front of me. I feel embarrassed to have him so close, remembering how warm he was last night. How his skin felt against mine.

I don't want to be so vulnerable.

I take the cup, letting it heat my hands through the cheap material. Ashton is right there, and he's so beautiful and so dangerous. Dark eyebrows and dark lashes, shots of Fireball and nights driving through abandoned towns.

This might be the last time I ever get to look at him, up close like this.

"You deserve a day of happiness," he tells me, whispers like a promise.

Maybe I do and maybe I don't. Honestly, what do any of us deserve?

• • •

The Grand Ole Opry tickets Ashton got us include a backstage tour. We walk together past the dressing rooms of the most famous country and bluegrass singers to ever take the stage. And the rooms are so unimpressive, like anyone could walk into them and then walk out onto the stage to perform. I take strange comfort in that.

Our tour guide brings the group to the area where performers prepare to enter the stage. I take a deep breath, my pulse racing like I might be next in the circle. Like I could be Patsy or Loretta or Miranda, even for a moment. Ashton stands behind me, and I've learned to sense him, the way his body leans toward mine, feels and feeds my excitement. But he doesn't touch me, and I feel like there's knowing in that.

And then I think, *God, I'm really losing my mind.*

I think, *Let him go.*

To wrap up, the tour guide leads us onstage so we look out over the audience. "And finally," the tour guide says, "we offer you all the chance to stand in the circle. This is a piece of the Grand Ole Opry floor taken from the original building. We want every musician who plays at the Opry to stand where the greatest country musicians of all time have stood and sung. And now you all have that chance, too." The tourists in their Nashville shirts all pull out their cameras, greedy to be in the circle. I hang back, letting all the other people on the tour go before me. I need to prepare for it, to accept that I'm really here. Finally, the tour guide looks back at us expectantly, just me and Ashton.

"Do y'all want to come on up?" the guide asks us.

Ashton glances at me and I shrug at him, a nonverbal language we are both learning every day.

We walk together into the circle and gaze out over the seats, hundreds upon hundreds of them lined up and empty, but where, later tonight, people might be, looking up with expectant faces and listening and clapping and lost in the music.

"You should be up here by yourself," Ashton whispers to me, and then he steps back and I am alone. I start counting the seats, breathing in the moment, imagining every face upturned, and it's silly, a daydream I had one time, but I'm also standing here in a place I never imagined I could be, and that's real.

I really left McNair Falls behind.

And isn't there power in that? I was so afraid of being stuck. Of becoming my mama.

I'd given in to it.

"I'd capture it for you," Ashton says, "if I could." I turn around and meet his eyes.

"That would ruin it," I say, and he nods.

I take one last look and then we go.

• • •

We grab gyros (*twelve more dollars down*, I think, even knowing it doesn't matter anymore) from a food cart and walk through Music Row, which has almost nothing to do with music. People stumble out of the honky-tonks, laughing like any and everything happening is the funniest thing that has ever happened. Brides-to-be stumble past wearing a bizarre number of penis accessories.

"Do you need a drink?" I ask Ashton. It's early still so the bars aren't teeming with life, but I see that shine he gets in his eyes when it's been too long.

"Not right now," he tells me, and he fakes a smile. I know he's trying, after last night, and that makes me sad. "You belong here, Evelyn."

"I don't belong anywhere."

"When you sang"—he shakes his head—"it was like nothing else existed."

"You're biased," I tell him.

"I'm biased to feel nothing," he answers.

"Oh, Ashton," I say, "you're biased to feel everything." He looks down as I say it, nodding his silent agreement almost to himself.

"What else did you do?" he asks. "What else did you love in McNair Falls? Besides music and your sister."

I sigh. "Nothing? I guess."

"Really?" he asks, raising an eyebrow as we dodge a Garth Brooks impersonator.

"Why do you care so much?" I ask, though I can't help but laugh.

He shrugs. "We're here together. You know so much about me, but I'm still not really sure I know you."

I think on it—on the little pockets of happiness I carved out for myself, something I can give him. "I used to read to Kara a lot," I tell him. "And sometimes to myself. When Matt hung out at our house, he'd have all these old-school fantasy books he'd read at night. I'd ask to borrow them when he finished, and I never gave them back. They're under my bed now." I stop, feeling that loss suddenly. Not just Matt, but Matt's fantasy books. "I guess they're not, actually. Shit." I shake my head.

"Sorry," he says. He stops at an open window, and we stand there and listen to someone crooning Reba.

"Nothing like performing for the noon crowd in the honky-tonks," Ashton says, and I can tell he thinks it's depressing.

"At least they've got a dream," I tell him. "That's what Mrs. Brewer used to tell me, you know? 'Get a dream, girl.'"

"I'm not sure she's the one who should be telling anyone to get a dream," Ashton says in a dark voice. "She ain't exactly got a lot going for her."

"She's had a hard fucking life," I shoot back defensively.

"She's still got a drug problem," Ashton says. "Though I guess it's not your phone she calls at three in the morning."

"What?" I ask.

He shakes his head. "It doesn't matter. C'mon, I've got another surprise."

"Ashton, wait," I say, standing there in front of the bar as he takes off. He looks back at me.

"Not *today*, Evelyn. I don't want to talk about it. Please."

And after a few beats, I agree and go with him.

We return to Ashton's car, and he drives through town until we get to a large shopping center. He pulls in, parking near the food court.

"What are we doing here?" I ask.

"*That* is what we're doing here," he answers me, pointing at a large steamboat docked on the river next to the mall. He grins. "The guy in our lobby sold me these tickets, too."

"Ashton," I say, "how much money do you have left?"

He doesn't answer me because we both know the answer. "They're nonrefundable," he says. "So we're setting sail now or we're flushing it all down the drain."

I'm angry and I'm not. At least he'll have plenty of time to think about it when he figures out how he's going to get back to McNair Falls tomorrow.

I shrug. "I've never been on a boat before," I tell him.

He opens my door, takes my hand with such new and casual confidence that I forget to retreat, and not twenty minutes later, the air is whipping through my hair as we sail across the Cumberland River.

We wander the decks, listen to a Dolly Parton impersonator performing on a stage in the belly of the ship. I find myself singing along to "My Tennessee Mountain Home." She finishes it off with a flourish, and we clap enthusiastically. She gets close to the mic and tells us we might be familiar with this one, though we may have forgotten it was a Dolly original.

Then the opening chords of "I Will Always Love You" ring out.

"Too bad," I say to Ashton. "A slow one."

He grabs on to my hand and pulls my body flush with his. "No time like the present."

I smile up at him. "You are one for a dramatic moment."

"I learned from the best."

His easy manner belies the truth. The way our pounding hearts are in sync. The way his fingers trace the small of my back, where he's looped his arms around me. I hum along with the words, and I feel him lean into me.

"How is it?" I ask, close enough to count his dark lashes.

"Different," he says, "than I remember." He takes a deep breath that I feel through his shirt.

"You have more practice than me," I whisper.

"You're a natural," he says, his fingers finding the end of my long hair, teasing out a few curls.

We step back from each other when the song ends, and I can tell how much it is. Maybe too much.

Finally, he says: "The sun is setting soon."

"Let's go watch it," I answer.

The two of us walk upstairs and to the railing on the left side of the ship—Ashton tells me it's called port. We lean out, gazing over the horizon. I watch as Ashton closes his eyes, the wind whipping harsh against his face, tossing his hair. It's cold out here, so other passengers are scarce.

"I never thought I'd feel like this again," Ashton tells me when he opens his eyes. "Happy. Wasn't sure I'd even still remember the feeling."

"Happy?" I ask. "That's what this is?"

I feel the way he's looking at me, imagine the way I must look with the wind blowing my hair on this boat on the edge of the river. I know I don't look anything like Reid, and I know how much he feels everything, even if he wishes he didn't.

He feels everything right up until it breaks him open and he spills out.

"I think so," he tells me. "I've half forgotten."

"The water," I can't help but say, "doesn't it remind you of her? Just a little."

He blanches. "I try not to think of her that way. The way she died. That it ever happened. Maybe it's getting easier." He looks over at me again.

"Ashton," I say, slow. "You know I'm not her, right? Reid."

I used to wish I could be her. Wish it until I felt like I'd forgotten myself. But maybe I was never wishing to be her at all; maybe I was wishing for her.

For something I didn't understand.

"Of course I know that," he tells me, and I only believe him a little. "Reid never wanted this. She didn't want happiness, not really. Couldn't find the ability to love inside herself. She lost the part of her that knew how to want those things."

This isn't love.

Or maybe it is. Maybe you kill someone and you run away and that's love.

"You know," I say, letting the words bubble up on my lips, "she kissed me. Once."

Shock doesn't even reach his eyes. He laughs. "Of course she did."

"You broke up with her," I say. We're farther apart now, I realize.

"I guess I did," he returns.

"But," I say, "she never really liked me. Not even as a person. She felt sorry for me. And she definitely didn't like me that way.

"I think maybe it was a game," I say. "I see it now, a little more clearly."

"And did you," Ashton asks me, "like her that way?"

"I don't know." I shrug. "Maybe. I still close my eyes sometimes and think about it. Her purple lipstick and dark eyes and the way she pushed my hair back. Is that what loving someone feels like?"

I look up at his face when he's silent and see the tears pooling in his eyes, and I remember just how deeply destroyed he is. "Yeah," he says. "Yeah, it is."

He leans his head down against mine and whispers, "I'm sorry," and I know he means for both of us, for loving a girl who can't love us back. For all of this. For the end we both know is coming.

And I hate myself a little for it because I know it's weak, but I wrap my arms around his torso and lean into him so tight against the wind and he holds me tighter and God help me, I wish we could make it last.

REID

Three Girls
One Year Before

It's the first day of school since Ashton broke up with me, and it's a shit day.

Every day is a shit day, but this one is the worst shit day I've ever experienced.

I failed a test that I didn't care about before Ashton and certainly don't care about after. I got detention for saying "fuck this" in front of my history teacher, which is apparently now a high crime in the halls of McNair Falls High School. I haven't eaten since Subway—I tossed the candy I bought from Evelyn directly into the trash—and I'm actually hungry, but everything looks like more shit.

So, the bell rings and this shit day is finally done and that's when I see it. Evelyn hanging back from her locker, waiting for Savannah to finish grabbing all her things, so she can avoid Savannah's constant torture. And that's it. I throw my book bag down and make my way over there.

"You have so much fucking nerve," I say to Savannah, cornering her at her locker.

"Can I help you, Reid?" she says, not flinching. "Did you lose something maybe? Your boyfriend?" And then she laughs. She's not scared of me.

Fuck. That.

I slam her into the locker. She freezes in shock, so I do it again, pinning her back against the locker with my forearm, pushing her farther into it. Her expression changes to complete terror, and she screeches, causing every face in the hallway to turn toward us. "I swear to God, Savannah, don't you ever fucking—"

"Reid! What in the hell are you doing?" And there's the knight in shining armor, Ashton goddamn Harper, riding in on his fucking steed.

"Don't worry about it, Ashton," I spit.

He easily pulls me off Savannah, and I massage the red from my arm where it pressed into her.

"I'm so sorry, Savannah," he's saying, touching her gently. "Are you okay?"

"She's insane, Ashton," Savannah says through tears. But they're real ones, and I revel in that, in the best part of my shit day when I shoved her and she cried.

Ashton says a few more placating words to Savannah—words I can't even hear over the buzzing in my ears—and then grabs me by the arm and drags me away, everyone in the hall watching us as we go.

We're through the front doors and out into the parking lot and then we're even farther away, out close to the road.

He takes several long breaths and he's looking at me and hating me and there's so much longing there that I don't know what to do with it anymore.

I almost laugh.

I knew it. I knew he loved me.

"Why, Reid?" he asks me, and I know he doesn't care that

I shoved Savannah. I know he'd be fine if I did it all over again because Savannah is Savannah, and me and him—we are us. He runs his fingers through his hair, staring down at the ground because he can't look at me.

"Eventually, you'll figure it out, Ashton," I say, and he looks up, his expression guarded. "I'm the villain in this story."

"Reid," he says, and his voice cracks. I grab on to the front of his shirt and pull him toward me because when I touch him, he knows. He relaxes into my touch and then his lips crush mine and we kiss like starving people, people who have forgotten how it even feels not to be hungry, his hands tangled in my destroyed hair like it's all he thought about since the first time he saw me this morning.

We kiss like it's the end.

EVELYN

$38 Left
Now

After the cruise, Ashton and I stop for hot chicken; we both know it doesn't matter anymore, the money. Any of it. We let the day run away with us. We engage in a spirited conversation with our waitress about the hotness of the hot chicken until we finally agree on an order. It comes out faster than I expected, and just like the rest of the day, I can feel the way time is running out.

"Are you having fun?" Ashton asks, pulling a piece of chicken apart with his fingers.

"Are you?" I ask him with a smile, dodging the question.

"It's nice," he says, "to see you actually look happy. Not, like, weighed down. Happy."

I tear into the chicken with my teeth, savoring it the way a prisoner might a last meal, and then chug the water in front of me when my mouth starts to burn. "That's another illusion, though." But I laugh while I say it like it doesn't matter at all.

"No, it's not," he tells me seriously. "Who you were before. That was what you put up to protect yourself, you said so yourself. Now, you can do what you really want—"

I cut him off. "You live in a fantasy, Ashton. You always have. *Today* was a fantasy."

"It's not a fantasy," he says. "It's a perfect day."

"A perfect day before what exactly?"

"Nothing," he says.

"No, tell me what," I return. "Does this end with the two of us going out in a blaze of glory, driving off a cliff? Is that what you want?"

"I didn't mean that," he says.

"Didn't you? Isn't that how you like things? Fireworks and drama?"

"Low blow," he mutters. He takes the straw in his drink and knocks the ice at the bottom of his cup around, watching it instead of me.

"You know this is over just as much as I do, so you either think we're going home or we're going to be dead. Which is it?"

He doesn't answer until I think he's not going to say anything at all. But then he begins, "You love being miserable and practical because you think that makes you superior. And you hang on to that so you can never get anything you actually want." The way he says it is like it interests him, like he's gone distant again and is processing some fact. "Reid used to tell me I loved being miserable, and maybe I did, but not like you. Maybe that's what Reid liked about both of us."

It hits me then. I cannot stand to hear one more thing about Reid Brewer, because everything is and always has been about Reid Brewer, and that's not fair anymore. This is *my* life.

So I stand up, my chair scraping across the floor. "I have to go to the bathroom," I tell him, throwing my napkin down on the table. I don't care if he has to crawl home after I leave him.

I make my way through the restaurant, past the bar area. A TV plays over the bartender's shoulder, attached to the wall behind him. A picture flashes on the screen, stops me in my tracks. The setting is familiar, a trailer back up against woods that stretch forever, but where the trailer once stood, a burned-out shell stands instead.

I swallow.

To my relief, the scene fades, replaced by something else. And then horror grips me. My and Ashton's faces are on the screen—old yearbook photos that make it so obvious side by side that we are two people who don't belong together.

The bartender has noticed me. "You need anything?" he asks.

"Can you—can you turn on the captions on that TV?" I ask him. He shrugs, presses a button on the remote, and goes to serve another customer. The words type their way across the screen. *If you have any information, please call the Crime Stoppers number below.* An impeccably dressed woman appears behind her news desk, and the captions say, *One man was injured in the fire. He has returned home and is expected to make a full recovery.*

"Excuse me," I call to the bartender. He comes back over to me. "Can I borrow your phone?" At the look on his face, I continue, "It's an emergency. Please. I'll leave you all the money I have." I hope he doesn't take me up on it.

He shakes his head. "It's okay," he says, reading the panic in my eyes. "Ain't the weirdest thing I've ever been asked." He unlocks the screen and hands the phone over. I step out of the bar and dial a number I know by heart.

"Helen Brewer speaking," she answers on the other end.

"Mrs. Brewer," I breathe into the phone.

"*Evelyn,*" she says, and hearing her say my name is like coming home. "Thank God. Where are you?"

"It doesn't matter," I say.

"Come home. *Please.*"

"Is Dane alive?" I ask her.

She pauses, and I know she knows what I did and knows why. She inhales sharply and then continues. "You need to come home, Evelyn."

"Please tell me what's going on there, Mrs. Brewer."

"Listen to me," she replies, a note of hysteria in her voice, "you have to get away from him. You can't trust him. You cannot trust him."

My eyes go to where I know Ashton is sitting.

"Why?" I return.

"I've already lost one girl to Ashton Harper," Mrs. Brewer says to me. "I can't take losing another."

At that, I hang up. I erase the call and hurry back to the bar, feeling the vibration in my skin like some sort of second heartbeat. I hand the bartender his phone, go to the bathroom, and return to the table.

"Took you long enough," Ashton says, and he catches the wild look in my eyes. "Evelyn. What's wrong?"

I stare across the table, calculating.

You can't trust him.

"Ashton," I say, "Dane is alive."

ACT 3
GUNPOWDER
& LEAD

EVELYN

As soon as Ashton looks over at me, somehow I know exactly what he'll say before he forms the words: "I know."

I'd been waiting for the betrayal to come—somehow, it always does. And from the first moment we'd locked eyes on each other, it had been too safe.

No one would do all of this for me.

"What do you mean, *you know*?"

He doesn't say anything at first, not meeting my eyes. He grabs a wet wipe, trying to clean off his sticky hands before he answers me, and the absurdity of the whole thing hits me.

I wait.

"Before I threw out my phone, Trey texted me. Said Dane was alive, and we should go back before it got any worse."

The world expands, opening back up to include Dane, and then contracts again until it's just the two of us sitting at this ridiculous table pretending to have a normal dinner and Ashton is staring over at me, his hand too close to mine on the table.

"I couldn't—"

"You lied to me!" I shout over him. People turn their heads and we could be any couple. Any couple in an argument in this stupid chicken restaurant. "You *promised me*, Ashton."

"Because I knew what would—"

"What did you do to her?" I ask him. "Reid. What did you do to her?"

He pulls his hand back from mine, shocked. "I didn't—" he starts, then stops. He swallows. "Do we have to do this here?"

"Do *what* here? I'm not listening to another fucking word you have to say until you tell me what happened to Reid." And I don't know why I'm so furious about Reid in this moment when he lied and Dane still exists, but it's all I can see and all I can hear and Reid is gone and I still don't understand why.

I see Ashton retreat; his expression becomes that same blank slate I saw the first night, like watching a painting fade in fast-forward before your eyes.

"I killed her," Ashton says. He stares down at the table and then says it again, "I killed her."

I don't know what to say to that, the words are so absurd. He won't look at me, and I won't look away from him. "Reid drowned," I say.

"When we hit that rock and she went over, she screamed for at least a minute. I still hear the way her voice sounded, you know? It's burned into my memory, clearer than my own face."

"So, what?" I say, the anger thrumming in my voice. "You didn't save her?"

"No, Evelyn," he says, and finally looks up at me, dark eyes holding mine. "I got as drunk as I could because I couldn't stand your precious Reid, and then I steered into a rock and I listened to her drown. Do you understand?"

"You killed her."

"Not consciously," he quickly amends. "I didn't mean—"

"You killed her," I say again. "And tried to make me feel guilty about killing Dane."

"I tried to tell you—" he begins, and he's trying to take it all back as quickly as he said it.

"You *lied*, you lied like you've been lying every day. They said Reid was the one who crashed the boat."

"So I was supposed to watch my family get destroyed?" he spits back. "Watch my parents lose their restaurant because I'm a fuckup who fell in love with a girl who made me an even bigger fuckup?"

"That's the thing about boys like you, isn't it? A girl is dead, but what about you? What about your life and how important it is? Who gives a fuck if some trashy girl from McNair Falls died as long as Ashton Harper can still achieve his dreams? She was just a body, right? Just something for you to have."

Tears well in Ashton's eyes as he looks across the table at me. "In case you haven't noticed, I haven't exactly been enjoying my life since then."

"It must be so hard for you," I reply, unmoved. "You would've left my sister to the wolves so we could keep living this little fantasy of yours forever, wouldn't you? We'd go out in a fiery crash and you'd finally be at peace, but what about me? What about *us*?"

"Evelyn, please," he says.

"You ruin *everything*," I tell him. "You ruined your life and Reid's and the Brewers' and you even ruined this stupid fucking Bonnie and Clyde idea you had because nothing matters to Ashton Harper. You say it was all a game for Reid, but I wonder if you were the one always playing make-believe. Because you could leave and go back to your old life whenever you wanted, couldn't you? She just inconvenienced you by dying in the process."

A tear runs down his cheek, but I realize he's angry, too. Good. I want a fight.

"Don't you talk about her like you understand. You kissed her once and look how it did you in. Try to multiply that by a fucking lifetime and you tell me how easy it is."

"And who could ever love a girl who's not easy?" I snarl.

"One day," he whispers to me. "One good day, and then I could finally end it—I want it to be finished. If I'm gone, once I'm *clean*, maybe that would bring me peace, maybe—"

I stand up, staring down at him. "This isn't your story," I say. "Not an epic adventure for *you*. This is my life. People like Reid and me? We're not props. Our lives are real, and we may not be as important as you, but this matters. *We matter*."

I leave the table and walk out of the restaurant.

REID

"What's wrong now?" Ashton asks me.

"Why do you always do that? Assume something's wrong? I'm happy," I say. This is what happiness feels like.

Ashton's arm is locked around my body, and we're in the back seat of his car down our favorite dirt road, looking up at the stars out of his sunroof, and all I can think is:

Why do I feel so fucking wrong all the time?

"Do you think maybe . . . something went wrong when they made us?"

"When who made us?"

"I don't know," I say. "Whoever made us. I mean, I know you believe in God and everything so I don't know, let's say it was him. He made us and some shit went wrong. He broke us. He fucked up."

"God doesn't make mistakes. That's kind of his whole thing."

"Well, that's bullshit," I say. "Everyone makes mistakes." I prop myself up on my elbow so I can look down at him. "No one would make us like this on purpose. There's something *wrong*."

"Reid, seriously, are you okay?"

No.

"Ashton," I go on, "*look at us*. You hate yourself for this. You hate yourself for me."

"No," he says. "I don't." But the look on his face tells me he's wrong. He can't help but think it.

"No sane person would want to be with me," I say. "I push people and I push them and push them until they break, but you can't stop. You can't stop hating yourself just enough to love me."

"Reid"—he closes his eyes, scrubs his face with his hands—"we just got back together after you did something truly fucked up. Why are you saying all this?"

"I'm trying to save you," I tell him because it's obvious. "I thought this was the answer. Find the perfect boy. Win the game. Whatever."

"What game?" he asks.

"I don't know. *This town's.*" I touch his face. Winning always meant staying, I realize. That's what my mom had been telling me all these years, even if she hadn't been saying it. And staying— maybe that was the only thing that was safe for a person like me. "It was never supposed to be like this."

He reaches up and pushes a dark piece of hair behind my ear. "Do you ever think about it? That day at your car with the tire? I thought I was happy. I thought I was fine, that life was great. But it wasn't. That's what I felt when I met you, like I'd come out of a deep sleep. Before, it was one long day with no end. No sunset or night or sunrise. *Nothing.*" He sounds pained and I know why.

He wishes he could've been happy in the sun.

Because I'm his night. Maybe sometimes, *sometimes*, I'm the sunset or the sunrise, but more than anything else, I'm his night.

"I would be your sun if I could," I tell him.

"I know," he says, and he sounds so resigned that I know it's true.

But I feel it in the air. This is the end of the longest day, and neither of us is escaping it alive.

EVELYN

Twenty-Three Hours Left

Ashton finds me waiting outside by his car.

He scrubs his tired face with his hands. "I'm sorry," he says. "I didn't mean—"

"Stop apologizing and let me in the car," I snap.

"I know you loved her," he says. "Reid, I mean. I shouldn't have said any different."

"I didn't love her," I tell him. "I didn't even know her."

"I know."

"Because you think I wouldn't have loved her if I'd known her."

He looks me over, eyes up and down my body. "I have no idea, Evelyn. I won't pretend to know anymore. But whatever else you think of me, I loved Reid—I loved her until it ripped me apart—so don't pretend you know more about it than me." He unlocks the car and I get in without saying anything else, but my eyes are glued on him. On all of him, and I imagine how he looked to Reid. She looked at me like a toy; she looked at him like the sun.

He doesn't deserve that.

We're quiet as we start the ride back to the motel. I can't hear anything but the buzzing in my ears—the sound of coming doom.

I have a picture of Kara stuffed into my guitar case. It was taken last year. Mrs. Brewer had invited me to ride to Table Rock with her for a picnic, and I'd asked if I could bring Kara along. She'd been delighted.

I'd asked Mrs. Brewer if she used to bring Reid along with her to Table Rock, looked for some stupid connection across time and space, and she said she had, when Reid was younger. But it had been years since they'd gone to Table Rock together when Reid died.

"It didn't make her happy anymore," Mrs. Brewer had said. "Sometimes, it was so hard to make her happy."

The three of us had piled into Mrs. Brewer's car and ridden up for the day for one of the most delicious lunches I'd ever had—fresh deli sandwiches and potato salad and cheese on crackers, with homemade cookies for dessert. Afterward, we'd watched the kids splashing around in the water and Kara had crawled into my lap. Mrs. Brewer snapped the picture on her phone.

She'd handed it to me a few weeks later, all printed out on nice paper.

"You're both so beautiful," she'd said.

I hadn't even known people printed pictures anymore.

"Evelyn," Ashton says, cutting through the silence. "Please tell me what you're thinking."

"Why?" I snap.

"I should've told you about Dane," he says, "but I was afraid."

Good, I think.

"Here's what I'm thinking," I say instead. "I'm thinking that we drive back to McNair Falls and we finish this once and for all. And I don't take any stupid fucking shortcuts like setting a fire this time. I *end* it.

"I'm thinking I make sure Dane never lays a hand on my sister again."

He doesn't answer me. We pull back up to our motel room, and I see the way Ashton grips the keys tight, slips them into his jeans pocket on the opposite side from me. "Will you please listen to me for a minute?" he asks.

"You're a liar," I reply. "Why should I believe anything you say? You killed Reid. And you knew about Dane and you told me he was dead."

It burns through me. Staying with him every minute and through every whim when my sister could've been suffering. When he never cared about any of us.

"Because I thought maybe I had a chance of saving you from yourself."

"I don't need saving," I return. "I need justice."

"Justice," he says, shaking his head, looking as if he's half laughing at the thought. "Does that include me, too?"

I swallow. "Maybe you can set it right. Maybe that's why you found me. Maybe that's why we have to kill Dane."

"Listen," he says, "I have an idea."

I don't answer.

He says, "I'll call my parents in the morning. I'm sure they'll be so relieved to hear from me that all will be forgiven."

"Aren't your parents going to be pissed?"

"Of course," he tells me. "But they'll care more that I'm back. That I'm okay." He takes a deep breath. "I'll promise them to go to rehab. It's all they've wanted for a long time." He shifts, stops, and shifts again, and it's clear how unmoored the thought makes him. "And then I'll ask them to get a lawyer. For both of us.

"We'll turn ourselves in and see what kind of deal we can make. And we can tell them about Dane. We'll save your sister. I promise."

"That's not a promise you can make," I reply. "Not really." I gaze out ahead of me. I learned a long time ago that no one was coming to save me. "Besides, I already know you don't keep your promises."

"I swear to God, Evelyn," he says. "And he's about the last person who believes in me. I will not let anything happen to you and your sister. I'd rather be dead myself."

"Like you're such a far cry from that already," I say, cold as I can be.

"Maybe so," he returns evenly, "but at least this way gives us a chance."

I sit with it for a second, rolling it around in my head. He has these big hopeful eyes, the kind that aren't giving up anymore, no matter how much the world tries to force it.

"So, you'd really do that?" I ask him. "You'd go back? You'd change?"

He closes his eyes, and in that moment, I see exactly how much it costs him. "Yes." Then he looks over at me. "And I'll tell them everything I did. I'll tell them what happened to Reid, if you'll just promise."

I swallow and our eyes are locked on one another's and I think maybe it's not too hard to fall into another person, to shape yourself around them.

It's Ashton Harper's favorite hobby.

I get out of the car and he breathes a sigh of relief.

We go into the motel room. I throw my pullover on the table beside the door and sit down on my bed, carefully unlacing my ratty old shoes. Ashton shrugs off his jacket. I watch him.

"You really wanted her dead?"

He pauses in the act of taking off his shirt. He finishes, tosses it to the side, and looks over at me, bare-chested and skinny, his necklace with Reid's ring hanging down. "That's not what I meant," he says.

"Yes, it is," I respond.

"Why are you doing this?"

"What?" I ask. "Asking you what happened? Could you have saved her?"

"Jesus, Evelyn."

"You didn't try," I say.

"If I'd tried, I would have gone down with her."

"Good," I respond, but I can't help but think the only thing worse than Reid drowning would have been Ashton drowning with her.

He stands there, almost overwhelmed by the thought, before his face changes into something meaner. "You didn't feel guilty about killing him, did you?"

"No," I reply. "He was dead the moment he laid a hand on my sister."

"That's your answer to everything. Burn it all down."

"Oh, fuck off," I tell him.

"That's what you do. You get hurt and you cut everyone and everything off. Resign yourself to misery. Give up on life and the world and then say you didn't have any choice.

"You burn things down because that's easier than trying."

"Says the boy with so many feelings, he thinks drinking himself numb is the only way to control them." I stare back at him defiantly. "I've never gotten anything but shit for trying my entire life. I've always been trash to all of them."

"Not me," Ashton says.

"So what? You think that means you've earned me as a prize?"

We size each other up in silence, both breathing hard. His face changes ever so slightly to something like defeat.

"Is that really what you think of me?"

That's what I think of everyone.

But he watches me and I hear a boy in my mind saying "burn it all down," and I shake my head. He lets out a breath, relieved.

"*Stop* pushing me away," he says at last.

It's so stupid, but I'm staring across the room at him with his pale skin shining in the dull light, and I ache everywhere deep down into my heart, and Jesus, something about that feels so good. Like the switch is flipped to *On* when it never has been for my entire life.

"I can't."

"What do you want, Evelyn?" he asks. He closes the space between us, and then he's in front of me, standing at the edge of the bed. He drops his hands to my face and I don't draw breath. I'm not sure what will happen when I do start breathing again. "What do you want?" he asks again.

We watch each other carefully across the distance. "I want to know why you're doing this," I say.

Ashton licks his lips in that slow, nervous way he does. I feel his heart beating in his fingertips. "Because I was standing in the woods four days ago and I didn't care about anything and all I ever thought was that maybe, one day, I'd finally not be such a coward and end this once and for all."

I raise my hand to touch him, fall short, and instead, it comes to rest against the denim covering his thigh. I run my thumb back and forth over the rough fabric because if I don't do something, I feel as if I might combust.

"And then I met you," he tells me, "and you needed someone to give a shit and that was something I could do; it gave me something else besides the hum of *just fucking kill yourself* in my head. Something like hope."

"One day and a blaze of glory?" I repeat the words from the restaurant back to him. "Have you really changed that much?" He looks down.

"We both know this is over. And I guess . . . I guess that's why, for all of it. Because for the first time in forever, there was *something* where before there had only been nothing. I'm so *sick* of nothing, Evelyn. I needed you, and once it was over, there was only one way to keep going . . . I needed to want to be close to someone again."

"I'm not her," I tell him. "I'll never be her." I blink away the tears that want to fall, but a single one escapes and rolls down my cheek. "I'm not Reid."

"Maybe I didn't know that then," he admits. "But I do now. I do."

Reid wasn't easy anymore, the way she always had been. She was *so much*.

I'm *so much*.

"We'll be okay," he says to me. "Both of us. We're going to be okay. I can save you. We can save each other."

It hits me then that I can see him again. His face is no longer blank; he's back, he's there, the burning in his eyes, the emotion in his beautiful voice, asking me to absolve him. He's what a boy should look like, sharp cheekbones and dark brows and with that small gap between his teeth that makes him, him.

"I'm not your hero, Ashton," I say. "I can't save you. I wish I could." Maybe that's what she wanted to say.

His face falls imperceptibly, and I wish he'd let me go, but I know he won't. "Then just touch me again," he says. "Touch me again like I'm more than worthless in your eyes."

I shouldn't. I wish I didn't want to. I wish I could ignore this longing, this desperate need inside me, because I know it will be both our destruction.

I point at the chain hanging around his neck, the ring shining back at me. The thing between us. The thing we both can't let go.

"Take it off," I say. He looks down, his face clouding, and fingers the ring carefully. Holds it up, looking at it one last time.

Slowly, he slips the chain over his neck, placing it on the bedside table next to him.

We stare at each other for a minute, over every terrible secret between us, my heartbeat echoing loud in my ears, and then, before I can lose the nerve I'm up and across the distance and we are kissing and his mouth is so warm, his body is so warm, it's like coming home to somewhere you've never been, like losing yourself in the addiction you've been fighting.

He presses his fingers against my back, the two of us colliding into each other. We fall down onto his bed and I think I've never felt anything like that before and then I'm pressing my hands into the contours of his collarbone and I think, this is why they do it, this is what it feels like.

"Can I—?" he tries to mumble between our mouths, and I pull off my own shirt and then we roll over so he is staring down at me. His hands trace my body and I can see why he's a believer, the way his hands are made for worship. And then his mouth is on my skin and we don't have to say anything, we never had to say anything.

I unbutton his jeans and slide them down and then he asks me if it's okay and takes mine off, and I can't believe that anything can be this way, that it's okay now, and then his mouth is moving down my body and I think of how entirely vulnerable I am and how I don't feel scared at all and is that what it means? To want?

"Ashton," I say, and he hears it in my voice, how all of it has changed, in the way I say his name like a prayer.

His fingers brush against the underwear I'm wearing and I feel sick and euphoric. His eyes are on mine and he asks the question. "Do you want me to?"

Of course, I think, but what if that's it? What if this is the end for me and I can never stop wanting again. If I can't remember how to be what I was before.

Can I really do this?

I push my hair back out of my face, afraid to say anything, trying to catch my breath. He is staring up at me, eyes still locked on mine, and I know he won't, not unless he hears it.

"Yes," I say.

He delicately slides my underwear down my legs and then his mouth is hot against my skin again, his hands splayed over my stomach, and I close my eyes and tilt my head back and it shoots through me like fire, destroying everything in its path.

I don't know—not really—how it's supposed to be. But it's so achingly tender and satisfying, the way control slips away from me, the way Ashton's mouth moves so slowly across my thighs like a promise. Like a reckoning.

The moment I realize, for the first time in my life, that all he cares about is how I feel. And then it's just the two of us.

His mouth and my body and nothing between us but an entire fucking world of hurt we're both so desperate to forget about.

Afterward, he climbs back up the bed and pulls me into his arms. It's the first time I've ever seen him fall asleep, when it hasn't been him seeing me.

He looks like a child.

I gaze up at the darkness and wait.

I try not to sleep.

REID

Twenty-Three Hours Left

Ashton pulls up beside my parents' lawn and looks out over the one-story brick house. We have dinner with my parents sometimes and then afterward, he sits down to watch the Braves with my dad and they talk about their abysmal bullpen or their promising young talent and sometimes I fall asleep on the couch leaned up against Ashton's body or sometimes I just pretend to.

Actually, come to think of it, we haven't done that in a long time.

"Reid," Ashton says, "I don't want to leave you." And I know what he means because I'm a little afraid to leave me, too.

I don't know how to tell him I've wanted him for longer than I can remember, but now that want is tied up in so many other fucked-up things between us, I don't know how to untangle it.

"I'm sorry I kissed Dante," I say instead.

He stares straight ahead, hands gripped tight on the steering wheel. "I know you do things sometimes just to be cruel," he tells me. "But I don't know why."

My eyes sting, but still, tears refuse to fall. "You'll never believe me, but I don't want to be cruel to you. It's only that . . . sometimes . . . sometimes, I get so tangled up in my head that I think the way to fix things is to destroy them. That if I do something with my whole heart, I can control it. I can make people act the way I want them to."

"But you don't need to control me," he says. *Of course I do*.

"You never would've fallen in love with me if I didn't," I answer him.

"Where did you get that idea from?" he asks. "I fell in love with you of my own free will." He says it like it's so obvious, and I realize he has no idea how wrong he is.

"No, you didn't," I say. "You fell in love with me because I crashed my car when you weren't taking me seriously."

"I needed a wake-up call," he says, his brow furrowing in confusion. "I thought it was moving too fast, that I didn't want a serious relationship. I was stupid and I was scared, but it was so much scarier to think about something happening to you."

"So I had to drive myself into a fucking accident to make that happen," I say, disdain in my voice.

"What does . . ." Ashton swallows. "What does that even mean?"

"And that fucking flat tire the very first day I got your attention. Even *today*, you didn't come to me, not the way I needed. You think you would've even remembered me at all if I hadn't gone after Savannah? Jesus, you make me jump through so many hoops."

"What the hell does that mean?" Ashton demands. "You got into that accident on purpose?"

"How stupid are you, Ashton?" I ask him.

He shakes his head. "Apparently stupid enough to think that you weren't completely outside of rational fucking human behavior."

"I would've torn Savannah Rykers apart to get your attention. That's how much I want you," I tell him, and I can tell he doesn't know what to do. I went too far and said too much and ruined everything, the way I knew I would.

Shit.

"I need you to go," Ashton says.

"Hang on," I say. "Wait."

"Reid, get out of my car," he says, raising his voice only slightly. *"Please."*

"No," he says. *"No."*

I resign myself, reaching for the door handle. "Your will won't last," I tell him. "It never does."

"Get! Out! Reid!" He does lose his temper then, and I feel it. I step out of the car and take a deep breath, watching him drive away into the night.

Then I walk into the house, letting the screen door slam behind me.

"Reid," Mom says. She's sitting in the kitchen in her old McNair Falls High T-shirt and a bathrobe, drinking some of her sleep tea. "Where have you been? You have school tomorrow."

"It's a teacher workday," I say.

She checks the clock on the oven. "It's still too late for this, hon."

"I was getting Ashton back," I tell her. She meets my eyes and nods, taking a sip of tea. I sit down next to her and lean into her shoulder. I feel her almost pull back in surprise. "I'm tired, Mama," I tell her, just like I used to when I was a child.

"Oh, sweetie," she says, putting an arm around me.

"I've been doing whatever it takes for so long," I say.

From the corner of my eye, I see her wince and I know she doesn't want to know what *whatever it takes* really entails. You're supposed to go as far as you can until you go too far, and she was always too afraid to go over that line.

I always knew that, so I never let myself be scared to cross it.

"It won't be so bad in the morning, baby," she says.

"Why'd you come back here, Mom?" I can't help but ask her. "Why'd you ever come back here?"

She frowns at me. "This is my home. *Our* home. You can never let them take that away from us, you hear me?"

"What if this isn't what I want anymore?" I ask her. Sometimes I wonder if Ashton was her prize and not mine, for all the girls who told her she was trash.

I wanted to have a boy and I ended up loving him instead, but maybe there was still hope for something after this.

Maybe there is hope beyond this.

"Reid," she tells me, running a hand through my hair. "It's never going to get any better than this. The sooner you accept that, the better. People go chasing happiness, and they end up just as miserable as the rest of us with less to show for it. Stay focused."

Stay focused, she says, and I have no idea what that means.

"Savannah's mama got everything she wanted until she didn't," I tell her. "It doesn't matter who you are or where you're born, it can happen. Your whole life can fall apart. It can always happen."

"Oh, baby," she says, running her fingers down my arm, so soft I feel goose bumps rise on my skin. "Of course it matters."

Twenty-Two Hours Left

Mom goes to bed. I leave the way I came, go to the store in my old red Honda. Daddy thought they should've totaled it after the wreck, but it survived. We have that in common.

Evelyn has already locked up, but I bang on the door anyway and she lets me in.

"What are you doing here, Reid?" she asks. "Is everything okay?"

"You wanna go somewhere with me?" I say to her.

"What do you mean?"

"I mean," I say, "get in my car and we'll drive till this shit town ends. It's not like you got anything better to do, right?"

She doesn't respond, and I know that means yes. I grab a bottle of cheap red wine off the shelf and take it. "Follow me," I say.

She does. She locks the door of my parents' store behind her and gets into the passenger's seat. I hand her the wine, which she accepts as if it's some sort of illicit drug, and we drive right into the full moon.

I turn up the music. She fidgets.

"How was work?"

"Borin'," she says.

Ashton's words echo across time and space. *Choose to be bored.*

"Did you hear Ashton and I broke up?" I ask her.

"I heard you got back together," she says, and I laugh.

"We didn't." Another lie, but none of it matters at this point. I already picked the wrong time to admit my biggest lie, so I'll let all the others stand.

"Oh," Evelyn says, like she feels stupid now. I didn't want that.

I drive too fast like I always do and swing hard onto an old dirt road I know well. I pull down my mirror and the lights shine at its sides and I reapply my favorite purple lipstick, pressing my lips together. I kick my shoes off in the driver's side floorboard and take the wine out of Evelyn's lap. "Let's go," I say, and just like that, she follows me.

Just like that, she's mine.

I walk down the dirt road for a bit and then cut down to a path through the trees, sticks and gum balls finding the delicate skin of my feet. At the end of the path, I hear water running downhill, right below the bank. I jump down into the creek bed, and the water washes over my bare feet.

Evelyn follows me until we get to the creek and she stops.

"Take off your shoes," I tell her.

"I'm okay," she says.

"God, Evelyn. Live a little."

She gives me a weak smile but doesn't move. I unscrew the cap to my wine and drink it out of the bottle. From where I'm standing, the wine is neither bad nor good but it's here and so am I.

"Do you want some?" I ask her.

She shakes her head.

I sigh, drink some more and drop myself onto the bank so my feet are dangling in the water down below. At that, Evelyn sits down beside me, crossing her legs.

"Do the thing to me," I tell her, "the thing I always see you doing to the boys at school."

"What thing?" she asks.

"When they're bothering you," I tell her. "I've seen the thing you do where you play with them until they leave you alone. It's amazing."

I see you, I don't say. *Why don't you see how much I see you?*

I want her to be happy. I just want one person in my life to be happy.

She shakes her head. "I don't know what you're talking about."

"Yes, you do, Evelyn." I laugh and her face relaxes. "I see you do it all the time. It's so good."

Evelyn raises an eyebrow, but then I see it. Something in her expression changes, the tilt of her head or her eyes or something, and her hair falls in her face all long and blond and curly. She smiles without any teeth. "I don't know what you're talking about," she says, and her voice even sounds different. She's so beautiful like that, the moonlight playing off her skin.

"That's good stuff," I tell her, pulling at a piece of her hair so it straightens and bounces back into a curl when I let it go.

"Maybe later," she tells me, and she's still doing it. Then she drops the face and she laughs, too.

I sigh and flop onto the grass. With some hesitation, Evelyn lies back beside me. I stare up at the stars overhead, the same stars Ashton and I had been staring at earlier that night.

"What do you think of me, Evelyn?" I ask her, and she stays quiet, goes still again, the way she can't seem to help, like a wounded animal.

"You're nice," she says after a few minutes.

I cackle at that. "Even you don't believe that."

"I do," she says. "That day I was at TJ's, you saved me. You looked after me when nobody else would."

"I felt sorry for you," I tell her, because I can't stand someone being so fundamentally wrong about something, but her words, they're so beautiful.

Maybe she heard what I was trying to say all along.

"And how often do you think someone wastes their time doing that?"

"They're scared of you," I say. "Savannah and those girls. They're scared of who you could be. Of who you are. They're scared you might not hate yourself as much as they hate themselves. That's why they treat you like they do."

"Scary slut," she says with a laugh that echoes hollow in the night.

"I used to think you were so fragile, Evelyn," I say, honest, "but now I see you. You're the strongest person in this whole town. The county, maybe the state."

Her voice goes quiet and she tells me, "I wish I could be more like you, Reid."

"No, you don't," I reply quickly.

I hear her swallow.

"I think there's something, like, really, really wrong with me," I tell her. I turn my head to look at her in profile. "And I tried to explain it to Ashton and it ruined everything."

She turns to face me, too. "I'm sure it can be fixed."

I take a deep breath. "I guess, somehow, I'd convinced myself it was a game and I could win. Or that I *needed* to win. But you know, eventually, you're too tired to keep playing and realize the other person never knew they were in the arena to begin with. It was someone else's game all along." I look away from her. "But what *I* really wanted, more than anything, was for him to love me. And when he did, I couldn't help it. I had to destroy it, bit by bit, piece by tiny piece until there was nothing left. Because, in the back of my head, I was always wondering, What if he kept me here in this terrible town forever?"

All I ever wanted was for somebody to love me.

I close my eyes and I know I might cry and I hate that part of myself, keep trying to erase it, to claw it out. Keep trying to move forward.

"Reid," Evelyn says after a minute. I look back at her and she has these stunning blue eyes, the kind that stop you in your tracks. She's so beautiful and small and lost and real.

I put my finger under her chin and tilt it up, pull her face close to mine, and gently, I kiss her.

I kiss her because I know she'll kiss me back.

And that's so fucked up, isn't it?

She does kiss me back and I know she means it. I feel it in my veins, in the blood pumping from where my mouth is on hers right back to her heart, and I know how wrong this is. That I saw her and I knew her and I knew what she wanted and I gave it to her so I could get something back.

And I'm not even really sure what that is.

Finally, she pulls away, like we're playing a game of chicken. She looks at me for a moment, turns red, and averts her gaze.

"I'm sorry, Evelyn," I whisper to her. I ruined it.

I always ruin it.

She doesn't say anything to me for the rest of the night, not even when I drop her off at her trailer. I watch her back disappear and wonder why I can't find it in me to hate myself more.

I punch my hand into the interior of my car door because I still don't know what the fuck's wrong with me and then I scream because it hurts. My eyes water and tears gather and I think I should cry.

This would be a normal time to cry.

Instead, I take another swig of wine and take off.

Twenty-One Hours Left

Ashton's window is in the back of his parents' house, tucked away in its own corner. It's the window you'd only give to a kid you trusted as much as Ashton's parents used to trust him.

I knock on it with my fist. The lamp next to Ashton's bed flicks on, so I knock again. He comes to the window and looks out of it at me.

I don't know what he's going to do. I don't think he does either.

I stare back at him, not moving a muscle. The resolve in his eyes weakens and weakens until he opens the window.

"Go home," he says. I climb in the window.

"I ruin everything," I say, turning to him. "I'm a tornado and I ruin everything. I play games with people but I think, like—that might be the only way anyone will ever love me."

"Are you even apologizing?" Ashton asks me.

"For what?" I ask.

He goes back to his bed and flops down, and I know he's too tired to do it. To talk about it or fight about it or *whatever*.

"You promised," I tell him. "You promised you'd never leave me."

"Can we just sleep, Reid?" he whispers. His eyes are red and I don't know if he's been crying or if he's really that tired. "I've been sitting here all night wondering if the fact that I love you is, like, proof that I'm not a good person. That you're right about me in some fucked-up way."

I entwine my fingers together, absorb the blow, try to curl up into the smallest version of myself.

It hurts.

"I'm sorry." He shakes his head. "Whatever, it doesn't matter. Let's sleep."

And that's it. That's all he can think to say to me.

He crawls under the covers, and I go in after him, sliding my ring off my swollen hand and placing it on his bedside table. He puts an arm around me and I know it's instinct and nothing else, but still, I curl up into his side and I try to sleep.

I try to remember before.

And there, with him yet somehow still alone in his bed, I hold out my aching hand, my fingers reaching for something that isn't there.

Always reaching.

EVELYN

Nineteen Hours Left

I'm awake before the sun rises, my fingers curling instinctively around nothing. Ashton has shifted in the night, so I slip silently out of bed—a silence I have spent my entire life practicing—and grab up my clothes, quickly pulling them back on.

I slide Ashton's keys free of his jeans pocket, pick up my guitar, and head for the door.

I creep out into the gray before sunrise, dew still heavy in the air, finally breaking into a run as the door closes behind me.

Sixteen Hours Left

I'm seventeen and I've spent so much time thinking about loneliness.

Not just the loneliness of being alone but the loneliness of having so many people around you and being invisible to all of them.

It's morning now. I have a guitar, an obituary for a long-dead girl, a picture of my little sister, one change of clothes, and twenty dollars.

There's a lot of blank space between Nashville and McNair

Falls. Fields and trees and nothingness. Too much space to think about what I've done and what I haven't done and what I still have to do.

I try not to think about Ashton, about vulnerability and pain and what it feels like for someone to touch you so tenderly. To touch you with no intention of hurting you.

I never have to see him again, and that's what is going to make this okay.

Besides, I'm out of choices.

Thirteen Hours Left

I'm pulling into the driveway of Mrs. Brewer's one-story brick house. I grab up my guitar case and take Ashton's gun from the console tucking it inside the guitar case in between a shirt and pair of socks. Then I go to the Brewers' door and I knock.

I hear someone shuffling around behind the door, and then it opens. Mrs. Brewer stands there, and she's so shocked, it even takes the shock a moment to register.

"Evelyn!" she says, and she wraps her arms tight around me, so tight I can barely hang on to my guitar case. She doesn't have any makeup on; she looks so tired. "Thank God. Come in, quick, it's chilly out here."

I do, and she leads me through the foyer and into the kitchen, sitting me down on a stool at the island. "You must be hungry." She takes a long, hard look at me. "You *must* be hungry," she repeats, and she opens the fridge and starts sifting through it. "I've got stuff for sandwiches, but you hate bologna, right, dear?" I don't actually, because in my house, you always ate what you had or didn't eat at all, but I realize that she's thinking of Reid. "Well, I could make some mac and cheese really quick. What about spaghetti? It's a couple of days old but probably fine. It's not as good as when Adam makes it, but—"

"Mrs. Brewer," I say. "You don't have to do all that. It's okay. I'm okay."

She stops her fidgeting and turns back to me. There are tears in her eyes. "I thought I'd lost you," she says. "I thought I'd lost another one of my girls." She hugs me again and she cries—cries more than I've ever seen her cry, and I still remember her face the days they spent dragging the lake looking for Reid's body. Maybe she was too broken then, resigned to what they would find when they found Reid. Maybe she'd repaired herself bit by bit since then and I'd almost ruined it all over again.

I'm worried she might not realize that I'm already dead, too.

"I'm sorry, Mrs. Brewer," I say. "I shouldn't have been a no-show to my shift."

She almost laughs between her tears. "A no-show? Evelyn, I thought you were dead. I don't give a shit about you not coming to work."

"That doesn't make it right," I return.

"I want you to rest, okay?" she says to me. "We can talk afterward. You need some sleep. No one needs to know you're here yet." She surveys my face and pushes my hair out of it, running her fingers through it lovingly.

That feels better than I expected.

"Where are they?" I ask, trying to sound as casual as I can. "My family? Where did they go?"

She looks at me sadly. "I heard old Mr. Donalds down at the Deer Run Park had a home he let them have real cheap for a few weeks. An empty one. I dropped by with some food, and it's not— it's not the best situation."

You poked an angry bear, is what she's saying. You made everything worse.

She reads it on my face. "It's all going to be okay, Evelyn," she tells me. "It won't seem quite so dire after you get some sleep."

She grabs up my guitar case for me and leads me down the hall, opening up a side door, and before we go in, I know it. I know it was Reid's room.

"She'd want you to have it," Mrs. Brewer says, and I doubt that very much.

"Thank you, Mrs. Brewer," I say around the unexpected lump in my throat.

"I couldn't save her, Evelyn," she says, "but I can save you."

She hugs me again and closes the door behind me and I stand there, in this place I've always imagined, and some stupid part of me wonders if Reid is standing right beside me.

She can't save me either, I imagine saying to her, and she'd laugh and say, *That's what I love about you, Evelyn. You're secretly so dramatic.*

But that wasn't Reid in my head, that was just the Reid I had wanted.

Reid's room looks nothing like I pictured. I thought it would be black or deep purple with posters of bands and art on the walls.

But it's blue and green and soft, and pictures of Reid and her parents are on the wall behind a plushy chair. Reid scribbled quotes from songs on pieces of paper in neater handwriting than I would have expected, and some of the lyrics are about being in love.

I spot something facedown on the floor half-hidden under the chair. I lean down, pick it up, and flip it over to see that it's Ashton and Reid and she's kissing him on the cheek just like any high school girl in love would do and she'd hung it up on the wall so she could see him whenever she wanted.

I imagine Mrs. Brewer tearing through the room and tossing it to the floor, intending to throw it away, but getting so lost in her sadness that she forgot.

Ashton looks the same and different in the picture, and it makes my stomach hurt so I flip it over and place it back down on the floor like it was when I found it.

I'll wait until tonight. Once it's dark, I can do what needs to be done.

I crawl into Reid's bed under her comforter and deep in her sheets, and I close my eyes. I don't sleep.

I'm afraid I might dream.

REID

Thirteen Hours Left

"Where were you last night?" Mom asks me when I come in the next morning. "When I left, you said you were headed to bed."

"I went to Ashton's," I say, snatching a banana from the counter.

"Reid, my goodness. People in this town will talk."

"Okay," I say, peeling my banana with unnecessary aggression.

She comes over to me then, puts her fingers beneath my chin, and tilts it up so she can survey my face. Her lips are pursed. "Are you sure you're all right?" she asks, and I imagine I can see the bags under my eyes reflected back in her own.

"How would I know?" I ask. "I never have been, right?"

She touches my cheek, cradling my face in her hand. "You're my girl," she says. "You're perfect. You've always been perfect. And fuck them if they say anything else."

I almost smile and I almost cry but instead I do neither. I go to my room and bury myself under the comforter and I wait.

I don't even know what for.

Eight Hours Left

Ashton picks me up to go to the lake later, like we had planned. It amazes me, the way we slip back into this without ever saying the words.

I know he doesn't know how to let me go, and I am, improbably, sad for him.

"You look sweet in your swim trunks," I tell him, reaching out and grabbing the fabric between my fingers.

"What does that mean?" he asks, his words sharp.

"Just . . . that you're cute, I guess. That I like you." I shake my head and turn away from him.

"I'm sorry," he says, and even he knows he's not sorry.

"It's okay," I say. "All I want is to be with you."

He glances over and smiles, but it never reaches his eyes.

EVELYN

Six Hours Left

I hear the car pull up, and before I even hear Mrs. Brewer hurrying through the house, I know someone has come for me.

I glance out through the blinds and see the police car parked out front.

"Evelyn," Mrs. Brewer says, sticking her head into the room. "I didn't call him, but it's the sheriff. He's here."

I blow out a long breath and peek back through the blinds to see Matt getting out of the car, kicking some gravel in the Brewers' driveway.

"Ashton called him," I say, and then the doorbell rings. "I'll answer it," I tell her. "You just stay out of the way. I don't want you dragged into this."

Mrs. Brewer touches my shoulder as I walk by her, and I almost hug her but then decide against it. No need to make this worse right now.

I open the door to Matt. He's rolling his hat around in his hands, but he stops when he sees me.

"Evelyn," he says. He sighs, and something passes over his face that I won't mistake for relief. "Girl, we were so afraid you were dead."

He wishes.

"Are you here to arrest me?"

"Not today," he says. "But you have to come with me. I can't risk losing you again."

Mrs. Brewer appears behind me, looking at the two of us.

"Helen," Matt says, bowing his head at her.

"Evelyn, do you want your things?" Mrs. Brewer asks me.

I shake my head. "I'll come get them later." I walk out the door past Matt. "Let's go," I tell him.

We walk to the car together. He hurries in front of me, opening up the passenger's side door to let me in. I sit down, and he gets in on the other side, settling into his seat and pulling the visor down to block the sun. When the car starts, some classic rock plays over his speakers, like he was always playing at Mama's house.

"What did he tell you?" I ask Matt.

"Just where he thought I'd find you," Matt replies. "He sounded worried."

"Asshole," I say. Matt barks out a laugh.

We pull up at his house, two stories and ridiculously tidy, and he grabs his hat and walks in with me.

"My office is this way," Matt says, "to the right."

He leads me into a small, windowless space off the foyer and closes and locks the door behind him. The office is the opposite of the rest of the house with papers strewn everywhere, notebooks arranged messily on shelves on the wall, and a Coke bottle full of dip spit set up on the desk.

It's Matt's space. The only thing that reminds me of him in this entire bright, cookie-cutter house.

"Sorry," he says. "Been working in here a lot lately. Haven't had a chance to clean up."

I shrug.

"Can you sit down, Evelyn?" he asks me, and I do, still staring over at him.

He sits down opposite me, loosens the buttons of his uniform, and leans back in his chair. He doesn't say anything. Takes a deep breath.

"I know I'm probably the last person you want to talk to, but we really need to do this here, Evelyn. We need to do it here so things don't get any worse for you. Can you tell me what happened the other night at your house?"

I glance around the office. It's so small, there's nothing left to see that I haven't already seen. I lean back in my chair, too. "You aren't supposed to do this, are you? Bring me here? Could this get you fired?"

"Probably," he says.

"Fine," I say. "I tried to burn the house down because Dane was in it and I wanted him dead," I tell him, stripping as much emotion from my voice as possible.

"See," Matt says, leaning forward and opening up the desk drawer. He looks a little peaked as he draws out a dip and puts it in his bottom lip. "That's the kind of thing I need you not to say at the station tomorrow." He looks back up at me.

Oh. So we're doing this.

"What does it matter to you?"

"Surely, you see why I'd like to keep you out of jail," he says.

"Are you really going to do this?" I hear myself saying, and I don't stop. "Pretend you care? Matt, you haven't talked to me in years. *Years.*"

"And you understand exactly why that is, Evelyn. You're not a child."

"So, that makes it okay?" I demand of him. "Because I know you had to save your stupid fucking marriage, I should be fine with having to go fuck myself? I should be fine with my sister living with that monster? Your daughter?"

Matt visibly flinches as I say that. "Evelyn," he says.

"Stop saying my *fucking name*!" I yell. "Take me to jail, Matt. It can't be any fucking worse than this house."

He doesn't say anything for a moment, rubbing his hand over his face.

"Can we focus on one problem at a time?" he asks me. I shake my head and don't respond. "What exactly did Dane Barkley do?"

"What he did all the time," I tell him. "He got drunk, hit me and Mama a little, and then . . ." I take a shuddering breath. "He turned on *her*, just like I always knew he would, and he gave her a nice little concussion for the road. And Mama took off with Kara and left me there, alone, so I knew she'd come back like she always does." My voice cracks, betraying me. "She left me there alone with him. That's what I was worth to her."

Matt doesn't make an outward sign of what he's feeling, but he flexes his fist a couple of times and holds it there until the skin on his knuckles goes pale.

"How long has he been hitting you?" Matt asks me.

I take a deep breath, search for a calm inside myself. "He thought about doing it for two months after he moved in, and then . . . well, then he got around to it."

"Okay," Matt says, and writes a note to himself. He spits his dip into his Coke bottle, and I see the lines on his face that weren't there all those years ago. "So you decided to burn down the trailer?"

"Decided." I shrug. "It was a little more impulsive than that."

"And Ashton Harper?" Matt asks me.

I stare down at my hands. "He didn't do anything," I say.

"So," Matt says, scribbling again, "an accessory after the fact."

"He didn't know," I say.

"You're a bad liar, Evelyn Peters," Matt says to me.

I lick my lips and remind myself of Ashton's tics, the way he gets when he's nervous. I don't even know why I'm lying for him. "Why does it matter?" I ask.

"Because I'm trying to figure out the best way to deal with this," he answers. He studies what he's written, scratching at his hair in a familiar way.

Matt used to do that all the time, the thing with his hair. He was always there. Sitting in our house at our table and eating meals with us, like we were all a family. I remember when my mama told me not to speak to Savannah at school.

I remember when she told me she was pregnant, how me and her and Matt and the new baby were gonna be a family. How we were gonna be happy; Matt had promised.

I remember after he was gone and she barely talked to me for days, except to yell. She was six months pregnant. That was a bad month.

"You ever think about her, Matt?" I ask. "Kara?"

He looks up at me over his paper. "I think about her every day," he says.

"Sounds like bullshit," I reply.

"I know it might sound like that to you," he says evenly. He sets down his pad of paper on the desk between us. "But I made a deal with your mama. I told her I had to go back to my family, and she told me that meant I didn't get any privileges. So I pay her child support and I stay out of you girls' lives. It's what she asked of me."

"Who the hell would make a deal like that over their own daughter?"

Matt rocks back and forth in his chair, the same way I've seen Kara do. The same way I've seen Savannah do. "Somebody who realizes just how badly they've screwed up so many different people's lives."

He grabs his bottle and spits.

"I'm sorry, Evelyn," he says then, and he stares up at the light, not fully looking at me, and I can't help but think what a coward he is. "I didn't know about Dane. I didn't know you needed me."

"You were the only dad I ever had," I tell him, the words spilling out of me hot and fast. "And you left. You left us with him. You abandoned us. *Everyone* is always abandoning me."

"Evelyn." He's still not looking at me.

"And worse, you abandoned *Kara*," I say, "and she's the only good person on this whole stupid godforsaken planet." He starts to open his mouth, and I cut over him—"*Don't* say you're sorry again," I tell him.

He trains his eyes on his desk. "I was going to say that you're right."

"And so much good that is going to do me now."

"Okay," he says, flipping to a fresh page on his legal pad. "Then let's work on that." And I know why he's doing it. I know why every person in the world is constantly moving, constantly *doing* because they don't want to have to think about what they've actually done. All the mistakes they've already made.

They want to be someone else. Someone easier.

Every one of us is out here chasing our own Reid Brewer and never actually knowing who Reid Brewer is if we catch her.

I try to explain Dane to Matt, be clinical about it, but once I start, the words tumble out of me, by turns angry and scared. I'm not even sure why. Maybe because the closest I've ever come to saying it is in whispered conversations in Alex's bed and even then, only in the dark, only the smallest fragments so he couldn't really see me. Couldn't see my raw hurt.

You can't be afraid if you never look at the monster straight on.

"I remember a couple of times," I'm telling Matt, my voice starting to go hoarse, "when he'd lock the door to his and Mama's room, and I'd hear her crying and him yelling and things breaking, and I used to just bang on the door until my hand went numb." A tear slides down my cheek. "But he didn't stop, he never stopped, and then I'd wonder if I made things worse, but I couldn't *leave her alone*. At least if I was trying, she'd know she wasn't alone. But she'd never look right the next day, not like herself, not in the way she moved or stood, and then she wouldn't meet my eyes.

"And sometimes, I couldn't even make myself feel sorry for her, because I'd resent her, knowing he'd lay off if she was hurt bad. He'd turn his attention to me. He always stopped for a day or a week or two or three, and Mama thought it was over, but I'd know it was nothing but a moment, an exhale. Sometimes that made it worse. Waiting for that moment to end."

Matt doesn't say anything.

"I've got more scars than I can count," I say. "Things that won't ever be right about me again, but I think that still hurts worse. Listening to Mama on the other side of that door, helpless.

"That's how it felt when he hit Kara," I say.

"Evelyn," he starts to say, but then he swallows. Wipes his eyes with the heel of his hand.

"I know what it takes to put someone like Dane away," I say to Matt, meeting his eyes with resolve. "I've googled police reports on the school computer. First and second and third violations. You keep going back and picking him up and you keep letting him out until one of us is dead."

"I'd never let that happen," he tells me. "Not now that I know."

Like he can do anything to stop it.

"You'll stay here tonight," Matt says, "and we'll go to the station first thing in the morning." He looks me over. "You need the sleep."

I nod and he stands up. "I'm sorry, but our only extra bed is in Savannah's room. She has a trundle," he says.

"Jesus Christ" is all I can manage.

"Mm," Matt replies.

"Can I sleep on the couch?"

"No way," he says quickly, and I realize that maybe Ashton told him more than he let on.

"So Savannah's been put on babysitting duty, then?"

"Just give me a little time," Matt says. He sounds sure. "We're going to figure it out."

It hits me that I can't tell the difference between promises and lies anymore because they're both the way people say things they wish were true.

"Lead the way," I say to Matt, and he takes me up the stairs to Savannah's room.

Two Hours Left

Savannah hasn't spoken to me since her dad told her I was spending the night in her room. I heard Mrs. Rykers yelling earlier, but then she'd offered me a warm meal and we'd all sat together in mostly companionable silence eating a Hamburger Helper meal.

I'd probably hate me, too, if I were Mrs. Rykers.

But Savannah had given her dad the exact same treatment she gave me. She'd refused to say anything to him, staring at him with that haughty face of hers. Then she'd gotten dressed for bed in a huge T-shirt and shorts and turned her back on me when she climbed into bed.

So now, here I am, in the dark of Savannah's room, my legs curled up in the sheets. I have on some of Savannah's clothes, sweatpants and a sweatshirt with Matt's college printed on it. I don't know if Savannah did that by accident or if she did it as a sick joke. I'm not sure which one would make me respect her more.

Matt and his wife had gone to bed early so we could get up and go to the station when his 6:00 a.m. shift started in the morning.

Testing out Savannah's alertness, I slide from under the covers of her trundle bed and to the door. When she doesn't react, I open the door and sneak down the stairs toward the kitchen for a glass of water. Halfway down, I stop when I hear voices whispering from the kitchen, where the oven light is on. I quietly make my way down the rest of the stairs, stopping next to the arch leading from the hall into the kitchen.

Someone is crying. And I think it's Matt. I tilt my face slightly so I can see the two of them, in their shiny, clean kitchen.

"What am I gonna do?" he's saying to Mrs. Rykers, his head bowed toward the counter, her arms on his. *That could've been Mama*, I think. *This could've been ours.*

"We'll get a lawyer," Mrs. Rykers says gently.

"Do you know how long that will take?" He rubs a hand over his face. "You should've heard the things Evelyn said." Suddenly, he pounds his fist into the counter. "And worst of all, she knows. She knows I'm useless."

His wife moves closer to him, as if she might warm him with her own body. "You're not useless. You're doing more for those girls than anyone else is. You're trying to figure out how to save them."

Save us.

"I did this," Matt says, still staring down at the counter. "All of this is my fault."

"We decided to forgive ourselves for everything in the past, remember?"

Matt nods, and Mrs. Rykers reaches up with the hand not against his to wipe away a tear.

"I'm sorry," he chokes out.

"Matt," Mrs. Rykers says, her voice as soothing as if she were talking to a child. "You need to go to bed. We will start dealing with this tomorrow. It's like you're always telling me. One foot in front of another, right? We gotta trust in God to get us through this one."

Matt places his hand over his wife's, where she's still touching him, and they stand like that, almost at peace.

It's that sight, more than anything, that solidifies my heart into stone. Because this night is nothing but a blip in time; they'll get through it, but Mama might not.

Kara might not.

They've got God, but all I've got is me.

The truth is, even before, I'd known what I had to do. I'd always known, from that night in the trailer when everything had changed. I'd taken a half measure, but that was over.

Now, all that's left to do is finish it.

One Hour Left

Back in Savannah's room, I listen for Matt and his wife to go to bed, and then give another forty-five minutes for them to go to sleep. Once the quiet is finally oppressive enough, I start lacing up my tennis shoes, the same ones that have been carrying me since that very first night. I straighten up and I go to the door, and that's when the light next to the bed comes on.

Savannah Rykers sits there, looking at me, and I know this is the moment she's been waiting for. She blinks at me, all clean faced and with a scrunchie holding her hair up out of her face.

I wonder if Kara will look exactly like her one day.

"What the hell do you think you're doing, Evelyn?" she asks, her voice hoarse from disuse.

"What do you care?" I ask her.

"I'm supposed to stop you from any more attempted murders, I assume," she tells me.

I walk back, closer to her, keeping my voice down. "Savannah, you know as well as I do that Dane isn't going to get charged with domestic abuse. Let's say Matt did manage to arrest him—how long do you think they could hold him? A day? Two? Before he got bail?"

Savannah blinks at me.

"He could kill Kara by then," I tell her, and even I hear the desperation in my voice. "Mama would let him. She can't stop him."

"So, you think any of this is going to stop me from telling Daddy?" she asks, her sweet voice dripping with poison.

"You could help me, Savannah." I cling to my desperation; this is so far beyond petty anger and broken promises—it's life or death. "We could stop him together."

"You know," she says, standing up. For one wild moment I think she's really going to go with me, that I misjudged her all along. "Ashton was supposed to be mine. He always was and it was going to take some time, but we were in the right place. He was staring at me when he thought I didn't see. He was touching my arm when we talked. Everything was going the way I always knew it would. And then Reid Brewer came along and destroyed him."

"What the hell are you talking about?" I ask her. "What does Ashton have to do with any of this?"

"What did you do to him? *With* him?" she demands. I flinch, the memory of last night creeping in. She doesn't miss it. "I knew it," she says. "Why did he burn down that trailer with you?"

"He's not destroyed," I say. "He's not some piece to slot into your life at leisure."

"You don't know him." She's angry—angry as she's ever been at me, always and forever.

"Is this really what you're worried about?" I ask, my voice slightly hysterical. "I'm talking about a little girl's life. Don't you care about *anything*?"

"You tried to steal my dad," she says, furious. "You tried to ruin my family."

"No," I say, "I didn't." And then I grab on to her hands and hold them both in mine because I can't help it. I can't fucking help it. "She's your sister, too, Savannah. Please."

Her eyes hold mine for a steady moment, and I see it for the slightest blip in time—the humanity. The questioning.

For a moment, she wants to go with me.

Then she pulls her hands away. "Go get killed," she says. "I don't care."

She climbs back into her bed and pulls the sheets up, turning off the light. I take one last glance at her form, her tiny body curled up under the covers, and then I make for the door, closing it silently behind me and escaping into the night.

REID

One Hour Left

"You ever wonder," Ashton says, looking over at me, "how fast the last day of your life would go by?"

"No," I say. "Don't be fucking morbid."

Ashton tilts his head back to the sky, laughing a little. He's so stupid fucking drunk, and I think, that's how much he hates me.

"Give me some of that," I say to him, and he passes the bottle of rum over to me. I chug it, and still don't have a prayer of getting as drunk as he is.

"Do you like it?" he asks.

"No," I say easily. I hand it back to him.

He shrugs. "I know," he says. "You don't like anything." Allen and his girlfriend have disappeared back into Ashton's uncle's house, but even as he went, he'd asked if Ashton would be okay. I'd told him I could handle it, but maybe I was lying.

"We don't have to be here, Ashton," I say. "Last night . . . I can let you go . . . if you want me to."

He watches me, his eyes glassy and far away now. I see him thinking about it, almost see the wheels turning in his head. "I could never stop loving you." He says it as if it pains him. "No matter what you did. You're all there is here. You're the only person who's ever really made me feel alive. I was sleepwalking through this shitty life, and then you saw me and wanted me and you saved me."

I blink, and I know he really believes this.

"Let's take the boat out," Ashton says, and I don't entirely recognize him. Not anymore. "Come on, Reid," he says. "Let's try to have fun."

And he doesn't say, *Let's try to be who we used to be*, but I hear it anyway.

EVELYN

Half an Hour Left

The Brewers live about an hour's walk from the Rykers. I swiped a pack of cigarettes I'd seen on Matt's desk earlier, and on the walk, I steadily smoke one after another, trying to keep warm. Matt lives on a lighted street, but soon, I'm back in darkness, pounding my way down a gravel road where houses are few and far between, little lights glowing far off the road, next to tidy double-wides with gardens out front. Plenty of discarded beer cans light my way.

The stolen cigarettes are just one more sin to add to a tally that's already too long to erase.

I go in the back door of the Brewers'. It's unlocked because no one ever locks their doors around here. I easily find Reid's room, see the map of it in my mind.

I tiptoe inside and open up the guitar case. Grab the gun and leave the rest behind.

I don't need it anymore.

Then it's back out to Ashton's car, still parked where I left it, and off across town to Deer Run Park. Deer Run is between McNair Falls and Ravensway, in the middle of nothing. I pull into the park and drive through. Mrs. Brewer had said the place was toward the back of the park, in a corner next to the woods. I ditch

Ashton's car in front of a mobile home with no lights on and set out on foot, the gun tucked into the back of my jeans.

There are streetlights lining the paths looping through Deer Run, but most of them are burned out, as if someone just didn't have the energy to care about this place. So I pick my way through the dark, following the gravel road next to the woods. I turn, my heart pounding, when I hear gravel crunch behind me and reach for the gun; a figure hurries toward me through the shadow and I consider running. But I see the face coming into focus and pull my hand away, almost positive I am hallucinating. I stop and he catches up, stopping in front of me, leaving a good bit of distance between us.

"Evelyn," Ashton says, leaning down and panting. "Jesus Christ."

"How are you here?" I ask, stepping closer to him, out of the light shining from the streetlamps overhead. I almost want to touch him to be sure he's real. But what if I start and then can never stop?

"I was waiting for you," he says, staring up at me from his crouched position, as if that's the most obvious thing in the world.

"You were waiting for me *here*?" I ask him. I shouldn't let myself get drawn into a conversation, but some part of me wants to. Some part of me wants to be free of this burden.

Luckily, it's the smaller part of me.

"Don't do this," he says, abandoning all pretense. "Please don't do this."

I decide not to play dumb either. "Why not?"

He steps closer to me, into a circle of lamplight. He's pale, and he tries to sound calm but his face is drawn. "I had to call my parents this morning when I woke up alone and with one less car than I used to have. I had to ask them to drive to Nashville, pick me up and bring me home, and God love them, they did."

He's getting closer every minute, and I'm not backing away from him, mostly because that's the last thing I want to do. And what a bizarre thought to have when you're on your way to kill someone—that the person in front of you could touch you and wouldn't that be the best feeling on the planet.

And with that, I feel the white-hot shame of what I've done, of exposing myself so fully—not just my body but my stupid beating heart. I feel the memory of last night burning on my face. And I do step back.

I can't trust him. And I can't trust myself when it comes to him.

He stops, holds up his hands so I can see them. "I don't mean you any harm, Evelyn," he tells me.

"Then answer my question," I say. "Why are you here?"

"Because I knew you'd come," he says. "As soon as I got back to my house, I got on my computer and messaged Allen to come get me. He picked me up, brought me here, the whole while asking what the fuck was wrong with me, and I've been sitting at the front gate for the past several hours, hoping I wouldn't miss you." He points to a dark spot in the trees. "Glad to see my car is still in working order, by the way. Needless to say, my parents know I've bolted and at this point, are completely fucking done with me, but I can't care about that right now. I can't let you do this."

I tilt my head. "You could call the cops."

His eyes bore into mine. "I don't have a phone, in case you've forgotten." A piece of his hair escapes and falls into his face. He pushes it back. "Do you know how terrible it was to wake up alone this morning? Naked and carless and hungover—"

"You're always hungover."

"You want to be cold," Ashton says, "but you're not."

"I just wanted to steal your car," I tell him. "I never wanted the rest of it."

"Yeah, you did. You wanted both. Remember, I've been playing mind games with people much longer than you have." He shrugs. "And you're right that you couldn't fix me and you're right that I want that, but also, we both really fucking want to be loved."

"You don't love me. Please stop talking."

"I want to," he says, sticking his hands in his pockets. "I'm trying to."

"You'd just ruin it," I reply, and he winces.

"I might," he agrees after the insult has rolled off him.

"What did you do with Reid's ring?" I ask him.

He blinks. "I put it somewhere safe," he says. He didn't put it back on.

"I should've told you," I tell him, and I don't let the tears fall, I won't, "she did love you, whatever else there was. She told me it was cruel, how much she loved you. Like having all the rawest parts of your soul exposed."

I say it, and I hear the words and see all the worst parts of Reid laid out in front of me.

The best, too.

I wish she hadn't hurt so much.

"I can't feel things that way, Ashton. Not the way she did."

He swallows, words hard to come by. "I don't need that from you. I *can't* do that again. All I need is for you to get out of here."

"What does it matter?" I finally ask. But he hears what I'm really saying: *What do* I *matter?*

He licks his lips, and this is how I like him best—when all his emotion is shining off him brighter than the full moon in the sky. He takes a deep breath and says, "I know you don't think I do, but I *see* you, Evelyn. You were right. I didn't at first. I saw who I wanted you to be and that was Reid, and back when Reid was Reid, I saw who I wanted her to be, and that's what I do. I look for someone to create an illusion for me.

"But you—you're not an illusion. You'd do anything for the people you love and you're always ready to run when things get too real and those things exist together, but that means you always see the exit the rest of us can't. And even when you don't care about yourself at all, you believe in yourself because that's all you've ever had."

I blink once, twice, lost, mesmerized by the words.

"You never needed to be reborn, Evelyn. You only ever needed to *try*, for yourself. Not for anyone else."

And then he takes that one last step to close the distance between us and I know what it will do to me so I instinctively move away before he touches me and convinces me of something I don't want to hear.

I may not be an illusion, but Ashton is.

"Get out of my way," I say, and I pull the gun out of the back of my jeans. He doesn't flinch, just stares at it. "Or I swear to God, I will shoot you."

"Can't swear to something you don't believe in." Ashton's eyebrows go up, and I think we could be talking about anything. It wouldn't matter. "You know getting shot isn't much of a threat to me, right?" he asks, and he's so smug that I point the gun at him and I cock the hammer.

"Move," I say again, my voice getting stronger. "I don't care how drunk you are."

"I'm not," Ashton says. "Believe me, I already feel like I want to die, so a gunshot wound probably wouldn't be such a bad distraction."

"This isn't funny."

"Am I laughing?" he asks. "I want you to get your justice, I do. But how does this end for you, Evelyn? What happens?"

"He's dead," I say. "And then it's over. Get out of my way."

"It's not over," he says. "Not for you. Your story, remember?"

"It was over for me, Ashton," I say. "It was over the moment we set that trailer on fire. And you knew that. This is *my* blaze of glory, my end. I have to do this." I stuff his keys into his hand. "Your car is parked back there. *Leave.* Maybe I'll see you in another life."

"Shoot me, then," he tells me. "I'm not leaving."

I hold the gun on him, my hand shaking. He knows I won't, and I know I won't, but we stand there together like that, like I might.

And then a branch swings up out of nowhere behind Ashton, and he stumbles forward, hits the ground with a thump.

I jump back, my arm giving way and dropping to my side, and a thin figure steps into the light where Ashton was standing. The lamplight glints off her thick, dark hair. Savannah.

We stare at each other, and then she glances down at Ashton, who is moaning and grabbing for his head.

"I'll watch him," she says.

"Savannah," I say, and when our eyes meet, I get it.

I understand.

"Kill him," she says, and nods at me, then she leans down over Ashton and touches his head softly, like a lover.

Realizing what's happening, Ashton pushes her away and struggles to get to his feet. "Evelyn, *wait*—" he pleads.

I turn away from both of them and hurry down the road.

Minutes Left

I feel wrong. Dizzy or broken or something. I move closer to the trailer, to my family. My feet follow the path to their temporary home, and then I see it—Mama's hummingbird feeder. I know it's their place, and I know the feeder survived the fire. There wasn't much Mama did for herself, but she loved her hummingbirds. She loved to stand by the window and watch them and smile to herself.

Dane hung it up for her last summer. The thought that she brought it makes me so happy and so devastatingly sad.

Makes me hesitate. Makes me think about Mama. That last kiss on the cheek. The way she snorts when she laughs too hard.

That almost does it. I start to turn, start to leave—then stop myself. I don't think, even on the way here, I fully realized that a line was being drawn between my life before and my life now. But I know it now. That I do this and I don't go back.

I pull two things out of my pocket: Kara's picture and Reid's obituary. I look at the two of them together, a tiny dark-haired girl who looks nothing like her sister or exactly like her sister, and a series of lies about Reid Brewer, trying to paint her into the tiniest little box.

That's not who she was. She's so much more. So much more good and so much more bad.

I think, maybe, they'll use this picture of me and Kara when they talk about what happened here or my school picture or something else, and under it, they'll write the story of a girl who fits an image.

A loner. A slut. Nobody.

That won't be me.

So, I stuff the paper and the picture back into my pocket. I take the steps forward, up to the door, standing on a cinder block sitting out front.

I curl my fist and I knock.

The door opens.

REID

Minutes Left

Ashton speeds the boat along, and I watch him. He's drunk, and he's never drunk, so I don't know what to make of him.

He smiles at me, and I think I'll save that smile forever, keep it in my back pocket to have when nothing else matters anymore because neither of us are who we promised each other we'd be.

But he sees who I was, the girl I wanted him to see. The girl who gave him magic. He still sees her because he wants to.

I hope that's how he remembers me when this is over.

EVELYN

October 11, 2019, 10:19 p.m.

Dane is the one who opens the door, and my first thought is that I didn't hurt him at all, that he's just fucking fine, and that strengthens my resolve, knowing he will be fine—forever fine—while the rest of us bleed.

He looks angry when he sees me, his face screwed up and contorted. But I don't give him the chance to get the first word in.

"Come outside," I say, and I let him see the gun in my hand, small and warm against my palm. He glances down at it and his eyes narrow ever so slightly.

He can't fool me. He's scared.

"Evelyn, what in the hell?" he starts to say, and I raise the gun and point it at him.

"I'm not asking."

"Okay, okay," he says, and puts his hands up in surrender. He walks out slowly, making his way into the small stretch of dirt in front of the trailer. I notice as he moves that he's limping, which gives me some satisfaction. If I couldn't burn him alive, at least he hurt himself running away.

"Before I kill you," I start to say to him, "I want to make sure you absolutely know why."

"Evelyn," he says, cautious.

"I'm doing this for Kara," I tell him, "because she doesn't deserve this. Because every day, you'll find another way to hurt her and she'll live in terror and I'm so fucking done with seeing people I love afraid all the time.

"But even more importantly," I go on, "I'm doing this *for me*. I've been getting beat down by men like you my entire life, and I don't have to anymore. I *don't have to*."

I try to hold the gun steady, try to hold myself steady. *Be someone else*. "So say your prayer to whatever god you think will save you and be done with it."

We stand there like that and he says nothing and he's in a T-shirt from Kmart and an old pair of dirty sweatpants and he's going to die like this.

"*Evelyn*." My name cuts like a knife through the night. I look back at the still open door to Mama with her bruised face and tired eyes. She is colored with shock and fear and I don't care.

I can't care.

"Evelyn, what are you doing?" she asks me, her voice going to that high frantic pitch that Dane causes sometimes.

"What you're too big of a coward to do, Mama," I respond, my eyes not leaving Dane.

"Evelyn!" That's when I hear her voice, her tiny, clear voice, and she appears in the door next to Mama. I feel her before I even see her, like an essential lost appendage. "Mama, what's Evelyn doing?" she asks, and I can't help but look over at her, where she's wrapped her arms around Mama's leg and is watching me, waiting for me to kill Dane. She can't see this.

"Kara," I say. My stupid voice breaks, gives me away, and the tears start to crowd at the bottom of my eyes. "Kara, go inside," I say. I look over at her. "*Please* go inside."

"Evie," she says. "I missed you."

It's that split second that does me in.

I look back just in time for Dane to crack me across the face with his fist.

That's when I hit the dirt. I drop the gun, and it falls out of my reach. I try to feel around on the ground for it, but I can't find it.

Kara and Mama both scream bloody murder, and the door of the trailer slams shut. I can hear Kara's wails as she tries to get away from Mama through the door.

I push myself up on all fours and spit out blood and I'm back on my feet, clawing at him, at his face. But he's bigger and he's stronger and he shoves me off again.

"I always knew you were just as crazy as your mama," Dane says, and when I try to run at him, he kicks me down. He's playing so dirty.

He kicks me when I'm down on the ground, too, and that really hurts. I finally see the gun and I twist and struggle to grab it, but he steps on my fingers when I do. I cry out.

I made it this far, but this is as far as I can go.

I wasn't *enough*.

I try to pull myself across the ground, grasping for something, anything, but my eyes water, making my vision blurry. It hurts. Everything hurts, and I wonder if this is it.

And all I can think is, if I'm going to die, don't let him be the one to do it.

Don't let him do it.

But he's over me and grabbing me with one hand, reaching for the gun with the other. I fall back, my head bouncing off the ground. The pain shoots through my skull, hard and fast as a whip.

And then.

Nothing.

REID

October 11, 2018, 10:19 p.m.

I don't see it happen, not really.

I'm perched up on the edge of the boat where we both know I shouldn't be, and Ashton hits something hard.

The boat bucks. I fall. He screams.

I get swept away so fast, I don't know how it happened. I can swim. I'm not a bad swimmer, so I try. I really try because my instinct is always to keep clawing.

For one hilarious moment, I think of my life jacket sitting up on the deck of the boat, probably wishing it could save me right now.

I flail my arms, kick desperately against the tide. I try to yell for Ashton, but I'm not sure if I actually manage to get anything out. I've never felt so powerless before, never felt my muscles grow so weak. Desperately, I try to pull air in my lungs as I bob in and out of the water.

The current tugs at me, determined to have me. I feel myself going down before my brain fully processes I'm going down. That I've finally gotten into a situation I can't get out of.

My whole life, I've been trying to live. Trying to live harder than anybody else, kicking and screaming, and maybe that makes this a fitting end. That I'm absorbed back into the world I came from.

But if I'd known this was coming, I would have liked to see Ashton's eyes one last time—not like tonight, but clear, and maybe seen that love in them. I'd have watched another Braves game with Dad and planned a picnic with Mom. I'd have punched Savannah Rykers in the face, but this time for Evelyn and not Ashton.

I'd have scared people and I'd have laughed and maybe cried one last time.

I'd have lived just a little bit longer, if they'd let me—this town and this world. If they'd *wanted* me.

My body starts to give out at last, paddling toward nothing, and I know what's coming. My vision blurs until I can't see anything, but the pain lets me know: I'm still alive. I can still hear Ashton calling my name through the night, the way it echoes off the water and the trees, bouncing around in my brain. He didn't jump in, I think.

He's afraid.

I'm afraid.

And then.

Nothing.

EVELYN

I open my eyes and I'm not dead.

Not yet.

Dane has the gun pointed down at me, though, so I couldn't have been out more than a few seconds.

"You really going to shoot me?" I ask, and even my mouth aches.

"Yes," he says, finger resting on the trigger. "You've tried to kill me twice, and even you've got to admit those aren't odds anyone would wait around to take a chance on."

"Then do it," I say. "Please, kill me, so they will put you in jail once and for all." I fight to keep my eyes open, but it's hard.

Dying will be easier.

"Self-defense," Dane says. "You think your mama won't back me up?"

A tear rolls down my cheek. Goddamn him.

Before, some part of me had forgotten that I had to fight and keep fighting every day. I had given up.

But I'm done with that.

I push myself up and wrap my hands around the barrel of the gun and the gun is in my hands and it's in his hands. He's screaming and I think I am, too, rolling back against the ground.

Then I hear the gunshot and I flinch, wait for the hot metal in my skin, but it doesn't come. My ears ring and everything is muffled like I'm hearing through glass. I think maybe this is exactly what death feels like, this easy, but then Dane hits the ground next to me.

It's the end, and I'm the one holding a gun.

AFTER

The broken-down old heater in a broken-down old country store tries to keep out the cold of a November evening in McNair Falls, South Carolina. A group of middle schoolers are grabbing things off the shelves, and I'm lost in myself all over again.

Being alive ain't as easy as they make it out to be.

But I still figure it's better than the alternative.

I'm standing at the counter in the front of the Brewers' store and the middle schoolers have been standing in the same place for a while, where they can watch me over one of the shelves, whispering to each other.

"She killed him," I hear one of them say.

I try to make myself look busy, cleaning the counter, unstacking and restacking the cigarettes behind the counter.

"The sheriff got her off."

"Burned down the trailer."

I guess I did do all those things.

Mrs. Brewer comes out from the back office and gives them a look. "If y'all aren't gonna buy anything, you need to get," she tells them.

"I was just looking at the chips," one of the kids, the leader from the looks of her, shoots back defiantly.

Mrs. Brewer clicks her tongue. She certainly isn't planning on losing out on a purchase, so she nods and walks past the four of them, stopping in front of me.

"It's that time, Evelyn," she says. "Once they buy something, go ahead and close up."

"I'm sorry," I say, "about all the attention."

"Girl, you think I give a damn?"

I shrug.

"Before you leave, do a quick sweep and see if anything needs to be restocked. Adam is coming in to do the floors in the morning. I'll see you at home, okay?"

I nod, and she gives me a wave with her keys in her hand. As she goes to lock the door, an older lady walks through. Mrs. Brewer lets her in, locks the door, and leaves.

The kids come up and buy their bag of chips, watching me. "Come again," I say as I hand the change back.

But one of the girls, wide-eyed and dreamy looking, stares at me. "Did you see him die?" she asks, and then her friend turns red and grabs on to her and drags her out of the store. The rest follow.

I take a shaky breath and train my gaze on the cash register. Close my eyes.

I should be dead, I find myself thinking so often these days. Maybe it would all be easier if I were dead.

But that's not what I want. That's never what I wanted.

Everything about that day always flashes by in my mind so fast, I barely remember it. I remember Matt there, running over right after I fired the gun, with his own gun drawn, and I was crying and he was crying. It took me so long to understand how he got there, until I did.

Savannah. Savannah Rykers, who didn't go back to sleep after I left. Who sat there stewing in guilt until she drove to Deer Run Park and made sure I finished the job. Who called her dad because she knew I needed him.

I hate her.

She helped me.

I still hate her.

But Matt told them that he saw the whole thing. That it was

self-defense; he said I didn't have a choice. He'd lied for me, and it'd hurt me a little bit to see the way it tore him up.

"But I'd do it again if I had to," he'd said to me one night after. "I'd go to jail myself. Not so sure I wouldn't deserve it."

And then I think about Mrs. Brewer looking at my bruised face, running her warm fingers over my cheek the next day, after they let me out of the police station.

"They know what I did," I told her. "They all know and that's all they see. What I did. Why," I asked Mrs. Brewer, "isn't there any justice in the world?"

"Oh, baby," she had said, tilting my face up to her, "you're still alive, and I consider that a hell of a lot of justice."

"But Reid's not," I told her.

She looked me in the eyes. "And we learn to live with that," she said. "A little more every day. We have to keep on because that's what we do. It's what I've been doing every day of my life."

"Am I going to be okay?" I asked Mrs. Brewer. I was still seeing blood pooling every time I blinked, drenched across my entire world whenever I slept. "And Kara? Is she going to be okay?"

Mrs. Brewer didn't say anything for a minute, and I saw in her eyes that she didn't know what that meant any better than I did. "I think you'll both be as okay as any of us ever are."

Mrs. Brewer thought routine would help. So I came back to work a week later. I don't know if it helps. I like to imagine it does.

Mama had met me outside the first time I'd gone back to the trailer park to see Kara. She'd been next to the beat-down little single-wide when I walked up, hanging laundry on a line. The trailer looked nothing like our old one had, nothing like a home. Just a husk to fill up with the few things she had salvaged and the hand-me-downs from local church congregations.

When the police had come to the crime scene and told her what happened right outside her front door, I'd heard her wailing "my baby," and I heard those words echoing in my head when I tried to sleep every night, and I'd wondered over and over again who she was talking about.

"Didn't think you'd show your face around here," she said when she saw me that first day after.

"I wanted to see Kara," I told her.

"Not me?" she asked. I didn't answer, and she leaned back against the post holding the laundry line, lighting a cigarette with shaking hands.

"The police have been asking me a lot of questions," she said. "They won't let Matt handle things, seeing as he's been so involved in the case. They've got an investigator working on it."

"What did you tell them?" I asked Mama.

Mama gave me a long, searching look. "What do you think I told them?" she asked me, puffing on her cigarette. "I said that last I saw, Dane had the gun on you. I even told them"—she blew out a plume of smoke—"he liked to fuck around with fire sometimes. Not so sure he didn't start the fire and blame it on y'all."

"Why'd you do that?" I asked.

She didn't answer for a minute, and I could tell what it cost her, sucking down her cigarette, her hands still trembling. I used to think she was so beautiful; I saw then how life had constantly been wearing her down. It didn't seem fair. "How'd you know I didn't have a plan, huh, Evelyn? How'd you know I wasn't already planning for us to get out? Why, since the time she's been born, do you think I'm not good enough to take care of my own daughter?"

"I'm your daughter, too," I told her.

"And that," she said, throwing her cigarette down and stepping on it, "is why I won't let them have you."

"I did it for you, too, Mama." I kept my voice low when I said it.

"No, you didn't," she returned. "You resented me. You wanted it to hurt. A little. You always did."

"Mama—"

"And why wouldn't you?" she asked. "I never gave you anything, did I? You always looked more like that daddy of yours than me, and I never much liked him. Don't think you would have either."

"Sometimes," I said, "I don't even think you love me at all."

"Lovin' somebody isn't as simple as you think it is, Evie."

"You think," I answered, "that I think loving someone is simple?"

"You think if it's not pure, it's not real. You never let anyone be messy. You judge us all as unworthy the minute we make a mistake. That's why you fixate on Kara. She's too young to fuck up as bad as the rest of us do. No one else will ever be good enough for you."

"Mama."

"She'll grow up one day and be scared to make a mistake in front of you, too. I would never have chosen Dane over you," she told me.

I didn't tell her she already did.

"You can't come home," she said. "There is no home." She wiped away at the mascara-streaked tears running down her cheeks. "There's nothing."

"But you're safe," I said.

"That was our home, Evelyn. That was my mama's home."

I nodded, absorbing the blow. "Do you think you—would you ever forgive me?"

"Why would you even want me to?" Mama asked me, her eyes on my face, letting out a weary sigh. "What good have I ever done you?"

"It was me and you, Mama. It was just the two of us for so long, until Matt came along. And I know I wasn't much for company, but I was still happier in those years than after."

She reached up then, pushed a lock of hair back behind my ear, her fingers lingering over my face. "I never knew I could love anything like that. Like the way I loved you the first time I saw you."

I felt the tears coming and put my hand over hers, holding it against my face. "Mama," I said, but then she dropped her hand and turned away, going back to the laundry.

"Kara's inside," Mama said without looking back at me. "She'll be happy to see you."

She had been, but I couldn't stay long. Not there.

The old woman makes her way to the register now. I'd almost forgotten her, she'd been moving around the store so quietly. She's holding a couple of cans of cat food. She pushes them across the counter to me.

"Having a nice night?" I ask her.

She nods, shy. I quickly scan the cans and push them into a plastic bag. I hand it to her over the counter, and at the last moment, as if she herself didn't realize she was going to do it, she grabs my hands. I almost jerk away, but her hands are so soft and her eyes so kind, I let her be.

"I used to have a husband who—" She stops, shaking her head. "I wish I could've done what you did," she says. "I wish someone would've done it for me. We're never the ones who get out alive. You did."

And then, without another word, she pulls away and hurries out the door. I stay there, frozen for a moment, before I can't think about it anymore without feeling like I might explode. Before I have to do something.

I go about restocking the store and doing some quick cleaning, trying to get lost in the ritual of it all. Finally, I lock the money in the back office and head for the door, turning on the alarm behind me.

When I walk into the parking lot, I stop in my tracks, my

breath catching at the sight of the car sitting out at one of the gas pumps. It takes me a second to make sense of who I'm seeing. He's propped up on the hood of his Range Rover under the shining light of the farthest pump, cradling the biggest bottle of soda I've ever seen. His eyes meet mine, and I wonder if my heart will pound right out of my chest at the sight of him.

Part of me is sure that I've thought about him so long, I've manifested him right in front of me. That's what it's like seeing Ashton Harper there, framed in the harsh light of the gas station.

Mrs. Brewer told me he'd stopped by, when I was still at the police station the day after Dane. But then he'd been gone. I hadn't seen him at all since the night at the trailer park.

I want to grab him and not let him go. I never want to speak to him again.

"You're here," I say, after it's too long to not say something.

He laughs at that and then I do, too, because it's ridiculous. There's a light in his eyes that I've been craving since the last time I saw it. "Did you specifically order one deeply traumatized boy to be sitting in the parking lot or . . . ?"

"Were you aiming for maximum dramatic effect?" I ask.

"More like efficiency," he answers. "To be honest, I was afraid you might be gone by the time I made it back."

I kick some grass growing up through the cement, distracting myself, before I look at him. "I thought about it. Running straight into the sun."

"Considered it myself," he tells me. "Now that I've got so much running-away experience." But then he averts his eyes, too, awkward. "I heard we were going to be able to plead our arson charges down to misdemeanors. Guess I have you to thank for that."

"You got Matt Rykers's conscience to thank," I tell him. "And liars in small towns."

283

"I knew they'd end up on my side eventually."

"I wasn't sure you'd come back to see me," I say, and I can't help but stare at his arms, deep tan lines on his skin where his T-shirt sleeves end. "Especially since the last time I saw you, you were concussed at Savannah Rykers's feet."

"Aw, you know me, Evelyn"—he levels me with his gaze—"I can't help but pick at a scab. Thanks for all that, by the way."

I take another step closer to him. "Are you fixed?" I ask him.

"Now, now," he says. "It's very important that we both acknowledge that there was never anything wrong with me. Hate the addiction, not the addict."

"Why not both?" I ask, and I feel myself falling back into it. Into a person.

"Why not indeed?" he returns with a grin. He holds up the soda bottle in his hand. "This is basically the same. Just gotta hold out."

"Ah, well, quittin's the easy part," I tell him. "It's the staying quit that's hard."

He laughs, and he's so magnetic, some part of me thinks I'd start that stupid game of Truth or Dare with him all over again. He pats the hood of the car next to him, indicating I should sit. I do. We stay in comfortable silence for a few moments.

"How do you feel?" he finally asks.

I glance at him, looking at me, and wonder if he sees me differently now. If something has changed.

"Sometimes," I tell him, "I feel wrong. Out of place in the world. Like I got dropped here on accident and forgotten. But that's not new, is it?"

"I guess not," he says.

"It's different now, though, than before. Like, sometimes, I get convinced there's still blood under my fingernails and I need to scrub my hands until they're clean, or I hear that sound, the way a gunshot echoes in your head when it fires until you can't hear anything else. I *smell* gunpowder, and I wake up not sure if Dane is alive or dead or if it's me that's dead or you or Kara." I take a deep breath. "But I guess I deserve that."

Ashton swallows. I tilt my face, forcing him to meet my eyes, expectant. "Would you have done it?" he asks. "No matter what?"

"Are you asking if I would've done it if he hadn't hit me first?"

He nods.

"I don't know," I say, choosing my words carefully. "I went there to do it. I thought I could, but . . . it's not nice, Ashton. To see how fragile we really are. Even him. And I never wanted to be what he was." I push my hair from my face. "But maybe I am."

"You get to choose who to be now," Ashton says. "Isn't that what all of this was for? So you could choose?"

"I just wanted to feel safe," I say. And I still feel like I'll spend the rest of my life chasing that undefinable feeling, because there's never enough of it: *safety*.

"Do you think that's enough?" I ask.

One side of his mouth quirks, almost a smile. "Who am I really to say?"

"I killed someone," I say. "Don't you think my soul is destroyed?"

"I killed someone, too, Evelyn," he says, staring up at the night sky overhead. "And I thought about it a lot since I've been gone—if there's one person whose soul I'm not worried about, it's yours." He locks eyes with me and his dark hair falls in his face and without thinking about it, I reach out and push it away. He doesn't move. "If you want forgiveness, God will grant it, and if you don't"—he shrugs—"I will."

"Forgiveness, huh? You gotten any better at forgiving yourself in rehab?" I ask him.

He grabs on to my hand and laces his fingers through mine, holding it tight, warm against him. "Where would the fun be in that? All that time, I thought, for some reason, you could absolve me; I thought losing myself in you might be the answer, but that was more cowardice, so I did the right thing. I told Mrs. Brewer what happened."

My thumb presses into the skin on his hand. "What did she do?"

"Nothing," he says. "She barely even blinked. She thanked me. Said that's all she ever wanted to know. She forgave me." He reaches up, wipes a tear away with the heel of his hand. "Been crying so much lately."

"A boy built for tragedy," I say, and he laughs, taking in a deep breath after it passes him by. "You didn't have to come see me," I can't help but tell him.

"'Course I did, Evelyn," he answers. "You said you couldn't feel about me the way Reid did. You were right."

"I had my own version of Reid, too, you know," I tell him. "The one I wanted. The beautiful, mysterious girl who saved me."

He doesn't say anything for a minute, and we sit there, together, our hands entwined. "I loved Reid, but I knew it had to end, the self-destructive relationship we had, and I think she did, too. And I wish so badly I'd had the chance to tell her that, but I never wanted her gone," he finally tells me. "And Dane, well, maybe that blood is on my hands, but I wish you didn't have that burden. I don't know. I'm still taking it one day at a time."

"I don't want it to be all I ever am. The girl who killed Dane."

"It won't be," he says, that simple. "You'll be the girl who saved herself."

That sounds nice, I think. Maybe one day, I'll see that version of myself, too. Maybe one day, I'll figure out how to save someone else.

"You're driving the old Honda?" Ashton breaks the silence, pointing to Reid's old car. "It's like seeing a ghost."

"You scared?"

"Every damn day of my life."

"I think I am leaving," I tell him, the words surprising me, but feeling true on my lips. "All of McNair Falls is a ghost for me, some place I'd resigned myself to, and I can't live like that. It's not right.

"I've faced my demons here, now. It's time to leave them behind."

"I think you're right," he agrees. "Where are you gonna go?" he asks then, easy as anything. Giving me permission to go, believing I'll be fine. Letting me believe it myself.

"For now, Atlanta. Maybe farther, one day. I've always wanted to see the Grand Canyon and the Rocky Mountains and that Pacific Ocean. I'll probably get my GED." I shrug.

"You'd leave Kara like that?" he asks.

"I think maybe I have to. Besides, she'll have more capable people than me watching over her," I say. "I love Kara more than anything, but I need to spend some time figuring out my own shit for a change."

"You and me both," he says.

"Well," I tell him, "if you're ever on the West Coast, look me up. Maybe I'll have made it that far."

"If I'm looking you up, maybe I will have, too."

"Another life, right?" I ask him, and slide off the hood of the Range Rover, ready to leave him behind—but he hangs on to my hand and I let myself be spun back around to face him.

"I'd rather it be this one," he tells me.

"Don't forget about me, Ashton, okay?" I ask him, looking up into his dark eyes.

"Like you have to worry about that," he says, and I move back closer to him, almost close enough.

He's really so beautiful.

"Your eyes kind of have that look," I say.

"What look is that?" he asks.

"Wild," I tell him, and his eyes flicker in the bright light with the same old danger.

And then he finally releases my hand and lets me go.

• • •

Before I leave for work the next day, Mrs. Brewer is out front working on her garden. It's cool in the November sun, but she's still worked up a sweat. She drops her spade and walks over to me as I come out of the house.

"How's the old girl treating you?" she asks, nodding toward the Honda.

"It's driving really good," I tell her.

"It better be," she says. "I just had it tuned up."

"Why?" I ask, leaning against the car. She pushes her hair out of her face and takes off her gardening gloves.

"You planning on staying here, Evelyn?" she asks.

"I hadn't really—" I start to say, but she waves it away.

"The car's for you," she says, easy as that. "Adam and I want you to have it. He thinks I'm crazy, but at least if I'm crazy, he appreciates that it's in your direction. He says you're a good girl."

I'm not sure Mr. Brewer really thinks that, but it's nice to hear her say it either way.

"Are you sure?" I ask her.

"I've watched this place kill so many people, Evelyn. It doesn't kill everyone, no, but—some of us aren't made for it. I watched it kill my mama and my daughter and—I won't let it take you. I won't let them take you.

"So go," she says. "Go and start living and stop being this. I won't let them wear you down.

"Go, Evelyn," she says. "And don't stop until you see something that makes you happy."

• • •

The night before I leave town, Ashton stops by the Brewers' house. He parks his car out front, and I go sit in the passenger's seat, right where we started. He hands me a new set of guitar strings and holds my hand a moment too long.

"Atlanta ain't so far away," he tells me.

I bow my head and smile to myself.

• • •

I pack up my things on a Saturday, and out in the yard, I hug Mr. and Mrs. Brewer goodbye. She cries and maybe I cry, too.

I tell them I'll see them again soon.

I drive the car over to Matt's, and Kara is outside playing with Mrs. Rykers when I get there.

"Evie!" she calls when she sees me, comes running over, jumping up into my arms. I cradle her to me. "Are you staying?" she asks.

"Not for long."

"Evelyn," Mrs. Rykers says, "we're about to eat dinner. Come in and stay." I've figured out that's what she does in any bad situation—tries to feed you.

I wonder if she's the one who told Savannah I was a slut or if Savannah invented that on her own.

"That's okay, Mrs. Rykers," I say. "I have to hit the road."

I'd told Matt I was leaving. My public defender had helped me out with my plea deal, and Mrs. Brewer had given me the money to pay my fine. I was cleared of all charges in the killing of Dane Barkley.

I am free to go.

I knew how much it had cost Matt to lie for me. And I lived with that burden just like I lived with so many other things.

"Okay," Mrs. Rykers says. "I'll give you two a minute." She goes back into the house, and I wonder how a man who loved my mama could love someone like her.

But it doesn't matter anymore. That was a long time ago.

"Where are you going, Evie?" Kara asks me as I set her down. "Have you seen my car?" she asks then. It's one of those little motorized cars, a ridiculous pink Jeep, and she hops into it and drives around the yard to show me.

"So cool," I say.

She gets out, looking impressed with herself.

It's a Jeep, just like Savannah has.

Savannah's, on the other hand, is a 2005 Jeep Wrangler. Her daddy had bought it for her off some man in Simpsonville.

That's what I'd heard her saying at least.

"It's not the nicest, but it's the best he can do," she'd admitted, and she'd looked at me like it was my fault.

I remember thinking at the time that it had been better than what I could do.

I guess that doesn't matter anymore either.

"How is it staying with Matt and Alice sometimes?" I ask her.

"Fun," she tells me like a secret. "Mama wants me to tell her I had a bad time whenever she picks me up."

"Smart girl."

"You're leaving again," she says. "How long will you be gone?"

I squat down in front of her. "Long enough to figure out how far I can go," I admit to her. "It might be a while. I've gotta see some places, get a real job. I'll be back to see you real soon, though, probably Thanksgiving, and Matt has promised you can call me whenever you like."

"But," Kara says, "I want to go with you."

"Nah, you don't," I tell her. "It would just be borin'. Mama's got that new little house closer to school, and then on the weekends, Matt and Alice and Savannah will keep you company and they'll be much more fun than I ever was. You know how much you hate all the time I have to spend at work. They'll be around more."

Kara glances back at the house. "They did give me a lot of toys," she says.

"You better be good then, right? Or else you might get 'em taken away."

She laughs. "I'll be sneaky if I'm bad."

"That's my girl," I say, and she laughs at that, too.

"Come on," I tell her. "I'll walk you in for dinner. You don't want to be late."

I grab her tiny little hand in mine, just like always, the way I did the day she was born and every day after, and we go into the pretty blue house together.

The whole Rykers family is in the kitchen, getting ready. We stand awkwardly on the threshold, almost a part of them, but not.

"I've got to get going," I announce, and I can't help but lock eyes with Savannah. She doesn't look away, nodding her head in acknowledgment.

"Be safe, Evelyn," Matt tells me. "And please call me before you get into any more . . . crime."

"Can I at least send you with some food?" Mrs. Rykers asks me.

"Mrs. Brewer packed me some sandwiches," I say, waving her off. I glance at Matt. "You have my new number."

"You really aren't going back to school?" Savannah cuts over them. "You're just going to leave?"

"Savannah, hush," her mama says.

"I know you're not stupid," Savannah tells me, and I think that's some version of sorry. It doesn't matter.

Girls like us have been taught our entire lives to hate each other, and we do it because there's nothing else to do. But when it mattered—when it *really* mattered—we did what we had to.

"We'll keep up with you," Matt tells me. He moves toward me, and for a wild moment, I think he might hug me and I think he thinks he might, too. But he stops himself and puts his hand on Kara's head lovingly, and she doesn't shrug away. "Me and the wild one."

She grins up at him with something like reverence.

"Let me know if you need anything," I say, and then there's nothing left to say. I wave goodbye to all of them. Savannah picks Kara up and holds her in her arms, giving her a warm smile I've never seen from her before. When I get in my car, I see both their faces in the window, Savannah encouraging Kara to wave as I back out of the driveway. Their matching hair is the last thing I see in the rearview mirror as I drive away.

• • •

I decide to go to Reid's grave.

I know it's morbid and ridiculous to even half believe the ghost of a girl you wanted to love is haunting you, but I do wonder it sometimes. Wonder if the wind blew me straight into Ashton and her spirit inhabited me and somewhere between here and there, she was.

I want her to be with me. I always wanted that.

She's buried in the First Baptist graveyard. Even I know she'd hate that—I bet Mrs. Brewer did, too. But I guess graves aren't for the dead people; they're for the ones left behind.

Some part of me knows she wouldn't stay if she didn't have to. She'd go.

Maybe that's the lesson, if something like that stood a chance of existing.

Reid's old car is tidy now, the way I'm sure Mrs. Brewer always wanted it to be when Reid was alive, but I know Reid didn't leave it that way.

It was a mess that last night when we were together. Like a half of someone's home.

Reid, I think. *You kissed me because you could. I didn't understand you, but you wanted to save me in the only way you knew how, and now I guess I've taken over your life.*

She'd like that, I'm pretty sure.

I park right outside the low stone wall surrounding the graveyard and climb over it, walking through rows of Douglases and Scotts and Michaelses. I see one gravestone that I recognize. Peters—Mama's mama.

My granny told me I looked like my daddy, and did I know what that meant.

No, I'd said.

You don't belong to this town, she'd responded, and when I was young, I'd thought that was bad. Our family belonged to this town. We were all cursed, stuck.

We never left.

But, now, I wonder if it wasn't her blessing, her wish for me.

Run away from all this, Evelyn. Maybe that's really what she meant.

I keep on walking past and end up in front of the Morgan family marker. Reid's buried next to her grandma—Mrs. Brewer's mama, Elaine Morgan.

Elaine. Mrs. Brewer had told me Elaine was a single mom, too, back before people looked the other way.

It was hard growing up like that, Evelyn, Mrs. Brewer had said. *You try and try to fit in and you never really do.*

They never really accept you.

It makes me happy Reid's next to her because I think Reid would've liked her.

I squat down in front of Reid's grave, and I run my hands over the grass that has started to grow here. She's six feet under, dead and gone for longer than seems possible.

"I'm sorry," I say. "I'm sorry they got you."

The breeze blows, and I'm not silly enough to take it as anything but an errant wind, but I still lift my face into it anyway.

"I won't forget you," I promise, and then there's not much left to do, so I sit there for a few moments and study her name and say goodbye.

Leaving is starting to get easier.

I slide back into the passenger's seat and lift up the console, looking for something to tie my hair back with. But instead, I find the purple lipstick.

I take it from its hiding spot and put it on.

When my eyes meet my reflection in the mirror, I look like me.

Finally, I crank up the car, put on Ashton's old sunglasses, and drive off. It only takes ten minutes to see the city limits. That's all it ever takes.

With the music blaring and wind blowing my hair through the open window, I turn my car west—right in the direction of the setting sun.

AUTHOR'S NOTE

On average, nearly twenty people per minute are abused by an intimate partner in the United States—equating to more than ten million women and men each year.

If you or someone you know is experiencing domestic violence or abuse, for anonymous, confidential help, 24/7, please call the National Domestic Violence Hotline at 1-800-799-SAFE (7233) or 1-800-787-3224 (TTY).

If you are afraid that you might hurt yourself or are feeling suicidal, the National Suicide Prevention Lifeline provides 24/7 free, confidential support over the phone at 1-800-273-8255 or online at suicidepreventionlifeline.org.

You can also utilize the following online resources for info and assistance:

- The National Coalition Against Domestic Violence
  ncadv.org
- The National Domestic Violence Hotline
  thehotline.org
- National Child Abuse Hotline/Childhelp
  childhelp.org
- The National Institute of Mental Health website
  nimh.nih.gov
- The National Runaway Safeline
  1800runaway.org

ACKNOWLEDGMENTS

This fact will never cease to amaze me: Holy crap, I wrote another book!

This book was without a doubt a project of intense passion and love and I am nothing if not grateful for those who saw me through it. First and foremost, there is not enough gratitude in the world for my agent, Diana Fox, for the many phone calls, brainstorm sessions, and rereads. I am forever indebted to you for all your work on making this book happen. I also cannot forget the outstanding team members at Fox Literary who joined us in reading this book until their eyes bled: Ari Brezina, Elizabeth Gallup, and Isabel Kaufman.

Much thanks also to my editor, Erin Stein, as well as her two fearless (former and current!) assistant editors who guided me through the editing process: Nicole Otto and Camille Kellogg. I cannot say enough wonderful things about Natalie Sousa for her incredible cover design and incredible patience as I asked for "just one more tweak." Thanks as well to the entire team at Imprint. I'm also exceedingly grateful for the work of Morgan Rath and Molly Ellis as well as the entire Fierce Reads team for getting word of this book out and to Jennifer Edwards and her team for getting it into your hands. Publishing a book truly takes a village, so I would be remiss if I didn't also mention Starr Baer, Elynn Cohen, Raymond Colón, Hayley Jozwiak, Allison Verost, and Jie Yang.

Writing is, interestingly, one of those jobs where you're constantly asking yourself if there's something wrong with you that drives you to do it. Luckily, I have some fantastic publishing friends who are always asking themselves the same question right alongside me. Huge thanks to Maurene Goo, Diya Mishra, and Kara Thomas for early reads, encouragement, and listening as I asked, "How the heck do I end this

book?!" One pandemic ago, I finished the first draft of *A Better Bad Idea* on a writing retreat in France with some truly wonderful author friends: Rachael Allen, Kate Boorman, Alina B. Klein, and Dana Alison Levy. Nothing motivates quite like wine, cheese, and good company. Also, I probably couldn't make it through a book much less a publishing career without Courtney Summers's pep talks, so thanks for the encouragement and the yelling at appropriate intervals. Also, Veronica Roth, I miss our Chicago writing dates, but thanks for being ready with porch mimosas when I visited. Huge shout-outs as well to: Rebecca Barrow, Somaiya Daud, Kate Hart, Michelle Krys, Amy Lukavics, and Kaitlin Ward. Y'all are the real ones.

I'm lucky to have incredibly supportive parents and other assorted family members. Very appreciative to Bob and Pam Devore for all the things. Shout-out to Drew just for being you—have fun telling people there's a published book dedicated to you. Also super grateful to everyone else in the Devore/Campbell/Woolbright crowd. And Aunt Jo of course! Thanks for reading, Aunt Jo!

Lastly, no one can stand alone in the publishing world without some friends who are like, "That sounds bad, but publishing is meaningless to me. Let's have a drink instead." I could not be happier to have had wonderful day-job crews in my writing career, which include both the former Centrons reading as well as all my fellow RMers. I'm always thinking about the various wonderful friend groups I have made along the way: from Clemson to Chicago to Charleston and everywhere in between—so blessed to have lived in so many excellent C-cities with all of y'all! Special shout-out to Sarah S., Sarah W., Jamie, and Erin. I appreciate y'all more than you know.

As always, thank you for reading. It's still incredibly strange to me that people I don't (and do!) know are consuming so many thoughts that came straight out of my head! This really cool dream of mine wouldn't exist without you—THANK YOU!

ABOUT THE AUTHOR

LAURIE DEVORE was born and raised in small-town South Carolina and graduated from Clemson University. After four years in the balmy Midwest, she returned to her home in the South, where she now lives and works in Charleston. In her spare time, she reluctantly runs marathons, watches too much TV, and works a "y'all" into every conversation. She is the author of *How to Break a Boy* and *Winner Take All*.